S0-EGS-075

PARADOX

Donald Gorman

AuthorHouse™
1663 Liberty Drive
Bloomington, IN 47403
www.authorhouse.com
Phone: 1-800-839-8640

First published by AuthorHouse 6/15/2009

ISBN: 978-1-4389-9031-6 (e)
ISBN: 978-1-4389-9030-9 (sc)

Library of Congress Control Number: 2009905275

Printed in the United States of America
Bloomington, Indiana

This book is printed on acid-free paper.

To my dear friend Ellen. You are an inspiration. Your friendship, kindness, optimism and faith in me and this project made this book possible. Without you, this novel might never have happened. This book is dedicated to you with love and graditude.

CONTENTS

BOOK ONE

CRAVE

CHAPTER 1

MISTAKES

The night seemed deeper and richer this far off the ground. The darkness looked blacker, or more concentrated. It was as if you were closer to the true center of darkness up here, away from the chaos on the streets below.

A trifling breeze blew by. There was a certain chill in the air.

She shivered as she turned away from humanity and all its blatant desolation.

Not that you couldn't hear the sounds reaching up from so far beneath her. Car horns. Shouting voices. Anger. People who were all more important than everyone around them. They demanded so much attention.

And each and every one of them really thought they actually deserved it.

How sad. How pathetic.

The breeze kicked up again, just for the joy of making her shiver.

And as it toyed with her long, flimsy shawl, she lit another cigarette. She shielded the flame from the lighter with her hand. She drew the smoke into her lungs. Then she exhaled, offering a gray cloud up to the wind which carried it away.

"Will you please come inside so we can discuss this?" he asked.

She glanced over at the door where he was standing. She quickly turned away before any misapprehension of interest could be given.

"There's nothing to talk about."

"Come on, Cassandra," he said. "I know you're angry. You have every right. But we need to talk about this."

"Why, Mark?" she asked. "What can you possibly say?"

"Jesus, Cassandra," he said. "You've been out on this balcony for over twenty minutes now. Will you come inside? I understand you're angry. I don't blame you…"

"You don't blame me, Mark?" she scoffed. "You sleep with my sister and you don't blame me for being angry? I have your permission, do I? Gee, thanks! That's awfully big of you."

"I didn't mean it like that," he said. "It was an accident, for God's sake! Now come inside and talk to me. It's cold out here."

"You think it's cold?" she asked. "That's funny. I think it's fine out here. In fact, I'm quite comfortable."

"Will you please stop?" he asked. "I can see the goosebumps on your arms from here. You must be freezing."

"I told you I'm fine," she repeated. "I like it out here. I want to stay out here for a while. Besides, I have nothing to say to you, Mark. Why don't you just go inside and leave me alone? If you need something to do, maybe you can go find some new slut to cheat on me with."

"Oh, for Christ's sake!" he rolled his eyes. "I'm sorry already! I'm sorry! How many times do I have to say it? It was an accident! It was a mistake! It was a moment of weakness and it never should have happened! I was wrong! I promise I'll make it up to you. Now will you please come inside?"

"Is it that easy for you, Mark?" she asked. "You're sorry? It was a mistake? And now it's all over and I'm supposed to forgive you? Would it be that easy if *I* had been the one who cheated? If I had gone off and fucked some guy, could I just say, 'I'm sorry, it was a mistake' and you would just forget the whole thing?"

"Of course not," he declared. "I'm not saying you have to just forgive me right away. But you can at least come in and talk to me about it. Nothing will get solved by running away and refusing to talk to me."

"And now I have to go to my mother's Memorial Day picnic and face that little whore!" she snipped. "This ought to be fantastic! Both of you will be there: my cheating husband and my sister the skank! What could be better? Do you two plan on slipping off somewhere private, or can you control yourselves for an entire day?"

"Will you stop it, Cassandra?"

"I can't talk right now."

"Look," he tried to calmly explain. "Stephanie and I both had the same problem. We were both lonely. Her husband is never around. Just like you, Trey always buries himself in his work."

"I said I'm not ready to talk to you yet!" she shouted with her back to him. She stared out into the darkness. After a pause, she continued in a more civil tone. "I can't even look at you right now, you bastard! I need some air. Just go inside and get out of my sight! I'll come in when I'm damned good and ready."

"Fine!" he dismissed her with an exasperated wave of his arm. "Do what you want! When you're ready to grow up and discuss this like an adult, I'll be inside."

She could hear him close the glass door to the balcony behind him. Another breeze blew by. She shivered against the chill.

Somehow, it seemed even darker outside. And it amazed her to think how clearly she could hear the sounds of the street so far below her.

She needed another cigarette. She took the pack out of her purse. She put the filter to her lips. Again she sheltered the flame from her lighter with her hand. The flame flailed and protested against the wind. However, it ultimately performed its necessary purpose.

She took a drag as tears flooded her eyes. The cigarette felt good. But it could not hold back a merciless attack of the sobs.

She surrendered to the tears as she cried into her hands. And after a minute, the lit cigarette slipped from her fingers.

It took a header off the balcony and fell to its death to the sidewalk ten stories below.

* * * * * *

He hated this part of town. It was too congested, too populated. There was a certain feeling in the air.

A person could almost smell the sleaze and the filth!

There were buildings and businesses that promoted and inspired decadence and moral decay. This was a very unclean, unholy place!

He knew this. Yet, the incident from the previous night had shocked him. It caught him off guard. He'd reacted poorly. He hadn't known how to respond.

That had changed, however. Since then, he'd been instructed.

Now he knew what he had to do.

The streets were dark. So dark!

Neon lights, glitz and depravity could not hide that fact. These sinners could not find sanctuary in the very callousness of their sins!

He drove slowly. These sights looked familiar. He was almost there. And he so hoped he would find that woman.

That same woman from before…

He stopped at a traffic light. He turned his head to the right. The enticements on the street corner caught his attention.

The man in the passenger seat startled him.

"Dad!" he gasped. "How did you…?"

"I've been here all along, my son," Dad said.

"No you weren't," he argued. "I was alone in this car! In fact, I still am! You're not really here! You can't be!"

"Now, son. Is that any way to talk to your father?"

"You're not my father!" he snapped. "My father is… he's dead! I know he is! I was at the funeral!"

"You're taking this all way too seriously, son," Dad said. "There's no need to get excited. This girl you seek. You've seen her before. On this street corner as well as in your dreams."

"Don't talk to me, you agent of evil!" he warned. "I won't listen!"

"I know you want her," Dad said. "It's only natural. Lust is a natural and purely human emotion. There's nothing wrong with it."

"Shut up!" he shouted. "You are not my father! I know who you are! You are The Devil himself! Why do you taunt me?"

"Calm down," Dad said in a soothing voice. "I'm only trying to reassure you that it is perfectly natural to want this girl. It's okay to do this."

"Leave me, Satan!" he growled. "You vile beast! The very fact that you choose to take the form of my father in order to goad me into depravity proves what a despicable, loathsome demon you really are!"

"I'm only trying to help you, my son."

"Leave me, Satan!"

"Very well."

The driver blinked a few times. He could still hear the street sounds around him.

Car horns blared from behind. The light had turned green. He turned to the passenger seat.

It was empty. He still had a tight not in his gut. It was very disquieting.

He stepped on the gas pedal. The car moved slowly into the next block. He could see her on the next corner. She stood out among the others.

There were three of them in all.

He recognized the hair.

The fake white fur coat...the legs...the shoes...the shamefully short skirt. She was such a cliché. It was disgraceful!

And yet...

His passenger side window was down. He pulled in slowly. He knew how. He was glad that she was the one who approached when he came to a stop.

Her expression was very suggestive as she gazed in through the window.

"Hey, sexy! You want...?"

She stopped suddenly. Her smile vanished.

"Oh. It's you."

"No," he said with a placating hand gesture. "It's okay. I promise."

"Aren't you that ass who called me a fornicator last time I saw you?" she recalled. "Didn't you call me a vile temptress who was going to Hell?"

"Yes, I did say those things the other day," he admitted. "But I changed my mind."

"You did?" she asked suspiciously.

"Yes," he nodded. "I was wrong. It was all a terrible mistake. I was just in a bad mood because of work."

"Really?"

"I promise."

"Are you saying you'd like to go for a ride?"

"With you?" he smiled. "I couldn't think of anything sweeter."

"Do you want to discuss rates first?"

"We'll work that out as we go along," he said. "I can assure you price is no object."

She looked him over. Nice suit.

Then, she pulled back.

"Wait a minute," she observed. "This isn't the same car you had a few days ago, is it? This looks like a brand new Cadillac."

"That's right, baby," he said. "I just got it."

"But, your last car was an old rust bucket."

"I'm moving up in the world," he said. "Now, do you want to go for a ride or should I call for one of your friends over there?"

"No, no," she quickly replied as she hopped in the car. "I'm the girl for you. Believe me. I'll treat you much better than either of those skanks. You won't regret sticking with me, sweetie."

His eyes quickly scanned over the young woman beside him. She was very attractive. But, she was dressed like a whore.

"Oh, I'm sure I won't," he said. "And I'm willing to bet you won't regret it either. I may even throw you something extra for your trouble. This should be an evening to remember."

"Sounds great, lover," she said. "Lead the way."

"Oh, I will."

He shifted gears and pulled away from the curb.

Meanwhile at the police station downtown, an officer answered the phone at his desk.

"Hello," he said. "Eighth Precinct. Sgt. Boyle speaking. How may I help you?"

"Yeah, I'd like to report a theft," said the caller. "Somebody stole my Cadillac. It's brand new, too. I just bought it last week!"

* * * * * *

They were in a dark booth toward the back of the restaurant. Soft candlelight cast sensuous shadows. It seemed to flicker to the gentle beat of the music playing in the background.

Even in this light, her sense of doubt reflected beautifully in her gorgeous blue eyes.

"I don't know, Joe," she said. "The college term is over. My parents are expecting me to go back to Fulton for the summer."

"What's the big deal?" he asked. "Tell them you have a job and you have to stay here. They should be okay with that. And what are you worried about? It's not as if you're lying. They should be happy you're doing so well."

"But, how do I explain what I'm doing?" she asked.

"Just tell the truth," he said. "Your internship turned out so well, your employer offered you a full-time job."

"But, they know I was an intern for a senator," she said. "I know they're going to suspect something. I just know it!"

"So what?" he rationalized. "Just deny it. They don't need to know. We'll keep it all a secret unless things get serious. Or should I say *until* things get serious. There's no reason to think they won't. You're happy, aren't you?"

"Yeah. Sort of."

"You seem unsure."

"Well, don't get me wrong, Joe," she said reluctantly. "You've been great. You really have. It just all seems a little cliché. A college intern having an affair with the senator who hired her. It all just feels..."

"I told you, Marissa," he said. "It's different with us. This is not just some cheap, sordid fling. My feelings for you are genuine."

"But, you're married."

"I already explained," he said. "When everything comes together and the time is right, I'll tell my wife. I'll even leave her for you, if you want. But we have to make sure this is the right thing to do first."

"You can't leave your wife for me," she said. "You're a senator, for God's sake. You have a career on the line. Your private life is under constant public scrutiny."

"Oh, people are a lot more forgiving than they used to be," he scoffed. "We can finesse our way through this when the time is right. Of course, it will have to be handled delicately. We'll have to keep things quiet for a while."

"Still, you're older than my father."

"Only by a year or two," he reasoned. "It's not that big a deal. Age is just a number, sweetheart. You can't make major decisions based on such trivialities."

"Well, I don't know..."

"Don't I make you happy?" he asked. "Don't I give you everything you want?"

"Yeah, I guess..."

"Don't overanalyze everything, Marissa," he advised. "You're an intelligent, beautiful young woman with your whole life ahead of you. You can have a brilliant career in law or even politics, wealth and the whole world at your feet. With me by your side, you can have it all!"

"But..."

"No buts," he interrupted. "I love you, Marissa. I love you deeply. You do believe that, don't you?"

"Yes."

"Then, there's nothing for you to worry about," he continued. "Of course, we'll have to keep everything secret for the time being. But you can stay in town for the summer. I'll get you a nice apartment right here in the city. I'll pay for everything. You'll be working for me. And nobody will have any reason to stick their noses in our business."

"Are you sure this is wise, Joe?" she asked. "My parents are expecting me to come home for the summer. They miss me. And I miss them."

"You can visit them on the occasional weekend," he said. "I'm not trying to keep you from seeing them. I just don't want you to be gone for the whole summer. It would kill me to be away from you for that long. Surely your parents would understand that you have a summer job."

"I guess."

She looked down at her fork as she toyed with her food.

"And wouldn't you miss me if we were apart?" he asked.

"Of course," she said. "You know I love you."

"Then it's settled," he said. "I'll get you that nice apartment I showed you right here in the city. I'll pay the rent. We can move you in there tomorrow. I'll take care of everything. And we won't have to be apart. We can see each other whenever we want."

"It sounds good on the surface," she said timidly. "I just hope we're not making a huge mistake."

"What mistake?" he assured her while taking her hand in his. "This is the right thing to do, Marissa. Trust me. We'll take it slow and keep everything confidential for the time being. But, we'll be together. Believe me, sweetheart. As long as we're careful, there can be no mistakes in a love like ours."

"Really?"

The vulnerability in her eyes was so becoming in the flickering candlelight.

"You do trust me, don't you?" he asked.

"Completely."

"Then believe in me now," he said. "We're doing the right thing. I'll be taking care of you, and you have nothing to worry about."

Her hand seemed so small and gentle in his loving grasp. He gave her delicate fingers a reassuring squeeze.

She glanced down at the table. When she turned her gaze up to meet his, her eyes were even more beautiful and vulnerable than before.

Her silence betrayed the depths of her fragility.

"I promise, my darling," he said softly. "Everything will be fine."

Her smile warmed his heart. He knew he was winning her over.

"You're right," she said. "I'm being silly. I should be pitying all those poor fools out there who have to *look* for a summer job…or for love."

"That's the spirit," he beamed. "You'll see. This will be a great summer. I promise. There's absolutely nothing to worry about."

She glanced shyly down at her plate. Her smile grew warmer when she looked in his eyes again.

"Now finish your food, sweetie," he said. "The evening has just begun."

"Where are we going?"

"The sooner you eat," he smiled. "The sooner you'll find out."

"Okay."

He watched her as she ate. Her renewed appetite filled him with confidence.

It was starting to look as if he might really enjoy the upcoming summer!

* * * * * *

"Come on in."

"Thanks for letting me come over so late, Danny," she said. "I really appreciate it."

"That's okay."

She walked in and glanced around the room.

"So, this is where you're living now?" she asked. "Nice apartment. Much bigger than the one we had."

"Yeah," he muttered. "It's a step up. Let me take your coat. Make yourself at home. Can I get you anything to drink?"

"Something warm would be nice," she said as she removed her coat. "Would tea or coffee be too much trouble?"

"Instant coffee's easy," he suggested while taking her coat.

"That sounds lovely," she said. "Should we hug or kiss or shake hands or something?"

"It's not necessary," he said. "Maybe when you leave. We'll play it by ear. Have a seat while I get your coffee."

She walked over to the sofa. "So," she inquired. "Where's your new girl? Krysten, is it?"

"She's asleep in the other room."

"Oh," she said while sitting. "Sorry again for calling so late."

"I'll admit it was a bit of a surprise," he said. "It's been a while."

He walked to the kitchen. It was close by. They barely needed to raise their voices as they talked.

"I know," she said sadly. "I'm sorry. Frankly, I'm sorry for everything, Danny."

"Don't let it bother you," he said. "Everything turned out for the best."

Her eyes were even sadder as she glanced down at the coffee table.

Finally, she asked, "So, what's she like?"

"Krysten?" he said. "She's a sweet girl. Very pretty, smart, classy, delightful to be with…she's a lot of fun."

"She sounds wonderful."

"She is."

"How long have you two been together?" she asked. She tried to ignore the sting.

"Almost six months now."

"Wow," she said. "Is it serious?"

He came out of the kitchen carrying a steaming mug. "Too early to tell," he said. "Could be. Here you go. A freshly-nuked cup of instant coffee."

"Thanks," she said. She took a sip. "Mmmm! Just the right amount of cream and sugar. You remembered."

"I was always good with the little details," he said. He plopped himself down in a chair.

"That's true," she said quietly. "You always were."

"So, what's this all about, Lindsay?" he asked. "I'm sure you didn't call me at nearly midnight on a Saturday just to chat. Especially the way you sounded on the phone."

"I just needed somewhere to go."

"What about Prince Charming?"

"Ethan?" she rolled her eyes. "He's not as charming as he used to be."

"I see," he grunted. "And you ran out of friends?"

"Everyone's either..." she began. "Listen, Danny. Will you please stop? I just couldn't go anywhere else or talk to anyone else. You were the only one who was ever really there for me."

"Of course," he nodded. "That's why you left me, isn't it?"

"Please, Danny!" she said with a hint of desperation. "Don't do this to me now. I know I was a fool to dump you for Ethan! It was stupid and impetuous and the dumbest thing I ever did!"

"How is that *my* problem now?"

"I never said it was your problem," she explained. "I just needed somewhere to go. I just needed to get away from him."

"Has he gotten physical?"

"Not yet," she said. "He's been drinking more and more. He yells at me all the time. Nothing is ever good enough for him. He threatens me, calls me a stupid bitch...or worse. He's very controlling. He's...I just can't take it any more!"

"Sounds rough," he said. "So, how did you get away from him tonight?"

"He passed out drunk on the couch," she said.

"And, what's he going to do when he wakes up and you're not there?" he asked with a stoicism that wouldn't go away.

"I don't know," she said with a tear in her eye. "I don't want to think about it. I just had to get out of there."

"Well, you can't stay here," he said. "I've moved on. I have someone else now."

"Please, Danny?" she begged. "I just need a place to sleep tonight."

"You've got to be kidding!"

"I won't be in your way," she pleaded. "I'll sleep on the sofa."

"How am I going to explain that to Krysten?" he asked. "I may not know a lot about women. But one thing I do know is that they don't usually like it when a guy's ex-girlfriend suddenly reappears in the middle of the night. Even if they just want to sleep on the sofa. Most women just don't like that!"

"I'll explain it to her in the morning," she offered. "I'm not trying to start any trouble. I just had to get out of that house!"

"No," he stated while shaking his head. "This is not a good idea."

"Please!"

She began to weep into her hands. A familiar knot tightened in his stomach.

"I don't blame you for not wanting me here," she cried. "I know it's all my fault and I brought it all on by myself! I was a fool! I was stupid! I was a flaming asshole! It was all a terrible mistake! And I was wrong, Danny! I was so wrong! You have no idea how sorry I am!"

It was hard to understand her as she sobbed into her hands. However, he could make out what she was saying. That certain sense of communication still existed between them. He could feel himself weaken.

But, he vowed to stay strong. For Krysten's sake.

"I mean it, Danny," she continued sobbing. "I am so very sorry for what I did to you! I don't expect you to forgive me, but please just let me crash on your sofa tonight. That's all I ask. I'll explain it to Krysten in the morning. Then, I'll leave and you'll never have to deal with me ever again."

"If only that were true," he muttered. "And will you stop blubbering? If you get snot on the sofa, Krysten will be even more pissed off."

She wiped her eyes.

"So, you'll let me stay?" she sniffed.

"Well," he sighed. "I guess I really can't just throw you out into the street in the cold of night."

"Thanks," she smiled. "You always were the best, Danny."

"Yeah, right," he scoffed. "This is just wonderful! As if I don't have enough to worry about this weekend. My mother's Memorial Day picnic is tomorrow."

"Your mother's Memorial Day bash!" she recalled. "I remember those. I love those."

"And she'll want us all to go to church with her first," he reminded. "She's still psychotically religious."

"I always liked your mother," she smiled. "How is she?"

"The same."

"I wish I could go to the picnic."

"Don't push your luck," he said. "I shouldn't even let you sleep on the sofa. God! I don't believe it's Memorial day already."

"I know," she agreed. "We're staring summer in the face, but the nights have been exceedingly cold lately."

"I hope it's not a sign."

"A sign of what?" she asked.

"I don't know," he shrugged as he rose to his feet. "Just a joke. I guess my mother is starting to get to me. Do you need a blanket or something?"

"No," she said. She stood as well. "I'll be fine. And thanks, Danny!"

She threw her arms around him. "I'll take that hug now," she beamed. "I really owe you one, honey!"

"One, at least," he mumbled. "I should have my head examined."

"Why?"

"I know I'm going to pay for this, Lindsay," he said. "I always tell Krysten she looks beautiful when she's angry. Well, I have a feeling she's going to be looking extra gorgeous tomorrow."

She laughed as she held him.

Yet, neither of them noticed a pair of beautiful, angry eyes watching from a barely open bedroom door.

* * * * * *

He was still a bit shaken as he walked through the front door.

He unbuttoned his long, leather coat. He slipped it off and placed it on the arm of a chair. There was still some blood splattered on part of his shirt and his pants. There was even blood on the backpack that he dropped heavily on the floor.

He sat down and allowed his nerves to settle. Nearly fifteen minutes passed. He didn't move a muscle.

Suddenly, a noise from the next room startled him.

He jumped up to his feet. "Who's there?" he called out.

There was no reply.

"Is anybody out there?" he shouted. He was growing tense.

Finally, a figure stepped into the doorway.

"Mom?" he gasped. "What are you…?"

"Hello, son," she said calmly. "I've been watching you."

"You have?"

"Yes," she said. "You've been a terrible disappointment to me."

"I'm doing my best, Mother," he said. "I'm trying to live a good and righteous life."

"Good and righteous!" she scoffed. "You don't know the meaning of those words! I tried to teach you, boy. I tried to instill a proper love of God in you. I tried to get you to reject sin and walk in the Glory of The Lord!"

"That's what I'm aiming to do."

"I tried to lead you down the path of righteousness," she continued as if she hadn't heard him. "And how do you repay me? How do you spend your Saturday evenings? I'll tell you how! By cavorting with prostitutes! Don't deny it! I saw you! I saw you with that woman of ill repute!"

"But, I didn't have sex with her, Mom!" he begged. "I was a good boy! I didn't fornicate! I killed her, Mom! I killed her in the Name of the Lord! I did my part to help rid sin from God's Earth! I was a good boy, Mom! I killed her for you! I killed her in the Name of God!"

"Don't lie to me!" she scolded. "You may not have fornicated, but you wanted to! You can sin by thought as well as by deed, boy! You are a sinner! You will always be a sinner! You are an unworthy son! And you are unworthy in the eyes of The Lord!"

"No, Mom!" he begged. "Please don't! I'm trying to be worthy! I'm trying!"

"Trying?" she chided. "The Lord does not tolerate failure when it comes to sin! Haven't I taught you that yet?"

"Okay, so I've made mistakes," he began. "Maybe I'm not perfect, but…"

"Perfect?" she taunted. "You're a liar and a thief! Not only were you lusting after that loose woman, but you stole as car as well!"

"I didn't want to get any blood on my upholstery," he defended.

"Poppycock!" she argued. "You could have stolen any car for that! You stole a Cadillac because you wanted to impress that trollop! You had every intention of soiling yourself by fornicating with that common harlot!"

"You don't need to impress…"

"Silence!" she yelled. "Don't you dare try to justify your unclean, unholy actions to me! You should be truly ashamed of yourself! You have disgraced your God, your family and your church! Aren't you ashamed?"

He was afraid to speak.

"Well?" she prodded. "Aren't you ashamed?"

"Yes, Mother."

"Go to your room and think about what you've done," she warned. "Think about what you can do to ask for and deserve God's forgiveness!"

"But, I'm sorry, Mom," he begged. "I'm really sorry for what I've done!"

"Don't you think God is The One you should apologize to?" she asked.

"Yes."

"Then, go!" She pointed in the direction of his bedroom. "And what's in that backpack? More bloody clothes?"

"Yes."

"Just great!" she grumbled. "I suppose I have to clean up after you again! Take that bloody mess with you!"

He lifted the dirty backpack. He hung his head as he slowly left the room.

"Pray for forgiveness," she sternly advised. "I'll be in to deal with you later, you wicked, depraved sinner!"

CHAPTER 2

TREACHERY

Sunrise over a big city can be a breathtaking sight. The jagged horizon like a crooked dark scar against the sky which lifts its orange globe above the early morning. The silhouette of tall buildings and skyscrapers gradually allowing the sunlight to penetrate their fortress of blackness. Bright yellow, pink and peach hues reflecting off the glass and steel structures...

...And a new day begins with the familiar bustle of urban life.

He was apathetic of the throngs of people hurrying to their various destinations on the streets below him. He just couldn't care less.

He had his own problems.

A coffee cup sat on the kitchen table before him. A plate offered a pair of untouched blueberry Pop Tarts. He leaned forward in his chair with his elbows on the table. He stared straight ahead.

His whole body felt heavy and pained. He was jittery. He wasn't hungry.

Suddenly, he grabbed a cell phone and hit the speed dial.

"Hello?" said the voice on the other end.

"Cassandra?" he said. "Where the hell are you?"

"I stayed at a friend's place last night," she said.

"What friend?"

"You're in no position to interrogate me, Mark."

"I'm your husband, dammit!" he snapped. "I think I have a right to know where you spent the night!"

"Why?" she asked. "Seems to me, I made things easier for you. You could've just run to my sister if you were lonely."

"Don't start that again," he grumbled. "I'm sorry about what I did. How many times do I have to say I was wrong? I'm sorry already, okay? I'm sorry!"

"Well, that just fixes everything."

"You don't need to get sarcastic," he said. "I know you're hurt. But you're still my wife."

"For the time being."

"What does that mean?" he asked. "I hurt you, so now you have to hurt me? Is that it? You just have to lash out with vicious threats? You got to threaten me with divorce? You're incapable of discussing this like adults? What happened, Cassandra? Did I marry a child?"

"No. Apparently, *I* made that mistake!"

"Alright," he sighed. "Go on. Lash out. Get it out of your system. The sooner you get over your juvenile little tantrum, the sooner we can try to move past this."

"Don't you dare patronize me, Mark!" she fumed. "Don't even try to condescend to me, you son of a bitch!"

"I only want to talk," he defended. "You're the one who's being unreasonable."

"I'm not the one who cheated!"

"I said I'm sorry," he reminded. "What do you want from me?"

"I want you to be the man I married!"

There was a burdensome pause. Her angry, sobbing voice tore his heart out.

"Listen, honey," he said softly. "Can you please come home so we can talk?"

"I can't," she sniffed. "I have to get ready for my mother's picnic. My friend's lending me some clothes, but I'm already running late. Mom's going to kill me for missing half of the church service. You know how she is."

"Okay," he said. "I'll see you at her place."

"You will?" she asked. "Why are *you* going?"

"It's my family too."

"It is?" she asked. "Oh, that's right. I forgot. My sister will be there!"

"Please don't start," he said. "Look. This could be a great first step. You can see me tell Stephanie face-to-face that it's over and I want to stay with you."

"I don't want to parade your lying and cheating around in front of my family," she said. "I don't want to advertise my sister's treachery."

"Treachery?"

"If you insist on going," she instructed. "I want you to keep your filthy mouth shut. Stay away from me. And definitely stay away from Stephanie!"

"Okay, sweetie," he agreed. "Anything you say."

"I'm still furious with you, Mark," she averred. "Just seeing you at my mother's is going to make me nauseous."

"I understand."

"I have to go and get ready."

"I'll make this up to you, Cassandra," he said. "You may not believe me right now, but I love you."

"I have to go."

There was a familiar silence on the phone. He knew the call was over.

He hung up.

He looked down at his breakfast. He sighed.

After a few moments, he hit the speed dial on the phone again.

"Stephanie?" he muttered. "It's me."

"What's wrong?"

"She knows."

"What?"

"Cassandra," he said. "She knows about us."

There was a pause, followed by, "How?"

"We were arguing about how she spends too much time at her boutique," he explained. "I got mad and it just sort of…came out."

"Oh, thanks a lot, Mark!"

"I'm sorry," he said. "I didn't mean for it to happen."

"I'm going to have to face her at the picnic today!" she complained. "And I guess I'll have to tell Trey before we go. I know my bitch of a sister won't be discreet about discussing this whole thing. Jesus!"

"I'm sorry."

"Well," she sighed. "What's done is done, I suppose. Damn! I knew this was a mistake! You're not going to this thing today, are you? You know what a hot-head Trey is. I don't want Mom's picnic to turn into a free-for-all."

"You're right," he said. "Maybe it's best if I don't show up."

"Alright," she said. "Well, I have to go. Talk to you later."

"Sure."

He hung up. He stared at his breakfast.

Somehow, he just couldn't eat.

* * * * * *

She was on the sofa. He was in the recliner. He could see the hall from where he sat. Every muscle in his body grew tense before he even saw the face in the doorway.

It was almost an instinctive reaction.

Those beautiful blue eyes narrowed as she folded her arms.

"Who's this?" she asked curtly.

"Not even a 'good morning', Krysten?" he asked.

"Not until you answer my question," she said without changing tone. "Who's this, Daniel?"

"Very well," he sighed. "Krysten Salinger, this is Lindsay Bainbridge."

"Hello," Lindsay said. "Nice to me you."

"Lindsay Bainbridge?" she said directly to him, ignoring the girl on the sofa. "Isn't that the woman who dumped you almost a year ago?"

"Well," he stumbled. "Technically, yes."

"So, what's she doing here, Daniel?"

"She just needed a place to stay last night," he explained. "So I just let her crash on the sofa. It's no big deal."

"No big deal?" she asked. "It's no big deal, is it? Are we letting our exes sleep over now and it's no big deal? Is that the story, Daniel? Is it okay if I invite some of my exes to come over and spend the night?"

"I didn't invite her over," he defended. "She needed a place to stay, so she slept on the sofa. Nothing happened. You have no reason to get jealous."

"Jealous?" she said sharply. "I'm not jealous. Why would I possibly be jealous? I love having your exes over to spend the night! We should do this more often!"

"Will you please calm down, Krysten?" he said. "Nothing happened."

"Why does she need to crash here on *your* sofa?" she asked accusingly. "Doesn't she have any of her own friends to impose on?"

"I didn't mean to impose…" Lindsay began.

"It was late," he jumped in to help. "She didn't have many options. She just needed someplace quick and easy…"

"Quick and easy?" she interrupted. "So why should she think that you're quick and easy, Daniel?"

"I didn't mean it like that."

"Then, what did you mean, Daniel?" she continued the attack. "What does all this mean? What did it mean when you said 'technically' she dumped you? Either she dumped you or she didn't!"

"We don't need to get into all this now," he began.

She finally addressed the girl on the sofa. "Listen, honey!" she said. "You're barking up the wrong tree here. Daniel is spoken for. He's mine now. And you're not coming in here and trying to weasel back into his life!"

"I'm not trying…" Lindsay began.

"Face it, sweetheart," she continued. "You screwed up and it's too late. Now Daniel's with someone who won't dump him every time an abusive drunk comes along!"

"How did you…" Lindsay started.

"Were you eavesdropping last night?" he jumped in.

"What 'eavesdropping'?" she argued. "I live here!"

"Still, Krysten…"

"I heard voices in the living room," she continued. "I opened the door a crack and saw some bitch crying and crawling all over my man!"

"She wasn't crawling all over me," he said. "She gave me a friendly hug to thank me for letting her crash on the sofa. Anyway if you were awake, then you know nothing happened. I came to bed right after. I thought you were asleep."

"Well, I certainly was in no mood to talk to you," she snipped.

"Listen, Krysten," Lindsay said. "I know this whole thing is my fault. And I didn't mean to cause any friction between you two. I'm sorry for this whole thing."

"Well, you should be," she announced. "Don't you have any friends of your own?"

"It was late when I called," Lindsay explained. "I was panicking. I didn't know who else to call."

"And an ex-boyfriend that you dumped a year ago is the first name that popped into your head?" she asked accusingly.

"Well, Danny was always so good at..."

Lindsay cut her sentence short.

"Good at what, dear?" she growled. "What was Danny good at?"

There was a heavy pause.

"Taking care of things," Lindsay finally said in a sheepish tone. She was looking at Danny as she spoke.

"And that's why you left him for an abusive drunk," she taunted.

"It wasn't like that!" Lindsay defended.

"Well, that's just too bad!" she declared sharply. "You already made your choices, sweetheart! Danny's not taking care of things for you any more! He has someone who appreciates him now! So why don't you pack up and get out? I don't want to see you around here ever again! And stay away from Danny!"

"Cut it out, Krysten," he said. "There's no reason to get hostile."

"Is that so?" she chided. "Well, just remember that when *my* exes come knocking on the door after midnight!"

"I should just go," Lindsay said. "I'm sorry to you both."

"Will you be okay, Lindsay?" he asked.

"Yeah. I'll be fine."

"And it's not your problem even if she isn't, Daniel!"

Lindsay stood and walked to the door. Danny followed her.

"Run along, little girl!" Krysten called behind her. "Go find somebody else to take care of things for you! Danny's not available anymore!"

When they reached the front door, Danny opened it for his guest. Lindsay turned to face him. She looked into his eyes. She silently mouthed a 'thank you.'

She lingered for a moment. Then, she left.

As Danny closed the door behind her, Krysten shouted a final, "Bitch!"

He spun around.

"What the hell, Krysten!" he scolded. "That was unnecessarily rude!"

"Are you kidding me?"

"It was just a quick emergency," he explained. "Nothing happened and it's over now. You didn't need to go ballistic."

"Don't hand me any of that bullshit!" she argued. "That was no quick emergency! And it certainly isn't over! I saw the way she looked at you!"

"What are you talking about?"

"That look that she just gave you at the door," she expounded. "It's the same look she gave you last night! I know that look! She finally realizes what a fool she was and she wants you back!"

"You're crazy!"

"Am I?" she argued. "Then why did she come here last night, Daniel? She could've gone anywhere last night! Why here? Why go back to someone she hasn't spoken to in over a year?"

"She was desperate."

"I'll say! She sure was!"

"This is ridiculous," he shook his head. "It's all over now. We don't have time for this. We have to get ready to go to my mother's. We're already going to be late for church. Mom isn't going to like that."

"Okay," she said. "But, I'm telling you that Lindsay wants you back."

"Will you please drop it, Krysten?" he insisted. "We have more pressing concerns."

She didn't say a word. She knew he was right. They had more immediate matters to attend. She didn't want to leave a bad impression with his mother on this occasion.

Still, she seethed in private. It was obvious that Lindsay posed a threat that was not going to disappear.

* * * * * *

There were already two squad cars blocking the alley. There were more officers on crowd control than there were investigating the crime scene. Even before you entered the alley, you could see it was a grizzly sight.

The alley was dirty and cluttered with garbage. Trash cans were overturned. Debris was strewn all over.

However, the horrific center of the crime was far enough away from the main road that it was impossible for spectators to make out the details.

Two men crossed over the yellow crime scene tape. They flashed their badges at the first officer they encountered.

"I'm Detective Paczecki," he said. "This is my partner, Detective Grogan. What do we have here?"

"We think it's a prostitute," the officer explained. "That hasn't been confirmed yet. She was sliced up pretty good. It's not a pretty sight. You might want to brace yourselves."

"We're hardly first-timers, Sergeant," he scoffed. "Just lead the way."

There were a few uniformed policemen and experts in suits conducting their duties. Still, they focused on the main attraction as they approached.

"Oh God!" he said while making a face. "That's a thorough job he did!"

"I told you," the officer reminded. "It ain't pretty."

"Oh man!" he observed. "Is that her heart? He just sliced it out and left it there like that? This guy is a psycho!"

"Didn't Jack the Ripper used to do things like that to prostitutes?" Grogan asked.

"Something like that," he said. "I think."

Suddenly, Grogan's eyes grew wide.

"Oh my God!" he gasped. "Angelica!"

The cops turned to look at him.

"You know her?" Paczecki asked.

"Just from the station," Grogan said. "Angelica's her work name. Her real name is Audrey Lindquist. She works the corner of 23rd and Fairdale not too far from here, I think."

"So, she *is* a prostitute, then?" Paczecki asked.

"Oh yeah," Grogan nodded. "She's been bounced in and out of the precinct a number of times."

"You even remember what corner she works?" he asked.

"I think so," Grogan replied. "Like I said, it's not too far from here."

"Leave it to you," he shook his head. "It looks like your depraved sensibilities will save us a lot of legwork on this case."

"Well, she was a nice-looking girl," Grogan said. "And a real sweet kid too."

"Yeah," he grunted. "I'm sure she was quite a little princess. Was she on drugs?"

"Not that I know of," Grogan said. "But I can't say for sure. As I told you, I only know her…"

"From down at the station," he interrupted. "Yes. I know. Do we have a time of death, Sergeant?"

"I think they pinned it down somewhere between 11:30 to 2:00 last night," the officer said.

"Who found the body?"

"An old wino found her about an hour or so ago," the officer said. "They're talking to him over there."

They looked over to where the sergeant was pointing.

"He probably won't have a lot to offer," Paczecki conjectured. "It looks like my most valuable witness in the case of a dead hooker is my own morally bankrupt partner, so far. That's just marvelous."

"Glad to be of service," Grogan smiled.

"There is one more thing," the officer said. "Did you notice the note that was pinned to what's left of her coat?"

"Not yet," he said. He bent down to take a look. "Oh yes. That's actually pinned to her coat. I thought it was just some garbage. There's blood on it. The boy's penmanship could use a little work."

"What's it say?" Grogan asked.

They both looked down at the note. They read:

I crave.
I am the Paradox that is All Mankind.
All sinners must be judged
And suffer the Wrath of God!

"Oh great!" Paczecki grumbled. "A religious fanatic. Just what we need. So this is probably not an isolated argument between hooker and john."

"You didn't really think it was an argument that got out of hand, did you?" Grogan asked. "Not with this brutality."

"I guess not," he said. "I was holding out hope. I suppose I'm just an optimist."

"Well," Grogan said. "I guess we better get started. And the sooner the better. I have a feeling we'll be seeing more of this guy's work before we're done."

"Most likely."

"Stan?" Grogan asked cautiously. "Do you believe in God?"

"Sure," he said as he stood. "I'm Polish. I was raised in a strict Catholic household. How about you?"

"Yeah," Grogan said. "I'm Catholic too. I believe everything I was taught when I was growing up. I know that God doesn't like sin. But God didn't ask for this!"

"I agree."

They looked down at the body.

"Such a shame," Paczecki commented. "You say she was a sweet kid?"

"Yeah. She was."

"Well, we might as well start here checking out the crime scene," he said. "Looks like your familiarity with the local hookers will come in handy."

"I really don't know that many," Grogan reiterated. "But, I'll use my expertise whenever possible."

"That's all I can ask, you pervert."

* * * * * *

"Mom," he said. "You've got quite a crowd here. What happened? I thought this was just supposed to be the usual family picnic."

"Danny!" she beamed. She threw her arms around him. "I'm glad you could make it. You look wonderful!"

As she released her son, she shot a judgmental glance at the girl beside him. "Hello, Krysten," she muttered.

"Hello, Betty," Krysten said with a hint of anxiety. "Thanks for inviting me."

"Well, you *are* my son's live-in girlfriend," she said. "You *are* still living together, aren't you?"

"Don't start, Mom."

"Well, I can't help it, Daniel," she said. "You know how God feels about people who live in sin. I don't want you to spend eternity in Hell. And God knows you need all the help you can get. I noticed you were half an hour late for church today."

"It couldn't be helped," he said. "We had unexpected company."

"Unexpected company?"

"Lindsay stopped over late last night," he explained. "She needed a place to crash. So, I let her sleep on the sofa."

"Lindsay?" she grumbled. "Lindsay Bainbridge? The last girl you were living in sin with? That little tramp? Didn't she throw you over for some hopeless drunk? What was his name? Evan…something?

"Ethan McIntosh," he said.

"Yes, that's it," she nodded. "So, Lindsay's back, eh? Stumbling drunks are losing their appeal, are they? Well, Danny. With two women at your place last night, it must have been quite the den of iniquity over there!"

"Stop it, Mom," he said. "Lindsay just slept on the couch."

"And, it'll never happen again. Will it, Danny?" Krysten added.

"No, dear."

"In fact," Krysten pressed. "He's never even going to talk to her again. Are you, Danny?"

"Let it go, Krysten."

"I just want to make sure we're clear."

"Mom," he said, desperate to change subjects. "I thought this was a family thing. It looks like half the church is here."

"I consider my friends from church to be family," she explained. "I figured, why not invite them to join us in this glorious celebration."

Two young men approached. Both had dark hair. Both were clean-cut, around thirty years old.

"Hello, Mrs. Stark," said the thinner of the two. "Thanks for inviting us. Looks like you've got quite a turn-out."

"Please," she said. "Call me Elizabeth. Actually, Betty to my friends. And you're most welcome. You look so dapper in your new suits."

"Thank you...Betty."

"This is my son Daniel," she introduced. "And his girlfriend Krysten Salinger. This is John Nelson and Jeremy Blackwell. They are regular attendees at my church."

They exchanged greetings.

"You've got quite a spread here," Jeremy spoke up for the first time. "You've done a great job! Congratulations. And thanks. Your husband must be proud."

Betty's smile vanished. "My husband died a few years ago," she said.

"Oh, I'm sorry," Jeremy said.

"It's okay," she said. "He was a lawyer who worked for the district attorney's office. That's how we could afford this big, beautiful house on the edge of town. Unfortunately, my husband made a lot of enemies in his business. The police think they know who shot and killed my husband. One of the many people he put away escaped shortly before my husband's murder. But the police never caught up to the escaped felon. The maniac is still on the loose."

"How dreadful for you," John offered.

"It's okay," she tried to smile. "We may not always understand The Lord's plan, but I know there's a purpose for everything He does. If nothing else, it has brought me closer to Him."

"I know the feeling," Jeremy said. "My father died a year or so ago. He was allergic to seafood. He accidentally ate some and had an extreme reaction. My mother didn't take it well. She moved up to Canada to stay with friends. I don't talk to her much."

"Oh, that's terrible," Betty said. "I'm sorry for your loss, Jeremy. But you should stay in touch with your mother. You're family. Do you have any brothers or sisters?"

"No," he said. "I'm an only child."

"In that case," she continued. "It's even more important that you stay in touch with her. Oh, here comes my youngest, Michael. He's only 21."

"Hi, Mom," Michael said.

"Hi, son," she said. She introduced everyone. "Michael still lives at home with me. He hasn't really found his way yet."

"Come on, Mom," he complained. "This is supposed to be a picnic. Besides, it's not as if I don't have a job."

"Oh yes," she said sarcastically. "That waiter's job will certainly take you far in life."

"It's a start."

"Yes, it's a start," she said. Her sarcasm was relentless. "And he doesn't have a girl at the moment either. Do you, Michael?"

"So, I'm in between girls at the moment," he admitted. "Is that a crime?"

"Don't say 'in between girls' like you're shopping for a car," she instructed.

"It's just an expression, Mom."

"Michael tends to be the 'dark and brooding' sort," she pushed. "Aren't you, son? Girls don't like the dark and brooding sort."

"Will you stop, Mom?" he complained. "Not in front of strangers!"

"Okay," she agreed. "You're right. This is a picnic. Have you seen either of your sisters anywhere around?"

"Stephanie and Trey showed up about ten minutes ago," he said. "I think they're out back. I haven't seen Cassandra yet though."

"Oh, here's Stephanie," she beamed. "Everyone, I'd like you to meet my oldest child, Stephanie and her husband Trey Wagner. Don't they make a handsome couple?"

"They sure do, Mrs. Stark," John said.

Betty introduced everyone. She also bragged a little about Trey's high-paying job.

"It's not that big a deal, Betty," he muttered.

"Of course it is," she smiled. "You and my Stephanie will be in a house that's even bigger than mine by the time you're 30."

"That's only two years away, Mom," Stephanie said.

"Well, I have confidence in you," she said. "Are you two enjoying the picnic?"

"Yes, Mom."

"That's nice, dear," Betty smiled. "And thanks for showing up on time to church."

She shot Danny a judgmental glance.

"That's okay, Mom," Stephanie said.

"There's Cassandra," Michael pointed out. "She's just getting out of her car."

"Wonderful," Betty said. "All of my children are here, finally. Why don't you all go in the back and grab some franks, chicken and burgers?"

Trey looked over at Cassandra. There was a certain sympathy in his tense gaze. Then he said, "I think I will go out back, now that you mention it. I suddenly feel like a burger."

With a bunch of 'thank you's, everyone started rambling toward the back of the house. Only Stephanie stayed with her mother in the front lawn. She nervously watched her sister make her way between a few groups of picnic-goers as she approached.

"Hi, Cassandra," Betty greeted warmly. "So nice of you to come. How are you, dear."

"Just lovely, mother," she muttered with a half-hearted hug. She gave her sister a lingering glare.

"Where's Mark?" Betty asked.

"I doubt he'll be here." Cassandra's voice remained quiet and simmering. "He's... not well."

"Oh dear," Betty frowned. "I hope it's nothing serious."

"We can only hope," Cassandra grumbled. She was still glaring at Stephanie. "Sister dear? Can I have a word in private, please?"

"Ah...sure."

Betty watched with curiosity as her two daughters walked off toward the house.

* * * * * *

"So, where were you last night, Lindsay?"

That look in his eyes frightened her.

"I stayed at a friend's house," she said timidly.

"Which friend?"

"Renee."

"Liar!" he barked. "You weren't with some girlfriend last night! You were with a man! I'm not an idiot! I can tell when you're cheating!"

"I wasn't cheating, Ethan."

"Then where were you…really?"

She tried to be brave. "I told you," she repeated. "I was with Renee."

"You lying piece of shit!" he growled. "Who was it? Did you go crawling back to that last little pisser you were with? What was his name? Danny Stark? Is that what you did?"

"No, Ethan," she persisted. "Even if I wanted to, that would be impossible. He's living with some other girl now."

"Is he?" he asked angrily. "So who was it? Have you been out clubbing again? Did you go home with some stranger like a common whore?"

"No!" she averred with a fresh surge of courage. "And you have no right to talk to me that way!"

"You're my girlfriend!"

"That doesn't make me your property!"

"Yes it does!" he argued. "That's *exactly* what it makes you! You're my bitch, darling! And don't you forget it!"

"See?" she shot back. "This is why I left last night! That shit right there! You act like you think you own me!"

"And if you ever do it again," he warned. "I'm gonna pound you!"

"This has got to stop, Ethan!" she pressed. "Look at you! It's not even noon on a Sunday and you're plastered already!"

"So what if I am?" he challenged. "What business is it of yours?"

"If I'm going to stay with you…"

"There's no 'if' about it!"

"Ethan," she contended. "You didn't used to be like this!"

"You still haven't told me where you went," he spat. He grabbed her purse from where it sat beside her on the couch.

"What are you doing?" she argued as she jumped up from her seat.

He took her cell phone from her purse and opened it.

"Here we go," he grinned. "Let's check your call history to see who you've been talking to."

"You can't do that!" she demanded as she tried to retrieve her phone. "You have no right!"

He shoved her back onto the couch.

"I have every right, sweetheart!" he simmered. "And don't you forget it! As long as you live under my roof… oh, look at that. You deleted your calls. Smart girl! You think you're smart, huh?"

"I'm not going to take this, Ethan," she threatened as tears filled her eyes. "If you don't stop, I'm leaving for good!"

"You're not going anywhere, bitch!" he snarled. "Who else would even have a good for nothing, fat, ugly bitch like you anyway! You're lucky I even keep you around!"

"I'm not fat!" she wept.

"Now make me some fucking lunch," he ordered. "Make yourself useful for a change. I'm hungry."

"Make your own damn lunch!"

He got that look in his eye again. He took one aggressive step toward her.

She leapt off the couch.

She was crying as she ran to the kitchen.

* * * * * *

Outside, it was warm and sunny.

However, it seemed so cold and empty in the big house. There was no sound except the shuffle of her sister's shoes on the carpet as the crossed the desolate living room. She wished her sister would speak as they entered the kitchen.

The knot in her belly grew tighter as she watched her sister silently open the refrigerator and extract a juice box. The silence grew heavier as her sister sat at the table.

It was unbearable. She needed to speak. She needed to hear a voice.

"So you know?"

Her sister just stared at her juice box for an exceeding long ten seconds.

"Why did you do it, Stephanie?"

"I'm so sorry, Cassandra," she said. "I swear I never meant to hurt you."

"You're my big sister, Stephanie," she muttered. "I've always looked up to you."

"I know."

"Dad was never there for us," she reminded. "He was always too busy working. And for the first eighteen years of my life, Mom was either drunk or hopped up on pills. The only way she could sober up was to wrap herself around The Bible. She's been even worse since Dad was killed."

"Listen, Cassandra..."

"We had two younger brothers we had to raise on our own single-handed," she continued. "I was only two years older than Danny. Hell! Michael's still a mess!"

"Please, Cassandra..."

"It was supposed to be you and me against the word, Stephanie," she muttered. "What happened? What the hell happened?"

"Will you please stop staring at your juice box and look at me?" Stephanie asked with tears in her eyes.

"I don't think I can."

"I got married to get the hell out of this house," Stephanie begged. "Trey was supposed to be my golden ticket...my knight in shining armor. He was supposed to answer all my prayers. But he's never home! He's always at work!"

"So you had to sleep with *my* husband?" she shouted.

"It wasn't like that."

"No?" she fumed. "Then, how was it, Stephanie? Tell me how if *your* life is so fucked up, then fucking up *my* life too solves all your problems!"

"It just happened," she explained anxiously. "Mark and I just got together to talk one night because we were lonely. You're always working. So is my husband. We were just talking, comparing our situations. We were lonely. And it just...happened."

"You were lonely?" she mocked. "I have to work all the time! That boutique won't run itself! Do you have any idea how much work is involved in running your own store? It never stops!"

"People need love, Cassandra," Stephanie reasoned. "I need it. You need it. So does Mark. Everybody needs to feel loved."

"So, you had to find it with my husband?"

"I told you," Stephanie repeated. "It just happened."

"'It just happened!'" she scoffed. "That justifies everything, doesn't it? I should just walk away and let you two have each other! You'd be perfect together! The worthless, horny dog and my big sister the whore!"

"Please don't be like that."

"You don't want me to be like that?" she taunted. "Then, what do you want me to do, Steph? You have all the answers! I'm sorry! I don't know what I'm supposed to do when I'm only 26 years old and my whole damned life is crashing down all around me!"

"We can fix this," Stephanie eagerly suggested. "I won't ever see him or touch him again. I promise!"

"You promise?" she ridiculed. "Well, I'm sure I can believe that coming from a slut! After all, you've never given me any reason to think I can't trust you!"

"You can trust me, Cassandra," Stephanie vowed while reaching out to her sister. "It will never happen again."

Cassandra pulled away.

"Don't touch me!"

"Please, Cassandra," she implored. "I'm your sister."

"Sister?" Cassandra growled. "I have no sister!"

"Please don't, Cassandra..."

The younger sister jumped out of her seat.

"You want him," she angrily offered. "You can have him, bitch! I'm through with the both of you!"

She slapped Stephanie hard across the face.

Stephanie sat stunned in her chair. After a moment, Cassandra turned to leave.

Stephanie jumped up and grabbed a handful of her sister's long, brown hair. She threw her onto the kitchen table. She shouted, "Don't you hit me, you tramp!"

The table overturned with a loud crash as they began to hit each other. In no time, they were rolling around on the floor, punching, kicking and yelling.

Another chair hit the linoleum floor in the scuffle.

They were still grappling on the floor a few minutes later when Michael pulled Cassandra off her sister. He held her back on one side of the room.

Danny held Stephanie on the other. They were still shouting obscenities and insults when their mother interceded.

"Girls! Girls!" Betty called until everyone was silent. "Who started this melee?"

"She hit me first!" Stephanie cried.

"You pulled my hair!" Cassandra shot back. "And you almost broke the table when you attacked me from behind like a punk bitch!"

"Now, now," Betty admonished. "There's no need for rude language. Now, what's this all about?"

"Ask your oldest!" Cassandra growled. "Ask her what she's been doing in her spare time!"

Betty looked at Stephanie as only a mother can. "Well, Stephanie?" she asked. "What have you been doing?"

"I already apologized!" she said defensively. "I offered to do anything I could to make it right!"

"What did you do, Stephanie?"

"She slept with Mark!" Cassandra shouted. "That's what she did!"

"Stephanie!" Betty gasped in genuine shock. "Is this true!"

"I told her it was a mistake!" she defended. "I told her it would never happen again! What do you want from me, Cassandra?"

"I want you to not be a whore!"

"It's enough of the filthy language," Betty scolded. "I think it would be best if you two stayed away from each other for a while. Can you both stay at the picnic without ruining everyone's day, or should one of you leave?"

There was an uneasy silence. Danny and Michael finally felt that it was safe to let go of the girls. The crowd who was watching from the door was growing larger.

"If only one of you has to leave," Betty added. "I guess it should be the one who can't seem to keep her hands off of other people's husbands."

"It wasn't like that!" Stephanie declared.

"That's enough," Betty denounced. "We will certainly discuss this later, Stephanie! Perhaps we should spend more time praying together."

"Mom!"

"'Mom' nothing!" Betty insisted. "If you were spending sufficient time in the company of our Lord, things like this wouldn't occur! Now both of you girls pick up the table and chairs and clean up this mess. No more fighting! And by the time you come outside, I expect you will both remember how to behave like ladies. Am I understood?"

"Yes, Mom," came the reluctant chorus of two.

The two brothers joined the sea of judgmental eyes that stared at the disheveled girls. After a few tense moments, the crowd began to disperse.

The motionless girls glared at each other as the onlookers slowly walked away. When most of the people were gone, Stephanie and Cassandra began to silently clean up. They each started by picking up a chair.

The only person who was conspicuously absent from the departing crowd was Trey.

CHAPTER 3

DEBAUCHERY

It was growing dark.

The bleeding stripes of orange, pinks and purples haloed the sun as it slowly sank behind the blackening horizon that was marked by spires, towers and high-rises. Lights sprang to life on the streets and in buildings like stars in the eerie, black sky.

Night life in the city was waking from its daytime hibernation. And a new breed of filth was coming out of hiding. Characters, freaks and all manner of human debris that seemed to vanish during the day were now crawling out of the woodwork like cockroaches. They mingled among the other people. They infested the streets.

Almost like a disease.

An unmarked car pulled up to the corner of 23rd and Fairdale. A scantily clad girl ran up to the passenger's side as the driver shifted into park. The girl wore too much make-up. It showed when she offered that sweet smile.

"Hi, honey," she cooed. "Would you like…"

The sweet smile vanished when she saw two well-dressed men displaying badges.

"Hi, Tanya," the man in the passenger seat said knowingly.

"Oh," she muttered. "Hi, Kyle."

"Can we talk to you girls for a second?" he asked as they got out of the car.

"Hey," she said while backing away. "We weren't doing nothing. We were just waiting for a ride."

"Calm down, Tanya," he said. "You know I'm not Vice. We're not here to ruin your work day."

"So, what's up then?"

The two men stood side-by-side facing the two young women.

"Detective Paczecki?" he introduced. "This is Tanya Alcazar, alias Desiree and Rebecca Heiden, alias Monique."

"Detective?" Rebecca said suspiciously. "This is another cop?"

"Relax, ladies," Paczecki said. "We're homicide detectives."

"Homicide?" Rebecca asked. "What do you want from us?"

"It's Angelica," he explained sympathetically. "I'm sorry, girls. Audrey Lindquist was murdered last night."

"Audrey?" Tanya gasped in shock. "Murdered?"

"It happened last night," he said. "Probably the last guy who picked her up. Do you remember when that was?"

"Yeah," Tanya said. "It was around 11:45, give or take a few minutes."

"Are you sure about the time?" Paczecki asked.

"Sure," she nodded. "I had just gotten back from..."

She paused nervously.

"Well, I checked my watch."

"What was he driving?" he asked.

"A black Cadillac," Rebecca spoke up. "It was a brand new CTS. It was a real nice one too."

"Are you sure about the model?"

"Yup," Rebecca nodded. "I'm a Caddy girl. Plus, in this job, it makes sense to watch for things like that. You know, business potential."

"Yeah, right," he said. "Did you see the guy?"

"No," Tanya said. "We've been on this corner so long, we got a system. It was Audrey's turn."

"So, neither one of you got a look at this guy?"

The girls shook their heads.

"Did you catch the license plate?" he asked.

"Are you serious?" Rebecca said. "Who's gonna be looking at license plates during working hours?"

Tanya just shook her head again.

"Alright," he said. "That's about all. We'll let you get back to...whatever. But be careful. If some whacko is targeting girls in your business..."

"Do you really think we're in danger?" Tanya asked with concern.

"It's too early to tell yet," Paczecki said. "Right now, that should translate to a yes."

"Okay," Tanya said. "Thanks for the warning."

"Good night, girls," he said. "Rebecca? Love the fishnets."

"Thanks."

"Tanya," he continued. "Don't do anything I wouldn't do."

"If I ever had to do something you wouldn't," Tanya smiled with a wink. "I'd have to charge extra."

Paczecki gave a quick wave before getting back into the car.

"Nice to meet you girls. See you around."

"Hope not," Tanya said. "Unless…"

"Well," Paczecki said as he started the car. "That lines up with the time of death. It backs up our suspicion that it was a john who picked her up on this corner. And it even makes that Cadillac with blood on the upholstery we found abandoned across town look like the murder scene."

"I just feel sorry for the guy who reported it stolen," Grogan said. "That car's brand new. Now it's evidence in a murder investigation. He won't be getting it back for a long time."

"Right," he nodded as he drove away from the curb. "This is going to be quite a case if we're going to be chasing around some religious nut who's targeting hookers. There's gotta be a zillion of those girls in this city. We'll never be able to cover them all."

"That's exactly what I'm thinking."

"Don't act like this is some big hardship for you," he said. "Those girls call you Kyle, do they?"

"That *is* my name."

"So is Detective Grogan."

"I promise," Grogan insisted. "I only know those girls…"

"…From the station," he interrupted. "Yeah, I know."

* * * * * *

The weather had been perfect. It was getting dark, but it was staying warm. There were lights on behind the house. The grill was still cooking. The air was still pungent with the pleasing aromas of a barbeque. Pop music played from a makeshift sound system near the back porch.

"So, how are you enjoying your first picnic at my mother's, Krysten?" he asked.

"It's been great, Danny," she smiled. "Your mother's a wonderful hostess. Aside from your sisters' little scuffle in the kitchen, everything went off without a hitch."

"My daughters have always been a bit willful."

"Oh, Betty," she said while turning to address their added company. "I was just telling Danny how much I was enjoying myself. Thank you so much for inviting me."

"You're welcome, dear."

"Seriously, Betty," she added. "Your brother did a terrific job running the grill. All the food is first rate."

"I'll tell him you said so," Betty said. "I'm sure he'll be pleased. He takes great pride in his cooking."

"He has every reason to be proud."

"Thanks," Betty said. "And I noticed you mentioned my daughters little tussle."

"I didn't mean any disrespect, Betty."

"No, no," Betty said. "That's alright. Everyone noticed their embarrassing little display. I can't fault you for that. I do find it distressing to find out the cause of such an altercation. The very thought that such infidelity is happening inside my family is very disturbing to me.

It seems that debauchery is running rampart in the Stark household."

"I wouldn't say that," she offered sympathetically.

Recognizing the look in his mother's eyes, Danny said, "Don't even get started with this, Mom. Krysten has been a gracious guest the whole time she's been here. You owe it to her to give her the same courtesy."

"I can't help it, Danny," Betty said. "Apparently, your father and I were too permissive in your upbringing. You're living in sin. And look at what your sisters are doing to each other."

"None of that can be considered debauchery, mother," he defended. "It's just life. It's just what everyone considers normal life in today's society."

"Yes," Betty nodded slowly. "That's the trouble with the world today."

Danny excused himself when he heard his cell phone ring. He stepped away to get some privacy as he answered. "Hello."

"Danny," she sniffed. "It's me."

"Lindsay?" he whispered so as not to be heard. "Is that you? Are you crying?"

"Yes," she said. "I finally did it. I left him."

"Well, that's great," he said. "Good for you. What happened?"

"He started again at lunchtime," she said. "Interrogating me about where I was last night. Accusing me of cheating. Threatening me, insulting me. He was drunk, of course. I told him I'd leave. He forced me to make his lunch. While he was eating, I snuck out the back."

"Well, congratulations."

"I'm scared, Danny," she said. "He's probably looking for me already. I'm sure he's furious. I don't know what to do."

"Yeah, well…good luck with that."

"I need to see you, Danny."

"What? Are you kidding me?"

"I just need to talk," she explained desperately. "I need to see a friendly face, or hear a sympathetic voice."

"Are you insane?" he asked. "You saw how Krysten reacted to seeing you this morning. What am I supposed to say to her?"

"I don't care," she said. "Make something up."

"No, Lindsay," he insisted. "This isn't my problem. You left me to be with that piece of shit. Deal with it yourself."

"Don't do this to me, Danny," she said, clearly on the verge of tears. "I know you're at your mother's. If you don't come out to see me, I'll go over there."

"Don't even think about it!"

"I'll do it, Danny," she threatened. "I promise I will."

"Don't, Lindsay," he averred. "We already had too much drama here today."

"Drama? What drama?"

"My sisters…" he began. "Never mind. Just don't come here!"

"Then, meet me at Chiffon's."

"Chiffon's?" he asked. "You chose that restaurant on purpose."

"Just meet me here. Please?"

"No, Lindsay!" he demanded. "Krysten's already furious!"

"Then I'll be over in twenty minutes."

"Krysten will kill the both of us!"

"I don't care," she wept. "She doesn't scare me. Not after what I've been through with Ethan. If you're not here in twenty minutes, I'm going over there."

"Damn it, Lindsay..."

"I mean it, Danny," she said. "Here or there, you're going to talk to me. Please?"

His mind was racing as she repeated her 'please' a few times.

"Alright!" he finally gave in with an angry sigh. "I'll be there in twenty minutes. But we're just going to talk."

"Thank you, sweetie," she said. "I love you."

"Yeah, right."

He hung up and went back to where his mother and Krysten were talking to a few people.

"I have to leave for a few minutes," he informed them. "I'll be right back."

"Where are we going?" Krysten asked.

"I'm going alone," he said. "But, I'll be back within the hour."

"Alone?" Krysten asked suspiciously. "What's going on? It's Lindsay again, isn't it?"

"No," he lied. "I just have to talk to a friend. I'll be right back."

"If you're seeing a friend," she inquired. "Why can't I go with you?"

"It would bore you silly," he said. "You're doing fine here. Just stay here 'til I get back. It'll only be an hour."

"It's Lindsay!" she growled. "I know it is! What's going on with her, Danny!"

"Nothing!" he said. "I don't have time for this. I've got to go. I'll be back. You two girls behave yourselves. And don't give me that look, mother. No more talk about debauchery. There is no debauchery going on with any of your kids. 'Bye."

He kissed Krysten. Then, he turned to rush off to his car.

"It better not be Lindsay!" Krysten called behind him. "If it is, I'll find out! I'll kill the both of you, Daniel! I swear!"

* * * * * *

The room was abuzz with activity. The desk sergeant had his hands full with aggravated citizens. Two or three officers were processing alleged offenders. Phones were ringing. Everyone was in a hurry.

Back in the Detectives Department, Paczecki sat at his desk. He frowned as he looked up from his paperwork.

"Hey, Kyle," he grumbled. "Any news on that autopsy?"

"Not much," Grogan said. "They found some skin and blood under her fingernails. It looks like she scratched the guy. He's A Positive."

"That's a common blood type," he said. "Not much to go on."

"Yeah," Grogan added. "No fresh prints in the Cadillac. Looks like he was wearing gloves."

"Oh, great," he said. "A careful maniac. This isn't going to be easy."

"Right," Grogan said. "We're not going to have much to work with before he strikes again."

"And did you see the headlines?" he asked while throwing a newspaper on the desk.

Grogan read:

'PARADOX' KILLER ON THE LOOSE!
CITY GRIPPED IN FEAR

"How did the press find out about the note?" he barked. "They quoted the whole note in here! We were trying to keep that bit out of the papers for now! They're really playing up the 'religious nut' angle."

"Just what we need!"

"Yeah," he scoffed. "Public panic…the religious community up in arms, getting all defensive…this case is going to be quite a circus before we're done."

"And a definite media frenzy."

"And without much to go on," he added. "We're going to look like the clowns."

"It certainly doesn't look good for us," Grogan agreed. "What kind of society are we living in when a prostitute can't even feel safe on her own street corner?"

"Don't be an ass," he grunted. "Just help me catch this scumbag."

"Don't worry, Stan," Grogan said. "I'm with you. Together, we're going to nab that goofball, even if we have to stake out every call girl in town."

* * * * * *

She still looked wonderful as she sat across from him in the booth.

"Are you going to order something to eat, Danny?" she asked.

"Of course not," he said. "I've been eating all day at my mother's."

"Well, how about something to drink?"

"No, just this coffee is fine," he said. "As much as I'd love something stronger, I can't right now. I still have to go back and face everybody. Now, what's this all about, Lindsay? I've been here for fifteen minutes, and all you've done is babble."

"I need to figure out what I'm going to do," she said. "Where am I going to go? Ethan is going to completely freak out on me."

"That's not my problem."

"Please, Danny," she begged. "You're the only person I can count on."

"Not any more."

"Please, Danny," she sniffed. "I need you!"

"No!" he insisted. "Don't start blubbering on me. It's not going to work. I'm with Krysten right now, and I like it like that."

"Alright," she sighed. "You want me to admit it? Fine! We both know why I called you here. I might as well confess. Sure, I have nowhere else to go. But I would've called you anyway. Danny? I was a fool to let you go. It was the stupidest, most unbelievably dumb asshole thing I've ever done! I know I deserve whatever happens to me. I know I don't deserve you. But, please take me back! Please?"

"Are you kidding me with this?"

"No, Danny," she begged. "Please! I'm dead serious! I've never been more serious in my life! I love you, Danny

Stark! I love you very much! I am so sorry for what I've done to you. Please forgive me! And please take me back!"

"And what am I supposed to tell Krysten?"

"Tell her whatever you like," she said. "I don't care! Just please take me back! I was wrong! It was all my fault! I'll do whatever it takes to make it up to you. Just give me a chance!"

"No, Lindsay," he muttered. "In fact, I gotta go."

"No, Danny!" she implored. "Please! You have to at least discuss this with me!"

"No I don't."

"You can't tell me you don't still feel something," she pleaded. "We were living together for over two years! We had something special, Danny! You know we did!"

"No, Lindsay," he shook his head. "If we'd ever had something special, you wouldn't have dumped me for a bumbling, asshole drunk like Ethan McIntosh."

"I made a mistake, Danny!" she persisted with tears in her eyes. "I'm only human! Aren't I entitled to make one lousy mistake? I love you!"

"I love Krysten," he said. "Sorry, Lindsay. You made your bed, now lie in it. Go back to drunk-boy, go to a homeless shelter or a battered women's shelter, sleep on the street…I don't care. You made your choices and I've moved on. Good-bye and good luck, sweetheart. I'm done."

He stood.

She jumped up from behind the booth. She quickly wrapped her arms tightly around him and trapped him in a long, smoldering kiss.

He was trapped…almost. He remembered this feeling…this connection to this beautiful, sweet girl. It seemed so long since…

The break had hurt so deeply…

He let it go longer than he should have.

Finally, he pulled away.

"That's enough, Lindsay!"

"I knew it," she beamed. "You weren't fighting it, Danny! You remember! You still feel something! I could tell!"

"No, Lindsay!" he declared. "Go away and don't call me again. Good-bye!"

He turned to leave. He threw some money on the table for the coffee he barely touched. Then, he marched hastily toward the front door.

She didn't move. She called after him, "I love you, Danny Stark! And I know you still feel something too! I could tell in your kiss! I'm going to get you back, Danny! You know we belong together! You'll be thinking of me! You'll think of me every time you touch her! I know you will…"

Her voice grew smaller and smaller as he hurried toward his escape. Her voice finally disappeared when he left Chiffon's.

Still, he knew she wasn't really gone.

* * * * * *

"You still make the best coffee, sweetie," he said. "You're a marvel."

"Thank you."

He put the cup on the table. He leaned back in the big, soft sofa and put his arm around her.

"Did you have a nice time tonight, Marissa?"

"Everything was wonderful, Joe," she smiled. "Thanks for everything."

She nearly turned away.

"What's the matter?" he asked with genuine concern.

"It's just all a bit too much," she said. "I'm not used to this. The attention, this apartment, the job…this bracelet is just too expensive. Those diamond chips…it must have cost a fortune!"

"Don't worry about it, sweetheart," he assured her. "You're worth every penny. You deserve everything I've done for you…and more."

"But, I don't," she insisted in that way that made her look so adorable. "I'm nothing special. I'm just Marissa Cosgrove, a simple college girl from Fulton. I don't deserve any of the special attention you've given me."

"But you do," he persuaded. "And don't say you're 'just Marissa Cosgrove'. You're not 'just anything'. You're a beautiful, intelligent girl with a bright and brilliant future ahead of you. What does it matter if I give you a little boost to begin with? Do you think I was always Joe Zanella, the senator poised in a position where I practically run the entire state? I started out as just Joe Zanella, the poor college kid. I had to work a lifetime to get where I am. And I didn't have someone 'like me' to help me along."

"I know, but…"

"No buts," he said. "You've got a brilliant career ahead of you. And there's nothing wrong with accepting a little bit of help from someone who loves you."

"A little bit of help is fine, but…"

"What did I say?" he reminded softly. "No buts. Everything's decided."

He kissed her.

"Are you staying here tonight?" she asked.

"If it's alright with you."

She was silent for a moment.

"What does your wife say when you're gone all night?" she asked. "Doesn't she miss you?"

"She knows I'm a busy man," he said. "She knows we just passed a tentative budget, with plenty of work still to do. She knows what this time of year is like for me."

"But, it's Sunday night on the Memorial Day weekend," she said. "The senate's not in session this weekend. Doesn't she expect you home?"

"Even if the senate takes a break in the session," he explained. "There are still meetings, committees, etc. There's plenty to keep me busy. You know that, and so does she. Don't worry. There's no problem."

"You're sure?"

"Absolutely."

She smiled. They kissed.

"Believe me, Marissa," he said. "You have nothing to worry about."

"I still feel a bit overwhelmed sometimes," she said. "I mean, this bracelet alone…"

"Ssshhh," he whispered. "It's nothing. Nothing to worry about. Everything is completely taken care of."

This kiss was longer and more reassuring.

"Still, you're my boss."

"Not here," he gently corrected. "In this apartment, I'm not your boss. And you're not my employee. Or my intern. Or whatever. Here, you are simply…my Marissa."

She could see it in his eyes. The compassion. The commitment. The longing and the confidence.

The paternal assurance that she needed. The assurance that would last forever.

Or at least until the morning.

And the kiss was the promise, like a signature in blood. A promise from the heart.

The kiss heated as their combined pulse quickened.

And he lifted her in his arms. He carried her to the bedroom.

And he stretched her out in that place where he would deliver the promise she so desperately needed him to keep.

* * * * * *

Everything seemed a little hazy. Everything felt a bit surreal.

He found himself walking down a long, brightly lit hallway. The walls were white, bleak, cold and clinical. The floor, the ceiling…everything was white.

He could here the stoic echo of his footsteps as he slowly trod over the shiny, clean linoleum floor. One footstep, then the next, as he made his way toward the stark, uninviting elevator at the end of the hall.

It was hot under those lights. He felt a few beads of sweat run down his face.

Still, he didn't know where he was…or why he was here.

He was still forty feet from the elevator when the bell sounded. The door opened with a loud clanging noise. It seemed dark inside. It was as if there was no elevator in the open shaft.

Still, a young woman emerged from the darkness. She stood before him in all her quiet glory. She looked just as she had appeared when he left her in the alley.

"You!" he gasped in shock. "It can't be! You're… you're…"

"My name is Angelica," she said.

"You're that whore from last night!"

"I came to talk to you," she said simply.

Her clothes were torn, sliced and dirty. Blood still lined the gashes where he had slashed her with the knife. There was no life in those once-beautiful blue eyes.

"I have nothing to say to you!" he declared frightfully. "You're, you're dead! I did God's work! I removed your sins from His earth!"

"But, God sent me to talk to you, lover."

"Don't you dare blaspheme in my presence!" he scolded. "God did not send a prostitute to speak on his behalf!"

"God is in all children," she reminded. "Is that not true?"

"Don't try to confuse me with your double-talk," he scolded. "Don't try to trick me by misrepresenting God's will!"

"You didn't kill me because of God," she softly corrected. "He knows that. You killed me because you wanted me! You killed me because you could not come to terms with your own lust!"

"Shut your filthy mouth, you foul temptress!"

"You can not fool God," she continued. "One sin can not mask another sin!"

"Shut your filthy mouth!"

"Don't listen to her, son," said the man who stepped out of the darkness. "You can kill whomever you want to kill. As long as you do it in His name. He doesn't mind."

"Dad!" he gasped. "You're with her?"

He pointed a shaky finger at Angelica.

"I took the elevator as it was going up," Dad told him.

"I took the elevator as it was going down," she said. "I'm coming from above."

Dad's eyes grew dark as he said, "And I'm coming from below!"

"No!" he screamed. "You're both trying to trick me! I can believe that Dad came from Hell! You were always a wretched sinner! But you can not tell me that God would ever speak through a common hooker!"

"You did not kill me in the name of God," she reiterated. "He knows that, you sinner. You wanted me! You still do."

"Don't you talk to me about sin!" he warned. "Don't..."

"God is in everyone, lover boy," she spoke gently.

"Don't listen to her, son," Dad disagreed. "God wants you to kill the wicked."

"You're in this together!" he stammered as he backed away. "You're both trying to confuse me!"

"You shouldn't have killed me," she said sweetly. "I only wanted to give you my heart."

She reached into the deep slash in her chest. She pulled out her heart. She held the pulsating organ out to him as blood dripped down between her fingers.

"Here it is," she offered. "Take it. It's yours."

"Take her heart, son."

"No!" he screamed.

"Take it, sweetie. I want you to have it."

Blood streamed out of the pulsing heart. Blood dripped and poured between her fingers and left red puddles on the linoleum floor.

"No!" he shrieked. "Leave me alone! No-o-o!"

He was still screaming when he woke up.

He was sweating. His breathing was heavy and labored. The room was dark. It took a few seconds to recognize his own bedroom.

It was empty. It was quiet. Everything around him was as still as death.

CHAPTER 4

EMOTIONAL DECAY

He could see the city from his kitchen window. It appeared to be a beautiful morning so far. A big, bold sun was erasing the darkness from the urban skyline. Perky clouds rolled past like commuters in lanes of bright blue sky traffic.

The kitchen was alive with sizzling pans on the stove. The air was fresh with aromas of bacon, eggs and toast.

He was enjoying this morning task. Cooking was something he didn't get around to as often as he used to. He missed it.

"Smells great."

He looked over toward the source of the voice. She was standing in the doorway. All she wore was an oversized football jersey that went down to her knees.

"I thought I'd do the cooking for a change," he said.

"Guilt breakfast?"

"What does that mean?"

"It means," she said. "Are you just making breakfast because you feel guilty about last night?"

"What are you talking about?" he asked. "Why should I feel guilty about last night?"

"Are you forgetting about your little pilgrimage to go see Lindsay?" she asked as she took a seat at the table.

"Not this again!"

"You haven't even had the decency to admit it yet, Danny," she said. "A relationship is supposed to be based on trust. If you want me to think I can trust you..."

"Jesus, Krysten," he interrupted. "It's Memorial Day Monday. We both have a free day off, and I was hoping we could go out and do something together. I just wanted to do something nice. I started off by making breakfast for my girl. And you can't even come into the room without starting a big ordeal."

"I'm not the one who went running off to see my ex yesterday, Danny," she said. "I'm the one who actually wants this relationship to work."

"Alright! Alright!" he said. "I admit it. It was Lindsay who called last night. Just spare me the 'relationship' speech, will you?"

"I knew it!"

"Oh, don't get all riled up," he said. "Nothing happened."

"So, if nothing happened," she inquired. "Why didn't you just tell me the truth last night?"

"Because I didn't want to go through this bullshit argument," he said.

"What's bullshit about it?" she asked. "I don't have the right to be mad about your ex trying to get between us?"

"Hey," he defended. "I'm an innocent bystander here. I didn't start any of this. I didn't offer her a place to stay the other night. And I didn't tell her to call me yesterday."

"But you *did* let her stay here the other night," she reminded. "And you *did* go to talk to her yesterday."

"She threatened to come to my mother's and ruin the picnic if I didn't talk to her," he explained.

"What did she want?"

"That reminds me," he said. "You never told me what you thought of the picnic. Aside from all the extra church people and my sisters brawling over stolen husbands, I thought it went rather well. Didn't you?"

"Don't change the subject," she said. "What did Lindsay want?"

He got all quiet. He scraped some eggs from the pan onto a plate for her. She waited for him to add a few strips of bacon before she continued.

She watched him busy himself at the coffee pot. She sensed there was a problem.

"Daniel?" she asked in that judgmental tone he hated. "What did she want?"

"She wants to get back together."

"I knew it!" she quietly seethed. "That little bitch! I should have killed her when I had the chance!"

"Don't worry about it," he assured her. "I told her I'm happy with you. I told her to get lost."

"I could see it in her eyes the other morning!" she grumbled. "I knew she was up to no good!"

"I told you, don't worry about it."

"What exactly did she say?"

"She said that leaving me was the dumbest thing she'd ever done," he informed her. "She still loves me and she wants to get back together."

He sat at the table with his plate of food. But that look in her eyes scared him.

"That little whore!" she fumed. "And what did you say?"

"I told you," he reminded. "I told her that I love you. I told her to get lost."

"Is that what you said?" she pressed. "Tell me. What were your exact words?"

"Oh, for God's sake, Krysten," he complained. "See? This is why I didn't want to tell you about her last night. What do you want from me? I didn't tell her to start this shit. She said she wants to get back together, and I told her to go away. Don't make a federal case out of it."

"And what did she say when you told her to get lost?" she continued.

"She didn't take it well."

"That's it!" she growled. "I'm going to kill her! I'm going to hunt her down like a dog! I'm going to tear her heart out! But first, I'm going to rip each and every bleach-blonde hair out of her big, fat head!"

"Calm down," he said. "She's just upset about her scumbag boyfriend. She'll get over it. You have nothing to worry about, Krysten. I love you."

"If she tries to contact you again," she said. "I want to know about it. Do you hear me, Daniel? I want to hear about it the moment that bitch calls!"

"Come back down to Earth, Krysten," he said. "Join the rest of us. I'm telling you. You've got nothing to worry about."

"I know I've got nothing to worry about," she warned. "Because if that skank Lindsay Bainbridge goes anywhere near my man again, it'll be the last thing she does in this lifetime!"

"Krysten…"

"I mean it, Danny," she insisted. "I'll kill her!"

* * * * * *

"Dr. Edmund Thorndyke?" he introduced. "Have you met my partner, detective Kyle Grogan?"

"Yes," the doctor nodded with a smile. "I believe we met once or twice before. How are you, Detective Grogan?"

"Just fine, Doctor," Grogan said. "Thank you for seeing us so early on a Monday morning. Especially on a holiday."

"Not at all," Thorndyke said. "It's no bother. It's all part of the job. And I realize this is a very crucial case."

"That's true, Doctor," he said. "And time is of the essence. We need to get a profile on the killer. He didn't leave a lot of evidence to work with. And my gut feeling tells me we haven't heard the last of this scumbag yet."

"That seems quite likely under the circumstances," Thorndyke agreed. "I've had a look at the case file. And it would appear that we are dealing with a very disturbed young man."

"You think he's young, Doctor?"

"Twenties or thirties probably," Thorndyke surmised. "Deep psychoses. He was most definitely traumatized as a child. Probably abused, extensively over a period of time. His religious affiliations were probably thrust on him by parents, maybe even his abuser. Parent and abuser may be the same person. And his psyche most likely developed by wrapping itself around his beliefs probably because it was all he knew while growing up, coupled with his needing these beliefs as a form of emotional protection."

"So, this guy's a real whack job, huh?" Grogan asked.

"Do you even doubt it?" Thorndyke replied. "Something set this guy off. Seeing that hooker, wanting her, being forced to deal with the conflict of confronting his desires, his opposing beliefs and coming to grips with the traumas in his past, which he still hasn't come to terms with."

"Sounds like a case of severe…" he searched for the right term. "Emotional decay."

"An interesting deduction, Detective Paczecki," Thorndyke said. "But emotional decay may not be the appropriate definition. It's more a lack of proper emotional development connected with violent tendencies caused by severe physical distress. People learn what they are taught. He learned violence, so he uses violence to deal with inner conflict. He knows what he learned. And he learned what he was taught."

"Violence in conjunction with religion," he said.

"Precisely, Detective Paczecki."

"So, you think he'll kill again?"

"I'm almost certain of it," Thorndyke said. "Of course, this is mere speculation at this point. But this doesn't look like it will be an isolated incident."

"More hookers?" Grogan asked.

"It's a bit early to tell what sets him off," the doctor said. "He may be on some crusade to rid the city of hookers. If he is, then he's even more screwed up than I gave him credit for. I have a feeling that he'll just react to personal stimuli...you know, just what he runs into in his daily life."

"Are you sure, Doctor?"

"As I said," Thorndyke reiterated. "With only one victim, it's impossible to know his motivations. He may well be on a crusade to kill hookers or sinners or whatever. We can't get a definitive profile on this guy 'til he develops a pattern. But we are dealing with a man whose 'emotional decay' as you put it...is in an advanced stage."

"So, how do we find this guy?"

"Churches, cults..." Thorndyke shrugged. "Any place with heavy religious activity."

"I'd rather stake out hookers," Grogan grinned.

"You would," he grumbled.

"It's not such a bad idea," the doctor said. "As I told you before, we don't know for sure what his intentions are. Hookers are all we have to go on so far. Even if you run into this guy in some cult, he's not likely to just come right out and say he's a murderer."

"What you're saying is," he deduced. "We pretty much have to sit and wait."

"He's bound to get sloppy eventually," the doctor said.

"I don't like sitting and waiting for killers," he grunted.

"There is one thing," Thorndyke suggested. "He may have been tempted by that girl before. Maybe he was a repeat customer, or maybe he'd seen her before."

"Maybe we should talk to Desiree and Monique again," Grogan said.

"Yeah, you'd like that," he said. "Should we go back to the street corner, or should we wait 'til the next time they get hauled in?"

"We don't really know when they'll get hauled in next," Grogan reminded.

"Leave it to you to think of that," he shook his head. "When it comes to prostitutes, your logic is impeccable."

"Just doing my job," Grogan said. "And remember, time is of the essence."

"Yes, of course," he said. "Thank you, Doctor. I'm sure we'll be speaking again."

"Anytime, gentlemen."

"Well, I'm guessing your friends only come out at night, Kyle," he said. "Will you be able to keep it in your holster 'til then?"

"I'll do my best," Grogan said.

"You do that," he said. "In the meantime, let's go check out that alley again. I'm not the kind of guy who likes to sit and wait."

"Sounds fine to me."

* * * * * *

"Cassandra?" he whispered. "Is that you?"

Even though he was being quiet, you could almost hear an echo.

"Michael?" she whispered back. "What are you doing here?"

"I don't really know."

"I never thought you were religious," she whispered. "What are you doing in church on a Memorial Day Monday?"

"I'm not very religious," he said. "I don't really know why I came here. I guess I just wanted to get away from Mom. I guess she rubs off on you with all her 'holier than thou' crap. I just needed to go somewhere quiet to think."

"Me too," she whispered. "This seems as good a place as any. I've got things I need to sort out. I've even considered talking to a priest."

"I guess you've had a rough week, huh?"

"Yeah," she nodded. "The whole thought of Mark sleeping with my sister kind of threw me for a loop. He swears it's over. But how can I believe him?"

"I see what you mean."

"And how can I ever trust Stephanie again?" she whispered. "I used to practically idolize her. Now I can hardly stand to look at her."

"You'll just have to work through it, I suppose," he whispered. "Is that why you're here?"

"Kind of," she said. "I don't even know if it's a matter of asking for God's advice. I just want to figure out if I should divorce Mark. Divorce is supposed to be wrong. But how am I going to stay with a man I can't trust? And why should I? How could God want that for me?"

"I know it's difficult to figure out what the grand plan is supposed to be," he agreed.

"Oh God, Michael," she gasped. "How did you get those scratches on your arm?"

"Oh," he stammered. "I got those working on my car the other day."

"You should get those looked at," she advised. "They seem nasty."

"Don't worry about it," he whispered. "They'll be fine."

"You know, Michael," she whispered. "You never told me why you came here today."

"Who knows?" he shrugged. "Maybe it was just to help you, Cassandra. I know you don't really want a divorce. Maybe you should at least talk to Stephanie first. I'll bet she feels terrible."

"I tried talking to her yesterday," she whispered. "You saw how that turned out."

"The wound was still fresh," he imparted. "You just found out what happened. You were still angry. Now you've had a day to let it sink in and absorb it. Maybe you can talk now instead of fight."

"Do you really think so?"

"Stephanie's our sister," he whispered. "She loves you. She would never do anything to intentionally hurt you."

"But she slept with my husband."

"I can't speak for her," he said. "Only she can explain what happened."

"What about Mark?"

"I won't even begin to try to justify his behavior," he replied. "If you don't want a divorce, you have to talk it out with them. I know Steph is a good sister. You shouldn't make any rash decisions 'til you at least talk to her one-on-one."

"I guess it couldn't hurt to try," she whispered. "Thanks, Michael. You're a good baby brother."

"I do my best."

She looked down at his arm.

"You know, you really should do something about those scratches," she reiterated. "And I wish you'd get rid of that old rust bucket. You can afford a better car. After all, you're still living at home."

"I'm saving up my money so I can move out," he said. "Living with Mom is driving me up the wall."

"I can see that."

There was a brief, uncomfortable pause.

"You know, Michael?" she smiled. "You really made me feel a little better. God! Talking to you was better than talking to a priest."

"And I didn't even wear my collar."

She giggled. She kissed her brother on the cheek.

"Thanks again, Michael," she said. "I will try talking to Stephanie again."

"I'm glad."

"I'm still not sure it'll work," she said. "She and Mark hurt me pretty bad. Still, it's a start."

"You have to start somewhere, sis."

"That's right," she said. "You really do."

She got up and marched confidently up the aisle to the front door of the church. He watched her go.

For a moment, it felt good to have helped someone.

For a moment, it felt satisfying. It almost made him feel holy.

* * * * * *

She rolled her eyes when she saw the name of the caller on her cell phone. She didn't want to take the call. She sighed with resignation.

"Hello?" she answered.

"Lindsay!" said the caller. "Where the hell are you?"

"I'm not going to tell you, Ethan," she said. "I'm done with this whole mess. We're through."

"We're not through until I say we're through," he grumbled. "Now get your worthless little ass home where you belong."

"It doesn't work that way, Ethan," she said. "You don't get to order me around. I told you we're through. Now don't call me again. Good-bye."

"Are you kidding me with this shit?" he growled with growing impatience. "I'm not fucking around, bitch! Come home *now*!"

"What part of 'we're through' isn't getting through to you?" she asked with her own sense of impatience. "I don't have to go anywhere just because you say. I'm done with you, Ethan. Now leave me alone!"

"Don't make me hunt you down, bitch!" he warned. "If I have to go looking for you, you're gonna be one sorry little tramp!"

"You don't get to talk to me that way, Ethan," she insisted. "This attitude of yours is exactly why I'm leaving you. I'm done! Now good-bye and leave me alone!"

"Lindsay…!"

She hung up. She instantly turned her ringer off.

"That was him?"

"Yes," Lindsay nodded with a sigh. "He's not taking this well. I'm worried."

"You have to be strong, Lindsay," she advised. "You have to stick to your guns and stay away from him."

"I know," she sighed. "I guess I'll have to get my cell phone number changed. And I won't be able to go to any of the places that he knows. And I really need to find a place to stay until I get things sorted out."

"It's okay, honey," she assured her. "You can stay here for a couple of days if you need to."

"Thanks, Vicky," she smiled. "You're the best."

"I'm happy to help, dear," Vicky said. "No girl should have to put up with that."

"I'm just hoping Ethan doesn't remember you," she said. "I don't want him harassing you. I think he only met you a few times. Hopefully, he's a drunk enough mess that he doesn't remember."

"That's a pleasant thought," Vicky said sarcastically.

"Well, I'm just thinking of you."

"Would you like some more coffee?"

"I don't want to impose."

"Nonsense," Vicky said. "You're not imposing. Here. Have another cup."

"Thanks," she said as she watched her friend pour.

"So, what are your plans?"

"Well," she replied thoughtfully. "To tell the truth, I was thinking of getting back together with Danny."

"Danny Stark?"

"Yes," she said. "Danny's the best thing that ever happened to me. I was an idiot to leave him for Ethan. But, at least my time with Ethan made me realize how much I really love Danny. And I really do, Vicky. I still love Danny very much."

"I thought Danny was living with somebody now."

"Yeah," she sighed. "Some homely little slut named Krysten Salinger. I'm not worried about her. Her hair is atrocious...a flat and stringy, shit-brown mess. And she's got no dress sense. You should see the outfit she was wearing. And all she does is bitch at him. She doesn't worry me. I can get Danny back from her. I just know it!"

"What makes you so sure?"

"I saw him at Chiffon's last night," she said. "I got him to meet me there. We kissed."

"You kissed Danny last night?" Vicky gasped.

"Yup," she nodded with confidence. "That's how I know I can get him back. I could tell in our kiss. He still has feelings for me."

"Really? That's great, Lindsay!"

"Thanks," she smiled. "Believe me. Getting Danny back won't be any trouble at all."

"How did you get Danny to meet you at Chiffon's?"

"That's not important," she said. "What's important is that I'm going to get him back."

"You're still going to have a difficult time getting Ethan to go away," Vicky said. "He's not going to disappear so easily."

Lindsay's smile vanished.

"You're right about that," she agreed. "He's going to be a problem."

"But you really think you have a shot at getting back with Danny?" Vicky asked.

"Absolutely."

"Don't you feel bad about trying to break up a couple?" Vicky asked.

"No," she averred. "He was mine first! Krysten is the home wrecker, not me! Besides, I love Danny more than she ever could!"

"Lindsay? Are you sure about this?"

"Of course I am," she grinned. "That kiss told the whole story. This will be no problem at all. And if Krysten decides to get in my way, then I'll just have to remove her from the picture myself!"

* * * * * *

"I don't feel comfortable being here," he said.

"Relax, Mark," she said. "Trey left for the day. I'm not expecting him home 'til dinnertime."

"Are you sure?"

"That's what he told me," she said. "He's running some personal errands. I asked if he wanted me to go with him. He told me he still can't face me yet. I think our news hit him real hard. He's still considering divorce."

"That's all the more reason why I shouldn't be here," he said. "Cassandra's talking the same crap. I don't know what to do."

"I don't want a divorce, Mark."

"Neither do I."

"So, what do we do?" she asked. "I love my husband. I want to save my marriage. I want…I don't know what I want."

"I know, Stephanie," he nodded. "I never expected anything like this to happen. It's just so unlike me. The way Cassandra and your mother look at me now. It's like I've been branded. I never thought I'd wear the label 'Mark Genovese: adulterer.'"

"I have the same feeling," she agreed. "'Stephanie Wagner: adulterer'. It's just not a label I feel comfortable with."

"You know, we've only made love a few times," he reminded. "I know we have to stop. It's the right thing to do."

"You're right."

"I guess I could live without seeing you," he said. "And touching you."

"Don't, Mark," she said. She pulled away as he touched her arm.

"Right!" he said as he pulled back. "I'm sorry. I have to be good."

"Mark," she scolded. "I invited you over to my place so we could discuss how to save both of our marriages. If you have anything else in mind…"

"No," he shook his head. He leaned back on the sofa. "You're absolutely right. I do love my wife."

"We have to be firm, Mark," she instructed. She was still sitting upright beside him. "We have to resolve not to see each other anymore."

"Of course."

"I'll admit," she said. "It won't be easy for either of us."

"It certainly won't," he agreed. "Even though it hasn't been long, I have developed genuine feelings for you, Stephanie."

She sighed without a word.

"I know it's inconvenient," he said. "But I can't just turn my emotions off."

"Please don't start, Mark."

He sat up again. "But it's true."

This time she didn't pull away when he touched her. She glanced down at her lap.

"I know," she said. "I sort of feel…but we can't!"

He touched her face. She couldn't help looking into his eyes.

"You're a beautiful, exciting woman, Stephanie," he said. "Our short time together has only confirmed what I felt when we first started getting close."

"I knew it was a mistake to invite you here."

He kissed her. She let the kiss linger. She allowed herself to feel.

"Was that a mistake too, Stephanie?"

She didn't reply.

After a few silent moments, he kissed her again.

She let herself feel again. So she finally pulled away.

"Maybe you should leave, Mark."

"That's not what you really want."

"I don't know what I really want," she said shakily. "But this isn't going to solve anything."

"Are you so sure?"

"You were just talking about Cassandra," she reminded. "How can you even think of doing this to her?"

"Because you're here."

"She's my sister, Mark!"

"And she's my wife."

"We have to be strong."

"That's easier said than done."

"We have to at least try," she advised. "We have to do it for ourselves. We have to do it to save our marriages."

"I don't want to lose my wife," he admitted. "But, losing you would kill me. And while I'm sitting here with you…"

"You really should go."

"Is this really so easy for you?"

"Of course not," she admitted. "I have feelings too."

"Then how can you ask me to go?"

"I don't want to," she said. "But it's the right thing. Please, Mark. This is hard on me too. But we have to resist temptation. I really think you should leave."

"I'd rather do this…"

He kissed her again.

As she kissed him, she wanted to say 'you're not even trying'…

…but she never reached that level of…

* * * * * *

"I don't believe it," he grumbled. "We've scoured this whole alley more than once. We can't find one single clue. Not even a hair that we can pin on this guy."

"Maybe he really did have God on his side," Grogan said.

"Don't be an ass," he grumbled. "God didn't have anything to do with this. Tell me again. Why didn't we talk to this girl's pimp. Seems to me, he'd be a likely suspect."

"A religious pimp?"

"Why not?" he replied. "Even some of history's most notorious crime bosses went to church every Sunday. Just look at Al Capone."

"I guess," Grogan said. "The thing is, I don't think these girls had a pimp."

"No pimp?" he asked. "How do three girls get a prime street corner like 23rd and Fairdale in a city this size without a pimp? And how did they learn to work together?"

"Who knows?" Grogan shrugged. "Maybe they have God on *their* side."

"You're quite the wise ass today," he said. "I thought you were a Catholic."

"I am," Grogan said. "But that doesn't mean I have to believe every word they teach you at St. Mary's. I'm devoted to my faith. But, I still think God has a sense of humor."

"Even about this sort of thing?"

"Well," Grogan considered. "I guess murder might be a bit outside his realm of acceptability. But this is an aggravating case. I'm just trying to lighten the load."

"How about lightening *my* load?" he suggested. "Go through that dumpster again. And take it slow this time."

"Again?" Grogan questioned. "What the hell, Stan? You're not going to find anything in that dumpster of all places. We can't even find anything near the spot where the body was found. I'm messing up my good suit!"

"Oh, that's right," he said. "You want to look your best for the hookers later."

"I always care about my appearance," Grogan corrected. "Face it, Stan. This was just a very careful and well-organized killer."

"Careful psychos?" he muttered. "Hookers with no pimps? It seems like the only side God is *not* on is *mine*!"

"You don't mean that."

There was a brief silence.

"Are you sure about there being no pimp, Kyle?"

"Not entirely."

"Because you only know the girls…"

"...From the station," Grogan said. "I swear it's the truth, Stan."

"Just search over there, will you?" he ordered. "I refuse to just sit around and wait for this nut case to kill again!"

* * * * * *

The first sound they heard was a loud gunshot.

The second sound they heard was glass shattering.

They looked up from the sofa.

"Trey!" she gasped.

He immediately pushed himself off her. He grabbed for his shirt from the floor. He never took his eyes off Trey as he leapt to his feet.

"Get the fuck off my wife!" Trey grumbled as he watched the disturbing spectacle unfold before him.

"Listen, Trey," he said. "There's no need to do anything rash."

"Trey," she bumbled. "This isn't what it looks like! We were just..."

"Put your fucking shirt on before you even try lying to me, you worthless whore!" Trey growled.

"Just put the gun down, pal," he said in a soothing tone. "We can discuss this like adults without anybody getting hurt."

Trey pointed the .38 Special at him as the man stumbled to button his shirt.

"I'm giving you ten seconds to get the hell out of my house while you're still alive," Trey threatened.

She was throwing on a blouse. "Calm down, Trey," she stammered. "This can all be explained."

"Just put the gun down, Trey..."

"One...two..."

"When did you get a gun, sweetie?" she asked. "Please just stop!"

"Listen, Trey," he said. "I'm leaving, okay? I just want to make sure you're not going to hurt Stephanie."

"Three...four..."

Trey's eyes were filled with loathing. They were as dark and vindictive as the low threatening timbre in his voice.

"Five...six..."

"I'm going, Trey!" he said as he quickly threw his shoes on. "Just don't hurt Stephanie, alright? That's all I ask. You can hate me forever and I don't blame you. Just don't hurt Stephanie!"

"She's my goddam wife," Trey growled. "I'll do whatever the fuck I want with her!"

"Trey!" she gasped in terror. "What are you saying? Please put the gun down!"

"I'm not going to let you hurt her, Trey!"

"Seven...eight..."

"I mean it, Trey," he warned. "You're not going to hurt her!"

"You're running out of time, Mark," Trey taunted. "Do you really think I would hesitate to kill you, even for a second?"

"Probably not," he admitted. "But I don't care what happens to me! This wasn't Stephanie's fault. She wants to stop. It was all me!"

Trey took careful aim at the interloper.

"Nine...I'll do it, you piece of trash!" Trey threatened. "I'd just love to kill you!"

"Mark!" she screamed. "Just leave! Please!"

"I can't leave you with this madman!"

"Just go, Mark!" she cried. "I'll talk him down! Go!"

"Last chance, Genovese," Trey grumbled.

"I'll call you, Steph," he said as he quickly circled around his assailant. "To see if you're alright!"

"Just go! I'll be fine!"

"Nine and a half, scumbag!"

He hurried for the door. As he reached for the doorknob, he called back, "I love you, Steph!"

She screamed as the loud gunshot echoed through the room. He heard the bullet whistle past his ear. He saw the crack in the wall where the bullet landed.

It had been a very close shot. Trey had missed on purpose. It was meant as a warning shot. But he was obviously very handy with that .38 Special.

The shot was very effective. Mark was out the door in a flash.

Trey walked slowly over to the door. She was afraid to move a muscle. She sat frozen on the sofa. She watched him close the door.

"I thought you were going to be out all day," she stammered.

"So you thought you'd fuck your sister's dirtball husband again while I was gone?"

"No! It wasn't like that!"

"You told me it was just a one-time thing."

She looked down into her lap. She was trembling.

He walked over to the sofa.

"First you wait to tell me until we're on our way to your mother's," he said. "We're on our way out the door to go to a picnic at your mother's house, and that's when you spring it on me. 'By the way, honey. I had sex with my sister's husband.'"

"Trey..."

"I'm supposed to swallow all that," he grumbled. He was waving the gun around recklessly as he spoke. "I'm supposed to have my heart ripped out and then go to that damned picnic and just smile like nothing happened."

"Please let me explain."

"You tell me you only slept with him once," he continued. "You give me a whole line of crap about it being a big accident and a mistake. You look me right in the eye and tell me you love me and expect me to believe your blatant lies!"

"I wasn't lying, Trey. I do love you."

"So we go to the fucking picnic," he persisted as his tone deteriorated into an angry growl. "I do my damnedest to smile through it all. Then the moment your sister shows up, you further humiliate yourself and me by getting into a catfight with Cassandra over her lowlife husband. I didn't watch, but I had to suffer the embarrassment of hearing about it all day long!"

"We weren't fighting over Mark," she expounded shakily. "It was just sister stuff that came to a head because of..."

"How many times did you fuck that piece of shit, Stephanie?"

"Please, Trey..."

"How many times?" he shouted. "Tell me the truth for once! You at least owe me that, you pathetic little whore!"

She glanced down at her lap again. Her whole body froze with fear.

"Three or four," she muttered finally.

"Three or four?" he yelled. "Seriously?"

"It started about a month or two ago," she explained with tears in her eyes. "We were just consoling each other because you and Cassie were never around. It started all very innocent enough. It just kind of…escalated."

"Escalated?"

"We both know it's wrong," she insisted. "We want to stop. I love you, Trey. I really do. But certain feelings rise to the surface in cases like this. There are emotions that get in the way. It's complicated."

"Emotions? Complicated? I'm your husband!"

"I know, Trey," she begged. "And I love you! I really do! I love you so much!"

"You've got a funny way of showing it, bitch!" he growled.

"It was just an accident," she insisted. "We were talking about ending it…"

"Ending it?" he scoffed. "You were both half naked on *my* sofa! The sofa I paid for! I came home and find my half naked wife lying underneath some scumbag in *my* house on the sofa I paid for with *my* hard-earned money!"

"I'm sorry, Trey," she wept. "I'm so sorry!"

"Then, prove it!"

A new wave of horror swept over her as she stared at the gun he was pointing directly in her face.

"Trey!" she cried. "What are you doing?"

"Well, you're half naked," he barked. "You're all hot and heavy. Prove to me you love me! Prove you're not just a worthless whore! You want to fuck somebody? How about fucking your own husband instead of someone else's?"

"What are you saying?" she sobbed. "Please put that gun down! You're scaring me!"

"Come on, bitch," he said. "You're still in the mood, aren't you? You haven't cooled off just because scum boy left, have you? Let's go!"

He grabbed her by the hair and yanked her off the sofa.

"Ow!" she squealed. "Trey! You're hurting me!"

"Like you didn't hurt me, you little slut?"

He half dragged her by the hair toward the bedroom. She struggled to stay on her feet as he led her from room to room.

"Ouch!" she cried. "Please, Trey! Stop this! Let's talk!"

"You didn't want to talk when loverboy was around," he growled. "You wanted it bad enough when *he* was here! What's the matter, sweetheart? I thought you loved me."

"I do," she implored. "But not like this! Ow! Please stop, Trey! Talk to me! This isn't right! You have to calm down! Please let's talk this over!"

"What's there to talk about?" he seethed. "You forgot who you're supposed to be sleeping with! I'm just going to remind you, so you can stop being a whore!"

"Please, honey!" she sobbed. "I know you're hurt and angry! But you need to calm down! We can talk through this!"

"The time for talking is over," he warned. "Now it's time for action!"

He dragged her into the bedroom. He threw her onto the bed. She was crying openly. She had never seen that look in her husband's eyes before.

"Please, Trey! Don't do this! Not like this!"

She had never been so terrified. She didn't want this to happen.

Still, she did what she had to do…knowing all the while there was a loaded handgun on the nightstand.

CHAPTER 5

CREEPY FEELING

The sun was setting over the city. It had to fight its way through a thick shield of clouds that were rolling in from the west. Any brilliant colors that would have painted the sunset in a beautiful light were hidden behind grim shades of gray.

The warmer weather brought with it the dreary threat of rain.

Two men marched through the busy precinct with a sense of purpose. The processing area was hectic, loud and crowded. Still, they made their way through the human debris on their journey to the front desk.

"I don't believe we had to come into the station for this," he said.

"It's a good thing Vasquez recognized the girls' names from our report," Grogan said. "I told him we were going to need to see them again. I'm glad he remembered."

They approached the desk.

"Hi, Vasquez," he said. "Thanks for calling."

"No problem, Detective," Vasquez said. "They're still getting processed I think. I told Hodges to put them in one of the questioning rooms for you when they were done."

"What's the story so far?"

"It looks like Alcazar was the shooter," Vasquez replied. "Black male, 28 years old, six feet tall. His name is Arnold Delaney. We got quite a rap sheet on him. Everything from pimping and attempted murder to possession with intent. It appears he was trying to move in and take over. He got two shots from a Glock in the chest at close range. We took him to County General. But it doesn't look good. He might not make it."

"Marvelous," he muttered. "Okay, Vasquez. Thanks again."

Vasquez nodded as they started over to the holding rooms.

"Well," Grogan sighed. "You wanted to know how those girls avoided pimps. I guess you got your answer."

"Yeah," he said. "But with all the scumbags waiting to take advantage of girls like that in this town, how many times could they get away with that crap?"

"I suppose only time can tell."

He got a glimpse of the officer he was looking for up ahead.

"Hey, Hodges," he called. "Wait up!"

"Detective Paczecki," Hodges said. "I was expecting you. Hi, Grogan."

"Where are those two hookers Vasquez told you about?" he asked. "Tanya Alcazar and Rebecca Heiden."

"Good timing, Detective," Hodges said. "We just finished with them. I put them in Room 6 a couple of minutes ago."

"Thanks."

They walked over to Room 6.

Rebecca was seated at the table. Tanya was standing with her arms folded impatiently across her chest.

"Good evening, girls," Grogan began. "Nice to see you again. Although I wish it was under better circumstances."

"Hi, Kyle," Tanya grunted.

"How long are we in for this time?" Rebecca added.

"Not so fast, girls," Grogan said. "This isn't your standard bust. Somebody got shot this time. And he might not make it. You could get charged with murder if this guy doesn't pull through. Either way, they're bound to hit you up for attempted murder at the very least."

"Hey, Tanya shot the asshole," Rebecca defended. "I didn't do nothing!"

"Shut up, Becky," she said. "I was defending both of us! You would've done the same thing!"

"Alright," Grogan said. "Calm down. There's no reason to get excited."

"But, I didn't do nothing," Rebecca repeated.

"So, what did they haul you in for?" Grogan asked.

"Trying to make a living!"

"Did they take a gun off you too, Becky?" Grogan asked.

"Hey," she argued. "It was registered. They had no right!"

"What do you usually do when they take your gun?" Paczecki asked.

"I always get it back," Rebecca said. "Eventually."

"Yeah, but this time somebody got shot," Tanya reminded.

"But, not by *me*!"

"So, you were both packing?" Grogan interrupted.

"A girl's got to defend herself," Tanya said. "Just look at that dirtbag we had to deal with tonight."

"Does that sort of thing happen very often?" Paczecki asked.

"Well, it wasn't my first time," Rebecca admitted.

"Mine either," Tanya added. "But when you've been out on the streets as long as I have, you learn how to survive."

"I see," Paczecki said. "And did Audrey have a gun too?"

"I think she had a .38 Special," Rebecca said.

"That's funny," Paczecki said. "No gun was found on the scene. The killer must have kept it."

"You don't think that guy from tonight was the same guy that killed Audrey, do you?" Tanya asked with sudden alarm. "I heard some of those guys can do that sort of…"

"No," Grogan interrupted. "Audrey scratched her guy. It was a white person's skin they found under her nails. This guy probably wanted to take advantage of Audrey's murder, though. That would account for his timing."

"Have you found the killer yet?" Tanya asked. "I'm not going to feel safe going back on the streets with that maniac still out there."

"Really!" Rebecca agreed. "I hope I get my gun back before they let me out of here."

"You don't seem to understand," Grogan explained. "You girls are in a lot of trouble. You shot somebody, and he may die."

"It was self defense," Tanya insisted. "You know that, Kyle."

"I hope your judge sees it that way," Grogan said.

"Can't you put in a good word for me?"

"I'll certainly try," Grogan said. "I know you're both sweethearts. But attempted murder carries a lot of weight with it."

"You know I'll make it worth your while, baby," she offered in a soft, sexy voice.

"That's awfully sweet of you, honey," he said. "But it's not necessary. I'll see what I can do. If you're telling the truth about self defense, you shouldn't have anything to worry about."

"I hope you're right."

"I'm losing business as we speak," Rebecca added.

"That certainly is a shame," Grogan commented.

"One last thing, ladies," Paczecki said. "Was Audrey's gun registered?"

"I wouldn't know," Rebecca muttered.

"I don't even know where she got it," Tanya said.

"Okay, I think we're done here," Paczecki said. "I'll go get Hodges. Wrap this up, Kyle. It was a pleasure to see you again, ladies."

The girls each said good-bye.

"I should go too, girls," Grogan said. "As always, it was a treat. And don't worry. I'll look into things for you."

"Thanks, Kyle," Tanya said. "You're the best."

Rebecca blew him a quick, half-hearted kiss.

A minute later, the detectives left the precinct.

"Charming girls," Paczecki commented.

"Well, I guess we learned a few things at least," Grogan added.

"The most disturbing thing is," he imparted. "Our Paradox killer took a .38 Special off his victim."

"That's hardly a comforting thought," Grogan muttered.

"We'll run a check on Audrey Lindquist's gun," he said. "If it's registered, it'll help us pin down the murderer when we find him."

"Wonderful."

"And it looks like your girls may be facing a little jail time," he said.

"Yeah, that's possible," Grogan sighed. "But I do believe they acted in self defense."

"You know them better than I do."

"Just the same," Grogan suggested. "Do you think we could grab a bite to eat before we go back to work? I suddenly feel a bit nauseous."

"Gee, I wonder why."

* * * * * *

Once again he found himself walking down a long corridor. Everything was white and stoic. Even the smells were clean, scrubbed, antiseptic hospital smells.

On some level, he sort of expected that it was a dream.

But, can people experience the sense of smell in a dream?

It was surreal. It was eerie. He could hear the faint echoes of each footfall as he took one step after another... walking slowly...

...walking so slowly toward that elevator. That dreaded elevator.

Just seeing that elevator put a lump in his throat. It tied his stomach in tight knots. He feared that cage...that receptacle of death. And he almost knew why.

There was a flash of memory. A taste of reality? A cold chill ran up his spine as the elevator seemed to grow larger as he approached.

He just kept walking up this white, sterile hallway, with only the echo of his footsteps breaking the almost sinister silence.

The doors of the elevator were made of ornate, hand-tooled brass. They must have cost a fortune. He recognized the design from before. And he was terrified at the prospect of who would be waiting for him behind those doors.

The silence became deafening as he stopped walking about thirty feet or so before those doors. His heart was pounding. The knots in his stomach somehow managed to pull tighter.

Then, he heard the bell ring. He wanted to run. He knew those doors were about to open.

But, it was too late!

With a swoosh, the doors slid open. He took a panicked step backwards as two grim figures emerged.

This time, the girl's clothes were sliced and torn. Blood drizzled all over her once-white faux fur coat. The old man appeared as he always did. He was well-dressed, neat and confident.

As they stepped out into the hall, he stumbled backward.

"No! Please!" he stammered. "Not you! Not again!"

"What's the matter, honey?" she asked with a deliberate tone. "Aren't you glad to see me?"

"B-but, you're d-dead!" he stuttered. "Both of you!"

"That's true, sweetheart," she said. "And I never got a proper chance to thank you. I never had a chance to return the favor."

"N-no! Please!"

"We've come to talk to you, my son," the old man imparted. "There are things you need to do."

"No, Dad!" he insisted shakily. "I know you're dead! Why don't you leave me alone!"

"We've come a long way to see you, son," Dad said. "I came up from so far below."

"And I've come down from above," she said. "We have a message for you."

"I am so proud of you, my son," Dad said. "You have sinned. You have forsaken your Maker. You have carved your path to the Kingdom Below."

"No!"

"God sent me to talk to you," she said. "He is angry."

"I won't listen!" he protested. "You are a liar! God would never speak to anyone through a woman of ill repute!"

"You haven't redeemed yourself," she continued as if she hadn't heard him. "Even after all that has happened, you still sin. You still lust in your heart. You still covet that which is not yours. You scorn the Holy Word of God."

"Don't you dare speak to me of God, you harlot!" he shouted. "You are an insult to all He stands for!"

"That's right, son," Dad coaxed. "Don't listen to her. She could not possibly have anything to say that you need to hear. You're fine just the way you are!"

"Stop talking to me!" he warned. "It is so immoral and repulsive of you, Satan! Speaking to me through my father is the lowest form of indecent behavior! I will not listen to your foul ravings!"

"God wants to talk to you," she said. "He still wants you to redeem yourself."

"Shut up, you whore!" he demanded. "You have both been sent by Lucifer: the lowest of the low! You can not trick me with your treacherous lies!"

She started walking toward him. He tried to back away, but he couldn't move. It felt as if his feet had been nailed to the floor.

"No!" he screamed. "Stay back! Stay away from me!"

She walked slowly toward him. "God is still angry," she imparted. "You haven't done enough to redeem yourself. You continue to sin even after all He has given you."

"I've tried to do good!" he pleaded. "I have tried to walk in the ways of God!"

He kept trying to retreat, but his feet wouldn't move. He began to panic as she drew nearer.

"Sure, you killed me," she said as she took another step. "But, is that really enough? Isn't there so much more you can do to serve The Lord? There is so much sin out there that must be expunged. There are so many misdeeds that must be atoned for."

"You can't make me listen!" he screamed. "Stay away from me, you agent of Evil!"

"Don't listen to her, son," Dad advised. "God told us 'Thou shalt not kill.'"

"It's not murder if you are helping God," she explained as she took another step toward him. "You are helping to erase the sin that has poisoned the world He made for you."

"That can't be right!" he argued. He kept trying to move, but his feet were still stuck to the floor. "Help me! Somebody help me!"

She took another step. "You are still full of sin," she averred. "God is angry. You need to atone. God wants to forgive you. But you must do his bidding."

"You can't be speaking for God," he insisted. "But if the Devil is speaking through my father, how can I know..."

"That's right," she said. "Your father speaks for Lucifer. God wants you to kill! For forgiveness!"

"No, son! Killing is wrong!"

"Please just stay away from me!"

She was only two feet in front of him. He was trembling with terror.

"Last time I saw you," she said. "I offered you my heart. You didn't accept it. This time, you will take my heart. And you will do what God asks of you."

She reached into her torn chest. She pulled out her heart. She held it up in front of his face. Her heart was still beating with a steady pulse. And blood spilled out all over her hand and leaked between her fingers.

He screamed in horror.

"Take my heart, lover," she offered sweetly.

"Don't listen, son," Dad called from behind the girl. "It is only human to sin. The Lord loves all sinners!"

"No! Please don't!"

She reached out with one blood-streaked hand. She gently pulled the lapel of his suit coat away from his body.

"She's just a prostitute, son!"

With her other hand, she dropped her pulsating, bleeding heart into the pocket of his white shirt. His trembling body was frozen as the heart spread a wet film of red over his crisp, clean shirt. He could feel the warm blood as it dripped and spilled down his chest.

"Take my heart," she repeated. "And do what God commands you to do."

"No!" he begged. "You can't make me!"

"It's what God wants," she instructed. "You're eradicating sin! Kill in the name of The Lord! Take my heart, and do as God commands!"

He could feel the pulse of her heart in his pocket. The whole front of his shirt was hot, wet, sticky...and very red.

"No!" he shrieked. "Please, God! *No*!"

He sat up in his bed. He was sweating. He couldn't breathe. He desperately gasped for air. Perspiration poured over his face.

Everything in the room was quiet. He could hear the patter of rain drumming a gentle rhythm against his window. It did little to comfort him. His mind was still racing. But, this had just been another bad dream.

It took a number of minutes to calm down. And he knew it would take a while before he would be able to fall asleep again.

Still, he fell back onto his mattress. He knew he needed to get some rest.

* * * * * *

A warming trend followed the rain over the next few days. It was as if God had chosen to go along with the calendar's unofficial beginning of summer.

By the time the lunch rush started on Thursday, it was nearly 70 degrees out in the blaring sunshine.

As three people perused the menu at the elegant eatery, a few people stopped at their table.

"Mrs. Stark," he smiled. "I mean, Betty. It's so nice to see you here."

She looked up from her menu. "John," she smiled. "What a pleasant surprise. I'm buying lunch for a few of my kids. You remember Cassandra Genovese and Michael, don't you?"

"Of course," John said. "Nice to see you both."

"Kids," she reminded. "You remember John Nelson and Jeremy Blackwell. You met them at my picnic last weekend."

They exchanged polite greetings.

"And, this is my girlfriend," John introduced. "Debbie LeClair, this is the Stark family."

"Nice to meet you, Debbie," Betty said. "Why haven't I met you before?"

"She's a waitress downtown," John explained. "She never gets weekends off. So she never gets to join me in church on Sundays."

"And I'm sorry I missed your picnic, Mrs. Stark," she said. "John tells me it was a fun time."

"That's very kind," Betty said. "Don't worry. I understand."

"Debbie and I get to worship together during the week," John said. "When her work schedule permits."

"It's strange running into you like this, Mrs. Stark," Jeremy piped in.

"Not necessarily," she said. "It is lunchtime. And The Manor House is one of the nicest restaurants in this part of the city. Why don't you join us?"

"We wouldn't want to impose," John said.

"Nonsense," Betty said. "I insist. We have plenty of room. And it's always nice to spend time with good, wholesome people. It reassures me there's still hope for the world."

"Okay," John said. "But you'll have to let me pick up the tab. It's the least I can do to repay you for last weekend."

"There's no need," she said. "I was happy to invite you. Besides, I can't ask you to pay for me and my children."

"We'll split the check," Jeremy offered.

"There you go," John said. "Jeremy and I will take care of it. I insist."

"Well, thank you, boys," she said. "Have a seat, everyone. Join us."

Luckily, their table was large enough to accommodate everyone. A waitress quickly reintroduced herself and handed out more menus.

"So, what made you take the kids here today, Mrs. Stark?" Jeremy asked.

"It just seemed like the thing to do," she said. "You know Michael is living with me. And Cassandra has been staying with me for the past couple of days. She's having a bit of a tiff with her husband."

"He's been cheating on me," Cassandra said.

"Oh, that's right," John remembered. "He's cheating with your sister. That's why you and Stephanie had that…"

He stopped suddenly. He looked away with embarrassment.

"What happened?" Debbie asked.

"It's alright, John," Cassandra assured him. "I don't mind talking about it. My sister and I got into a brawl at my mother's picnic over my cheating husband."

"Your sister and your husband are…" Debbie began cautiously.

"Yes," Cassandra nodded. "I had considered a divorce. But he told me it was a one-time thing. Then, her husband caught them together on Monday."

"Your sister's husband?" John asked. "Trey Wagner, isn't it? I met him at the picnic. He seemed like a nice man. It's a shame I didn't meet your husband, Cassandra."

"You're not missing much," Michael muttered.

"Michael!" his mother scolded.

"Anyway," Cassandra continued. "Trey is not such a prince. He shot at Mark twice with a gun. He chased him out of the house."

"With a gun?" John gasped. "Is Mark alright?"

"He's okay," Cassandra said. "But I left him after that. It's my sister I'm worried about."

"Why?" Debbie asked with genuine concern.

"According to Mark," Cassandra explained. "Trey was a raving madman when he shot at him."

"Well," Jeremy reasoned. "His wife was cheating on him."

"We were worried about what he might've done to Stephanie," Betty said. "I've called her a few times. She seems a little quiet and withdrawn. She refuses to come out and talk to me."

"If that scumbag hurt my sister," Michael grumbled. "I swear I'll kill him!"

"Now, Michael," his mother instructed. "I understand you're worried. I'm worried too. But, The Lord will take care of your sister. And He will bring her to us when she is ready. I told you she sounded okay on the phone. She was just upset about having an argument with her husband. I'm sure we're worried for nothing."

"I still want to see for myself," Michael insisted.

"He has a point," Jeremy said. "An angry husband can be capable of some pretty ugly things."

"Even so," Betty said. "I don't want him taking matters into his own hands. If Trey needs to pay for anything he did, the law and God will take care of it. Remember, 'Vengeance is mine sayeth The Lord.'"

"Still," Jeremy continued. "God sent us here to help and protect each other. Sin and temptation exist to make us stray from His path. God wants us to choose, and make the right choices. And if someone chooses unwisely...especially if it hurts others, He may call upon us to help right the wrong. And He may choose us as the vessel through which He achieves His ends. In fact, isn't that why we're here?"

"I couldn't have said it better myself," John agreed.

"Eloquently put," Betty commented. "You seem like such a bright young man, Jeremy. Have you ever been married?"

"No," Jeremy said. "In fact, I'm not even seeing anyone right now. I just haven't met the right girl yet. But I know someone will come along when the time is right."

"That's why we invited him to lunch," Debbie added. "We figured he could use the company."

"I'm sure The Lord will provide," Betty said. "Have you talked to your mother recently?"

"I talked to her on the phone a day or two ago," Jeremy said. "She told me everything is fine. I may be going to visit her in Canada at the end of next month."

"That will be nice," Betty smiled. "Give her my regards."

"Have you two been going together long, Debbie?" Cassandra asked.

"It's been nearly a year," Debbie said. "We met in church."

"That's wonderful," Cassandra smiled. "How often do you see each other?"

"We try to get together three or four times a week," John said.

"You're not living together?" Michael asked.

"No," Debbie declared. "We refuse to live in sin. We do all we can to resist temptation. We are determined not to have sex until after we're married. It's what God expects of us. Isn't that right, honey?"

"That's right."

"I think that's marvelous," Betty said.

"I think that's sick," Michael muttered.

"Michael!" Betty admonished. "Behave yourself! That's very commendable, you two. You should be proud."

"We are," Debbie said. "And I'd love to be married one day. To enter into the holiest of unions..."

"It's not always that holy," Cassandra muttered. "Believe me, sister!"

"Cassie!" her mother scolded. "I'm sorry. I don't know how often I have to apologize for my children."

"Don't worry about it," John said.

"So, you live alone, John?" Betty asked, hoping to change the subject.

"Not quite," John said. "My mother has been staying with me for the last few months. She's been kind of lonely since Dad died. She hasn't been well, either. Some sort of degenerative muscle disease. She is sometimes confined to a wheelchair. It's very painful. She gets cranky a lot."

"I'm sorry to hear that, John," Betty said.

"I've even considered putting her in a home," he said. "But I couldn't afford it. Plus, I feel God wants us to bear our burdens and take care of those who raised us."

"How true," Betty agreed.

"There are a lot of widows represented at this table," Michael pointed out.

"We all spend our time on this earth," John imparted. "But only those who spend their time wisely and walk in the ways of Our Lord can look forward to moving on to a better place."

"Still," Cassandra added. "You can't always do what everyone says is right. I'm very strongly considering divorcing Mark."

"Oh no," Debbie averred. "You shouldn't do that. Remember the vows you gave: 'For better or worse. 'Til death do us part.' God expects you to honor those vows."

"That's what I mean," Cassandra said. "How can I keep those vows with a man who won't stop cheating on me?"

"Remember what I just told you," John reminded. "We all spend our time on God's earth. And only those who have walked in His light and who have served Him can look forward to moving on to a better place. Your husband's sins are his own affront to God. And God will see fit to punish him in His own way."

* * * * * *

Later that day, the sun was setting over the city. It had not yet reached the point where it was painting beautiful patterns across the urban horizon. The sun was just lowering itself in the blue sky between high wisps of clouds.

Inside, she sat in the booth in the back corner. She played with her napkin.

"I still think The Robin's Egg is a strange name for a restaurant," she commented. "Especially for a place that almost never serves eggs."

"It's still one of the nicest places in the city," he said.

"It is a nice place," she agreed. "But I think you like coming here just to see your brother. Or at least tease him. I like the way they always seat us at one of his tables so he can serve us. And I'll admit Michael looks cute in his little waiter uniform."

"You should tell him," he said. "I'm sure he'd love to hear it. Anyway, I'm glad I saw him tonight. It was nice to hear Cassandra went back to Mark this afternoon. Some of Mom's church friends convinced her to at least try and talk things over."

"I don't know how she could ever trust that lying cheater ever again," she said.

"That's true," he sighed. "Part of me doesn't like the idea. I still think Michael and I ought to take that little Mark Genovese out 'behind the barn' and teach him a lesson for messing around on my sister. I think Michael works 'til midnight tonight. I wonder if he has any plans afterward."

"Don't start," she said. "Beating up Mark won't solve anything."

"It would make me feel a lot better."

"No it wouldn't," she said. "Anyway, your other sister is partly to blame. I can't believe she did that! Not only to her husband, but to her own sister! I swear sometimes Stephanie reminds me of your little friend Lindsay Bainbridge. She has a thing for other women's property."

She stopped suddenly. She looked at him with curiosity.

"What was that, Danny?" she asked suspiciously.

"What was what?"

"That nervous little twitch," she said. "As soon as I mentioned Lindsay, you got a nervous twitch and looked away as if you were guilty or something."

"What? You're crazy!"

"Don't lie to me, Daniel," she said in that certain way. "You know how I feel about that. I had a sneaking suspicion you had a reason for taking me to a place like this on a Thursday. I still have a creepy feeling you have something going on."

"Well," he ventured cautiously. "I guess I do have an ulterior motive of sorts. I want to thank you for being so patient. I know you're aware that Lindsay has been hounding me all week. She's been trying to get back with me."

"She's lucky she's still alive!"

"I know you feel that way," he continued. "And to achieve her devious ends, she's been threatening to tell you something all week. And I just wanted to give you the real scoop before she gives you her version."

"What is it, Daniel?" The look in her eyes was almost as scary as the quiet tone in her voice.

"Well," he stammered with the appropriate fear. "The other night...the night of the picnic...when I saw her at Chiffon's...well...she sort of...kissed me."

"What?"

"She surprised me with it," he defended. "She kissed me. I did not kiss her, I swear. I'm an innocent victim. I had nothing to do with it."

"She kissed you?" she asked with an anger that resembled a pot that was ready to boil. "Why didn't you tell me this before?"

"Because I was innocent," he said. "And I didn't think it was worth making you mad over nothing."

"Nothing?" she seethed. "You call kissing my man 'nothing'?"

"Well, of course she's trying to start something," he admitted. "But, there's nothing for you to worry about. I promise."

"That's it!" she growled. "I'm going to kill her!"

"Don't get excited, Krysten," he said. "Let me handle it."

"Let you handle it?" she scoffed. "I let you handle it all week, Daniel! And you handled it by kissing that slut behind my back!"

"It was just the one time," he defended. "And she kissed me, not the other way around. I wasn't going to tell you because I knew you'd overreact."

"Overreact?" she argued. "First, you let that little skank stay overnight in *my* place!"

"That's *our* place."

"Then," she continued furiously. "You go off to your ex's favorite restaurant so you can make out with her... while you're supposed to be with me at *your mother's picnic*!"

"Will you keep your voice down?" he coaxed. "You're making a scene."

"Making a scene?" she shouted.

"This is why I wasn't going to tell you," he argued. "I knew you would fly off the handle. I promise you, nothing happened!"

"Fly off the handle?" she spat. She was almost in tears. "Well, I'm sorry, Daniel! I don't know how to act at a time like this! I don't know how to act when I find out that the man I love is still sneaking off to make out with some tramp!"

"You're making more out of this than there is," he said. "I'm telling you nothing happened! Don't you see? That's why she did this. Yes, she kissed me, but I pulled away. She wants to tell you it was more than that, because that's her plan. She's trying to drive a wedge between us. Don't let her win. Don't let her get what she wants."

"She wants *you*!" she argued. "Are you so easy to get?"

"Of course not!"

"That's it!" she declared. She threw her napkin down on the table. "I'm leaving!"

She stood up.

"But, our food hasn't gotten here yet," he reminded.

"I'm not hungry," she snipped. "Are you coming, Daniel?"

"Please don't do this," he begged. "Don't reward her for pulling this crap. Don't believe her lies or let her get to you. Show her you're a better woman than she is."

"If I'm a better woman," she asked with tears in her eyes. "Then why are you going off to kiss her behind my back?"

"I'm not!" he insisted. "Don't let Lindsay do this. I love you, Krysten. You know I do!"

"I wish I could believe you."

"You can. I promise."

"Yeah, you're full of promises," she sniffed. "You were always good at talking."

He didn't know what to say.

"I'm leaving, Daniel," she snipped. "You stay here! I'll call a cab! Maybe you can find some other whore to fool around with while I'm gone!"

She stormed out of the restaurant.

"Krysten! Wait!" he called after her. "At least let me pay for the food we ordered before you go!"

It was too late. She was gone.

Michael saw her leave. He rushed over to his brother.

"What's wrong?" he asked.

"Lindsay," Danny said. "Lindsay's what's wrong."

"Lindsay? Lindsay Bainbridge?"

"I don't have time to explain," Danny said. "I have to go catch Krysten. Sorry we didn't stick around for the food. Can I just get the bill please? Hurry."

"Don't worry about it," he said. "Get out of here. I'll take care of this."

"Are you sure?"

"Go on. Go catch her."

"Thanks, little brother," Danny said. "I owe you one."

He ran through the restaurant and out the door.

* * * * * *

The late hours of the evening were appropriately deep and dark. It was a crisp, sharp darkness that drew the dregs of society out of hiding. It was the time when the lowest of creatures roamed free…

…and ruled the night.

She sat on a sofa in a luxurious room. The lighting was intentionally set to romantic. She had a wineglass in her hand. She leaned back to allow his arm to be around her shoulders.

"Oh, Joe," she smiled. "I always loved your apartment here in the city. It's just so big and glorious and grand."

"Well, I need a place to relax while I'm down here in the city," he explained. "Now that the budget is essentially passed, the session is almost over for the year."

"And you'll be going back home to your wife."

"Don't think of it like that," he explained. "Sure, I'll have to go up to see her for a while. Wives expect that sort of thing. But I promise you, Marissa. I won't touch her while I'm home. I really have no use for her anymore. Now that I've found you, she means nothing to me."

"So, you'll leave her?"

"Not right away, of course," he admitted. "I'm a public figure. My life is not my own. I have a reputation and a career to think about. These things have to be carefully finessed. But don't worry. Our time will come."

"I hate the thought of her even touching you."

"She won't," he vowed. "I already told you. I'm all about you. I love you, Marissa."

He leaned over and kissed her. They kissed again.

"And I love you too, Joe," she said. "You've been great about everything. Tonight was even special. I loved that restaurant. An elegant late dinner. The food was spectacular."

"That's one of the best restaurants in the city," he commented.

"I know," she agreed. "It was superb. My only problem is…I had this weird sensation that we were being watched."

"Are you serious?"

"Yes," she nodded. "The whole time we were having dinner I could've sworn someone was watching us. In fact, I still can't shake that creepy feeling that something is wrong."

"It's just your imagination," he assured her. "Maybe you're just tired. You've been working hard lately."

"No," she insisted. "There's more to it than that. I can't quite put my finger on it, but there's something that just…isn't right."

"You're being silly," he said. "Nothing's wrong. It's been a long day. You just need some 'down time.' Would you like some more wine?"

"Don't patronize me, Joe," she said. "I really feel…"

"I wasn't patronizing you, honey," he interrupted in a tone meant to calm. "You're just nervous. It's all in your mind. You just need to relax. Let me get you some more wine."

"Well…maybe just…"

This time she was interrupted by a noise.

"What was that?" she asked.

"I don't know," he said. "It sounded like it came from the bedroom."

"What could it have been?"

"There's only one way to find out," he said. "Stay here. I'll go take a look."

He stood. "Hello?" he called. "Is anybody there?"

There was no reply.

"Okay, stay here, Marissa," he advised. "I'll have a look."

"Be careful," she said shakily.

"I will." He began to walk slowly toward the bedroom.

Luckily, there was a deep, shag carpet covering the floor. He made one step, then another. He deliberately stayed as quiet as possible.

"Hello?" he called out. "Is anyone out there?"

There was no response. The silence was gut-wrenching.

He took a few more quiet steps. The silence seemed to grow in intensity. His heart was pounding like a bass drum as he neared the bedroom.

She watched as he approached the door. The lump in her throat grew bigger. She felt a bit nauseous.

She watched as he reached for the doorknob. He stayed slow and cautious. He turned the knob in his sweaty hand. He pushed the door open slowly and carefully.

He turned on the light. He stepped inside. All was quiet.

The silence quickly began to drive her crazy. Her heart was thumping away. Her nausea was getting worse.

"Joe?" she finally called out. "Are you okay?"

"There was no reply.

"Joe?" she called. "Don't do this to me! You know I'm scared! Answer me!"

The resulting silence made her even more jittery.

She slowly stood up. She began to slowly make her way across the carpet.

"Joe?" she called out. "Please answer me!"

She heard a thud coming from the bedroom. She started to panic.

"Joe?" she cried.

That silence was just too much to bear. Finally, she raced to the bedroom.

She looked down on the floor. Joe was lying still and lifeless near the bed. His body had been tossed to the floor like a rag-doll. His eyes were wide open. The deep gashes in his neck and torso were spewing blood down his shirt and over the carpet.

She screamed.

Then, she looked up. All she saw was a dark figure and a long knife. Light reflected off the only part of the blade that wasn't dripping blood.

She shrieked in horror.

An hour or so later, a young man walked in through his own front door. As he passed by his kitchen, he heard an aggravating voice.

"Where were you, son?" she asked. "You were late coming home from work again."

"Leave me alone, Mom," he grumbled. "I'm tired."

"You've got blood on your clothes," she observed. "Have you killed someone?"

"I was doing The Lord's work," he grumbled. "He told me to."

"The Lord told you to kill again?" she asked impatiently. "I don't believe it. I taught you better than that! That hooker was one thing. But to go on killing? That's a sin, son! What in God's name is wrong with you?"

He spun around with a crazed look in his eye. He held the bloody knife in a threatening manner.

"I told you," he snarled. "The Lord wanted me to do it! He asked me specifically! Now that's the end of it, Mom! Or you're next!"

The anger in his eyes frightened her. She was afraid to move. She stood frozen in the kitchen doorway.

After a few moments, he turned and walked out of the room.

BOOK TWO

COVET

CHAPTER 6

LUST

The gray haze over the city seemed to forecast the type of morning it would be for everyone. It was dark, dreary, damp and an unpleasing introduction to the day.

Two sisters sat in a modest kitchen in a standard suburban dwelling on the outskirts of the city. The mood in the house matched the gray mood outside.

"Thanks for seeing me, Stephanie."

"I know I owe it to you, Cassandra," she said. "I guess I owe you an apology again."

There was a moment of silence.

"What's going on, Stephanie? Tell me the truth."

"What do you want me to say, Cassie?" she said. "It started a few of months ago. We'd just have an innocent dinner to keep each other company. I guess I thought we could handle it. But the plutonic thing? Coupled with the loneliness that started it all? It just didn't work. We connected and found the comfort and solace we were lacking in our lives."

"I see."

"It's complicated, Cassie," she continued. "We didn't mean any harm. But you can't stop your emotions any more than you can stop a runaway freight train."

"So," Cassandra muttered. "Emotionally, we're speaking freight trains?"

"Not really," she shook her head. "It's not that bad. But there are emotions. We tried to keep them in check, but…"

"How many times, Steph?"

"What?"

"How many times did you sleep with my husband?" she asked with a touch of impatient anger.

Stephanie glanced down at her coffee cup with a twinge of guilt.

"Four or five. Maybe six."

"Maybe six?"

"It's not like…" she began. "I mean, we didn't plan…"

"Do you love him, Steph?"

"Well…sort of, maybe."

"What does that mean, 'sort of, maybe'?"

"We want to end it, Cassie," she explained. "We really do. But it's not as simple as all that. We can't just shake hands and say, 'no hard feelings.'"

"You know what?" Cassandra said sharply. "Keep him!"

"What?"

"Keep him. He's all yours."

"You must be joking."

"No," Cassandra shook her head with finality. "You want him? You can't just walk away? Then, keep him with my blessing. I'll get the divorce and *you* can put up with that little fucker and all his idiosyncrasies and habits and moods and all his bullshit. Keep him and all the headaches that go with him. I'll be getting the better end of the deal."

"You can't mean that, Cassie."

"I've never been more serious in my life," she declared. "I don't know why I ever married him in the first place."

"But, he..."

"You know, when you first decide to get married," she theorized. "Everything is just all happy and roses and rainbows. I don't know why we girls put ourselves through all this shit. We meet a guy, we paint a rosy picture of him in our heads, we ignore all the bullshit that goes along with the package. And it's all about how we *just have* to get married! It's what we all want, and who the guy is doesn't matter. We get a guy, we convince ourselves we're in love...'cause we're *nothing* if we're not in love! We justify everything about him in our heads. And then we just have to rush out and get married. It's what we're born to do! It's what we want! It's what we're *trained* to want!"

"Cassie? Are you okay?"

"I'm fine," she said as she grabbed a tissue. She wiped her eyes.

"I'm so sorry, Cassie."

"It's alright," she sniffed. "I was furious when I found out. I went to stay with Mom for a few days. I wanted to kill you. I probably would have killed you, if I'd seen you right away. But, I've had a few days to calm down and think about it. Now, I just want to walk away from it all. You can have him and all the crap that goes with him."

"Everybody needs to be loved, Cassie."

"Apparently," she said. "I need to keep looking. I kind of figure you should too. By the way, I love the bullet holes in the wall out there. Nice decorative touch."

"Yeah," Stephanie almost smiled. "I didn't even know Trey had a gun. God knows where he got it. I asked him. He wouldn't say. He hasn't been the same since… well, you know."

"Mark said Trey was a good shot," she told her. "And that Trey was like a madman, too. Are you okay, honey? What did Trey do after Mark left?"

Stephanie glanced downward. "I don't want to talk about it," she muttered.

"Come on, Steph," she coaxed. "You've been real quiet the last few days. What happened?"

"Well," Stephanie said slowly. "Trey was like a crazy person. He was waving the gun around, pointing it in my face, insulting me…"

"He pointed the gun in your face?"

"Then, he pulled me up off the sofa," she continued. "He pulled me up by the hair and dragged me into the bedroom. He told me that I'd forgotten who I was supposed to fuck and he was going to remind me."

"Oh my God, Steph!" she gasped. "He raped you?"

"I don't know," she muttered. "I never thought about it like that. I mean, he is my husband."

"It doesn't matter, Stephanie," she said. "You say he dragged you into the bedroom and forced you to have sex with him?"

She nodded.

"That's rape, Stephanie!" she announced. "Husband or not, that's rape!"

"I never really thought about it," she said. "At the time, I was just terrified. I was just hoping he didn't kill me. He was so insane! And so furious!"

"Oh my God, Steph," she said. "I'm so sorry! Are you okay? Did he hurt you?"

"Not that I know of," she said. "I'm fine now."

"How's Trey been since then?"

"I don't know," she muttered. "Kind of quiet, angry and brooding. We haven't talked much. He went out last night and didn't come home."

"Have you been to the police?"

"About what?" she asked. "You mean the gun thing? The other day?"

"Of course!"

"No," she shook her head. "Like I said, I didn't even think like that. I mean, he's my husband. And I did sort of bring it on myself."

"You didn't ask for what he did to you," Cassandra corrected. "Cheating or not, husband or not, he did not have the right to rape you."

"I don't want to do this now, Cassandra."

"You're going to have to face this sometime, Steph."

"I'm not in a mood to discuss it."

"Oh God," Cassandra gasped. "What will Mom say?"

"Don't you dare, Cassandra!" she said. "Don't you dare tell Mom!"

"She deserves to know."

"You're making too much of this," she said. "Trey is my husband. So we had sex while he was angry. It's not that big a deal."

"So why don't you want me to tell Mom?"

"Because she going to do what you're doing," she said. "She's going to blow it all out of proportion."

"Stephanie!" Cassandra argued. "He's dragging you around by the hair, pointing guns in your face, threatening you…"

"It's over, Cassie," she said. "Just let it go."

"What did Mark say about all this?" Cassandra asked. "As much as I hate to drag my husband into this…"

"I'm not going to tell him."

"But…" she began. "Well, it's probably for the best. I don't even know why I would want him involved. What are you going to do?"

"I know I have to see Mark again," Stephanie said. "I'm sorry, honey. But we have to talk. I want to end it. I really do. You're my sister. You mean more to me than this sordid mess. And as for Trey, I don't know. I love him, but I just don't know. I think we can get past all this."

"Are you sure you want to?"

"Yes! He's my husband!"

"He's a lunatic."

"Be fair, Cassandra," she said. "He was angry because he caught me…well, you know. He'll get over it. At least, I hope."

"I don't understand you, Stephanie," she said. "If Mark had ever…"

"Mark's done enough," Stephanie said. "To both of us. Or we've both done enough to *you*. I wish you knew how sorry I am."

Cassandra just stared silently at the kitchen table.

"Incidentally," Stephanie added. "I'm surprised you came over this morning. How did you manage to drag yourself away from your boutique?"

"Tiffany, Alyssa and Ellen are all in today," she said. "They can handle things for an hour or two. Mom and I were worried about you. Michael, too. I had to check on you and see that you're okay."

"Thanks."

"Besides," she added. "This whole mess has me thinking. Maybe I need to get away from that shop more often and spend time on things that are more important."

"Sometimes it takes something like this," Stephanie imparted. "To make you take a step back and look at things a little more clearly."

"Yeah," Cassandra smiled sadly. "Well, we certainly are a pair, aren't we? I'm married to a scumbag. You're married to a lunatic."

"Life couldn't get any sweeter."

* * * * * *

"What do you got, Sullivan?"

"It's not pretty in there, Detective," Sullivan said. "It looks like our buddy the Paradox killer finally struck again."

"Wonderful," he grunted. "So, one of the victims is Senator Joe Zanella?"

"Yes," Sullivan nodded. "That has been confirmed. It appears the senator was having an affair with his intern. She was a college girl attending State. Her name is Marissa Cosgrove. She's 20, majoring in Political Science and

Law. She's over here from Fulton. Must've been a smart girl, very pretty. What a waste!"

"Well, Kyle," he conjectured. "It looks like Paradox doesn't only limit himself to prostitutes. Looks like he's stepped up to politicians. Zanella was a big name in the senate too. Oh great! They'll probably bring the state cops in on this."

"Just what we need."

"What's the matter, Kyle?" he poked. "I figured you'd love the help. Now that we know Paradox isn't just targeting hookers, I thought you'd be losing interest in this case."

"I've got to admit this case is losing its appeal," Grogan said.

Sullivan and the two detectives crossed the yellow crime scene tape and entered the plush apartment.

They followed as Sullivan continued, "They're in the bedroom. The window was open. Apparently, the killer cut through the screen. He was waiting for them when they entered the bedroom. Seems he killed them at the door, then dragged the bodies to the bed. Sliced them up real well, cut out their hearts, left a note…the whole nine yards."

They looked over at the bed. They winced.

"God!" he commented. "He does like to go into detail with the bodies, doesn't he?"

"He does enjoy his work," Grogan agreed.

"His aide had the superintendant let him in around 10:00 this morning," Sullivan said. "He got suspicious when Zanella didn't show up for a committee meeting. The aide and the super are in the other room talking to

Officers Kilgallon and Weinberg. We place the death at somewhere between midnight and 3 AM."

"We'll need to talk to that aide and the super," he said.

"I figured as much," Sullivan said. "Be careful stepping on the carpet as you approach the bed. There's blood everywhere."

"I can see that," he said. "Thanks, Sullivan. Any fingerprints yet?"

"Only Zanella and Cosgrove so far," Sullivan said. "We're guessing Paradox wears gloves. But we're still working on it."

"Good. Thanks."

They cautiously made their way to the bed. They looked down at the corpses which had been carefully laid out. The blood-smeared note was pinned to what was left of the senator's shirt. It read:

I lust.
I am the Paradox that is All Mankind.
Those who so willingly flaunt their sins
Incur the Wrath of God

"Well, that sloppy handwriting looks familiar," he said. "It looks like our boy is back."

"That's just lovely," Grogan muttered.

"I wish we could just dump this whole case off on the state cops," he suggested. "I don't want to be involved in anything that has to do with senators and infidelity."

"That's right," Grogan said. "Zanella's wife ain't going to like this."

"That's for sure," he agreed. "But we still owe it to him to give the state boys as much info as we can. Let's comb through everything. We need to find the connection between an important state senator and…one of your friends."

"You mean Angelica."

"Exactly."

"I swear, Stan," Grogan defended. "I only know her…"

"Don't even say it," he interrupted. "Just find me some clues. I want to stop this nut as soon as possible!"

* * * * * *

"Wow, Betty," she said. "This is so nice of you. And so unexpected. Thank you."

"Believe me," Betty said. "It's not all that nice. I have my motives."

"Listen, Betty," she said. "I know we've had our problems in the past. And I fully realize they are all my fault. You don't like me very well. And I can't blame you. You have every right to feel the way you do. And I am truly sorry for all the trouble I've caused. I can't tell you how sorry I am."

"I'm pleased to hear you say that, Lindsay," Betty said. "That's very big of you. Feel free to order anything on the menu. It's my treat."

"Thank you," she said. "I can't tell you what this means to me. I know I've been a pain this last week or so. But I don't mean to be. I promise. I'm only doing this because I love your son. Danny and I were meant to be together. And I'm glad I have an ally in his family.

Together, you and I can get that Krysten Salinger out of the way and get things back to normal. Trust me, Betty. I may have made a mistake, but I've learned my lesson. I will never, ever hurt Danny again."

"Just order your food, dear."

A young waiter was standing at the table. He took their order and left.

"I'm so delighted that you called me, Betty," she said. "And this is such a beautiful restaurant. I just know I'm going to enjoy our lunch together."

"I'm not so sure you will," Betty said. "You see, Lindsay? I had a reason for wanting to talk to you. You've been causing quite a stir this last week with my son. Calling him at work and at home, bothering him, staying at his place last weekend, interrupting my picnic…and I gather there was something about a kiss?"

"Yes," she said. "We kissed last weekend. When he came to see me during your picnic. For a moment, it seemed like the old days. It was the kind of kiss that reminded me of when we were together. I know he felt that way too."

"That's not the way he sees it, Lindsay."

"I'm sure he won't admit it," she allowed. "Especially in front of that prissy little Krysten. But just between you and me, woman-to-woman, it was the kind of kiss that spelled out Danny's feelings. He wants me back."

"While we're speaking woman-to-woman, dear," Betty said. "Let me fill you in on a few things. Danny does not want you back."

The sudden look on Lindsay's face made it all the more enjoyable for Betty to continue. "You see," she went on. "Danny is very happy with his new girl Krysten. And this instigative behavior of yours is not in anyone's best interest. Not even yours."

"Are you telling me you like Krysten?"

"She's not the first girl I would have chosen for my son," she admitted. "And I certainly don't approve of their current living arrangement. But she's basically a good girl. Danny loves her. And there's a certain potential for a happy life together. And I just want to see my son be happy."

"All Krysten does is bitch at him."

"Well, your profanity aside," she said judgmentally. "She didn't start getting snippy until you resurfaced. She would be fine if you would just go away."

"Betty!" Lindsay gasped. "I thought you were on my side!"

"I'm on my son's side," she said. "That's the only side I'm on."

"Me too," Lindsay said. "I'm only thinking of Danny. We were happy together once. We can be happy together again. Isn't that what you want?"

"Danny is happy with Krysten," she said. "If you had been happy, you wouldn't have dumped him for that drunken what's-his-name. Evan McIntyre."

"Ethan McIntosh," Lindsay corrected. "Anyway, that was a mistake. I know that now. I made a mistake, I learned my lesson and I'll never do anything stupid like that ever again."

"Whatever happened to your little drunk?"

"Well, he still harasses me at work," Lindsay sighed. "They've thrown him out of the building more than once. I've considered getting a restraining order. I've been staying with a friend of mine named Vicky Needlebaum. Luckily, Ethan doesn't know where she lives."

"A restraining order, huh?"

"Betty, don't you dare even think it," Lindsay said. "I see that look on your face. It's different with Danny and me."

"Ethan's harassing you," she observed. "You're harassing my son. It's a wonder you get any work done. How do you keep from getting fired?"

"Betty, I..."

"And if the drunk is harassing you," she continued. "Then you know how Danny feels when you bother him."

"But, Danny and I were meant for each other."

"If you really feel that way," she asked. "Then why are you wasting your time with drunks?"

"It was a mistake! A terrible mistake!"

"Lindsay," she said. "Let's cut to the chase. You threw Danny away and you're not getting him back. So let's make this easy on everybody. How much will it take for you to go away and never bother Danny again? Just name the amount."

Lindsay gasped, "You're trying to buy me off?"

"Seriously," she said. "Money is no object. Danny's father left me quite well off when he died, thank The Lord. Name your price."

"Betty," she said. "This isn't about money. I love Danny. And no amount of money is going to change that."

"You'd be surprised, dear," she said. "Love comes and goes, but ten thousand bucks lasts forever. Or at least it'll keep you warm 'til the next man comes along."

"Betty, I could never..."

"Sure you could," she interrupted. "All you need is to meet a nice young man. Hopefully, a good, wholesome, church-going man. Someone to get you back on track."

"Hello, Mrs. Stark...I mean Betty."

She looked up with surprise. "Jeremy!" she smiled. "Fancy meeting you here."

"I was just stopping in for some lunch," he said.

"How wonderful," she said. "Lindsay Bainbridge, this is Jeremy Blackwell. He's a friend of mine from church."

"Nice to meet you," he said.

"Why don't you join us?" Betty offered. "We just ordered. I'm sure the waiter could set a place for you."

"Well I..."

"I won't take no for an answer," she said. "There's no need for you to eat alone. And it would be nice to have a handsome young man to keep us company. Wouldn't it, Lindsay? What do you say, Jeremy? Would you like to join us?"

He looked down at Lindsay. "I think it would be delightful," he said.

Lindsay could smell a set-up. She glared at Betty as Jeremy took a seat beside her.

* * * * * *

In another part of town, a young couple was already eating in a more modest restaurant.

"I'm glad you stuck around for the food this time," he said.

"You haven't blindsided me with any devastating news yet," she said. "Why? Do you have any more surprises for me?"

"No."

"And don't trivialize kissing that slut, Daniel," she said. "It never even would have happened if you hadn't run off to see her when we were at your mother's."

"It *was* trivial, Krysten," he insisted. "And I told you I only went to see her because she threatened to come over and ruin the picnic. We'd already had one catfight at that picnic. My mother didn't need to go through seeing another one. My mother's starting to get used to you. I'd like to keep things moving in a positive direction."

"Well…thanks…I guess."

"Don't let Lindsay get to you," he advised. "She's just being a manipulative, conniving little bastard. I told you she's just trying to drive a wedge between us so she can swoop in and break us up. Don't play into her hand. She is no threat to you. I promise I love you, Krysten. You've got nothing to worry about from her."

"I still want to wring her scrawny little neck," she said. "We still have to do something about her, Danny. I'm not going to put up with her shit forever. What are we going to do about her?"

"Don't worry about it," he said. "My mother's on the case even as we speak."

"Your mother?"

"Yes," he said. "I think she took Lindsay out to lunch today. They're probably out somewhere right now."

"Your mother is taking Lindsay to lunch?" she asked. "What on earth for?"

"I don't know," he said. "She wouldn't tell me. After she heard about our argument last night, she offered to step in and talk to Lindsay."

"How did Betty hear about our fight?"

"I called her this morning," he said. "I was still mad until we talked."

"And Betty's stepping in and talking to Lindsay?" she smiled. "I wonder what she has in mind."

"Who knows?" he shrugged. "But don't let her easy-going, religious demeanor fool you. She can be a shrewd, calculating, sharp old lady when she wants to be. She's pretty good at getting things done."

"And you think she's working on our behalf?" she asked. "Working to keep us together and get rid of the slut?"

"Mom knows I'm crazy about you," he said. "My happiness is her main concern. And like I said, you're growing on her. She's starting to warm up to you."

"Do you really think so?"

"Trust me," he said. "Mom's on the case. And when my mother steps into the fray, things get done and battles get won."

"Wow," she said happily. "Betty's starting to like me? That's sweet. I wonder what she has in mind for that little trouble-maker."

Seeing her sweet smile brightened his lunchtime. His appetite was already returning to normal. The morning's headache seemed like a distant memory.

Even at that moment, he was considering ordering dessert.

* * * * * *

"So, how'd everything go?"

"You're not going to believe it, Vicky."

"What happened?"

"Danny's mother only offered to buy me lunch," she explained. "Because she's trying to get me to leave Danny alone. Do you believe it? She actually tried to buy me off."

"She did?" Vicky asked. "How much did she offer?"

"We didn't get too much into details," she said. "But I think I heard the number ten thousand being tossed out to me."

"Are you kidding?" Vicky gasped. "She offered you ten thousand dollars to stay away from her son?"

"Not specifically," she said. "We didn't get into the numbers to any great extent."

"Why not?" Vicky said. "With numbers like ten thousand floating around, I would have been all ears."

"I love Danny," she declared. "You can't put a price tag on that."

"For ten thousand smackers," Vicky said. "I'd be willing to negotiate."

"You have no soul, Vicky."

"Soul is all very well and good," Vicky stated. "But it doesn't pay the rent. I like Danny too. But you're a fool if you passed up an offer like that to move along."

"One day you'll find true love too, Vicky," she said. "Then you'll know how I feel. Anyway, none of that mattered. Betty also tried to set me up with one of her little church friends."

"She did?"

"Yeah," she laughed. "Do you believe it? She tried to pass it off like a 'chance meeting' as if the guy just 'happened to accidentally' show up in the same restaurant as us. But Betty's not much of an actor. She let the guy join us for lunch."

"So, what's he like?"

"Not too bad," she said. "He could lose a few pounds, I guess. But overall, he's not bad looking. His name is Jeremy Blackwell. He's 29. Clean cut. I could do a lot worse. He's kind of religious, though."

"What does he do?"

"Get this," she smiled. "An uncle died about five years ago and left him a tidy sum of money. He's getting monthly annuities 'til he's thirty. Then he gets the rest in a lump sum. Also, his father died a year ago. He's supposed to inherit some of that, plus even more when his mother dies. But, she lives in Canada now, so it's hard to say how long it's going to take to sort out all the legal work."

"So, you're saying he's rich?"

"Well," she considered her response. "Let's say he's comfortably well off. I don't know if he really does anything in the way of a job. But, who cares? He told me he's invested in a few local businesses, but he hasn't even gotten used to having the money. He's been sitting on most of it. He still drives around in an old pile of junk, for God's sake! Isn't that a riot?"

"If he's still driving an old, beat-up car," Vicky asked. "How do you know he's telling you the truth about being rich? You know, some men lie about stuff like that, Lindsay. You know what guys are like."

"Betty backed up his story," she said. "She's known about his money for a while."

"Really?" Vicky brightened. "Sounds interesting. So, are you going to give him a try?"

"I told him I'd go out with him tomorrow night," she said. "I figured, why not? It's a date for Saturday. It might be fun. I'm sure it'll make Danny jealous."

"Wait a minute," Vicky said. "Are you just doing this to make Danny jealous?"

"Sure," she shrugged. "Why else? Nothing else has worked. Danny's still playing hard to get."

"He's with another woman!"

"For now," she said confidently. "But wait 'til he sees me with one of his mother's rich church friends. It'll drive him nuts. I just know it."

"Lindsay," her friend said. "Are you just playing with this guy to get back at Danny? That's not fair. In fact, it's kind of mean, don't you think? You shouldn't intentionally hurt this guy's feelings."

"Oh, stop!" she said. "Everybody has an agenda in dating. Everybody. That guy tries to pass himself off as being so religious. But all the time we were talking, I could see the lust in his eyes. He knows what he's after, just like I know what I'm after. It's all a game, sweetheart. Everything is just a game."

"Oh God, Lindsay," she said. "Just be careful. Those kinds of games can always backfire on you. Aside from the fact that it's wrong to just hurt this guy, you can never tell what kind of a nut he may be."

"Jesus, Vicky," she scoffed. "Not everybody's a nut. What are the chances this guy's going to end up being a whacko? I usually can tell a whacko when I see one."

"Then how do you explain Ethan?"

"You've got a point there," her smile vanished. "But only one guy in a million can be that much of a maniac. I've already had my fair share. I'm sure this guy's fine. Besides, we're just having fun."

"Okay, just be careful," Vicky advised. "That's all I'm saying."

"I'm *always* careful."

"If that were true," Vicky reminded. "You wouldn't be staying here with me now."

* * * * * *

"Stan! Kyle!" he called. "Can I speak with you for a moment please?"

"Sure, Chief," Paczecki said. "What can we do for you?"

"Stanley Paczecki?" he introduced. "Kyle Grogan? I'd like you to meet Ray Spapper and Patrick Van Leer. They're detectives for the State Police."

"Excuse me," Grogan interrupted. "Did you say 'Spapper'?"

"That's right."

"They've been called in to help with your Paradox case," he said. "Now that a prominent senator is involved, big names have expressed an interest. I believe you boys have seen the latest headlines?"

"Indeed we have," Paczecki said. He looked down at the newspaper on his desk. The blaring banner read:

PARADOX STRIKES AGAIN!
NOTED SENATOR LATEST VICTIM!

"I expect you gentlemen to give Detectives Spapper and Van Leer your full cooperation," he said. "And every courtesy. We are grateful to have The State Police lend us a hand in this very important case."

"Of course, Chief," Paczecki said. "It's nice to meet you, gentlemen. And we're delighted to have your help."

"And we'll be glad to share everything we have so far on the case," Grogan added politely. "Have a seat, gentlemen."

"Thank you," Spapper said. He and his partner sat down.

"So, I can leave you alone to get started?" the chief said. "I don't need to tell you that big names want progress to happen in this case rather quickly. Fill these guys in fast! Then get them out to the latest murder scene... pronto!"

"Leave it to us, Chief," Paczecki said. "We've got you covered."

"We'll be glad to share everything we have," Grogan said. "But, would you give us a moment alone first?"

"Sure," Spapper said.

The two city detectives stepped away a bit for privacy.

"Do you see these two guys," Grogan whispered. "They're a bit stiff and stodgy."

"Yeah," Paczecki agreed quietly. "I guess you have to be like that when you work for The State Police. Man! I was expecting they'd send someone over eventually because of the senator. But they sure didn't waste any time, did they?"

"Watch your back," Grogan advised. "These guys will stick a knife in you quicker than our friend Paradox."

"I think you're right," Paczecki whispered. "All of a sudden, this kind of help doesn't sound so appealing. We're going to have to crack down hard on this case. I refuse to be outdone by a guy named Spapper."

CHAPTER 7
LUCIFER

Rain continued to fall during the early evening. It was a steady, dark and gloomy rain that dampened moods as it soaked the streets.

However, one girl was determined to remain optimistic.

"Where are we going tonight, Danny?" she asked.

She was still running from room to room in the apartment. She was in a mad dash to get ready.

"Didn't you say you wanted to see that new action film?" he called after her as she sped into the bathroom. "You know, the one with that goofy little guy you've always had a crush on?"

"I never said I had a crush on him," she called back. "I said he was nice looking."

"You said you and your friends were all 'gah-gah' over him in school," he reminded.

"We were kids then," she replied. "And he's not goofy-looking."

"Anyway," he continued. "That movie opens tonight. I figure we can start out going to that seafood place you like over on 41st. Then, we can hop over to The Cineplex and I can watch you go 'gah-gah' over your boyfriend."

"He's not my boyfriend," she said as she came out of the bathroom. "But it does sound nice. I do want to see that movie. What times does it start?"

"If we leave soon," he said. "We'll be able to eat with plenty of time to catch the 9:30 showing."

"Sounds good," she said. "I'll be ready in just a few minutes. And you're taking me to The Bayside for dinner? What's with all the special treatment?"

"Well, it is Friday night," he pointed out. "And I know it's been a rough week for you with all this Lindsay business. You've had your bad moments, but overall you've been very patient. And I want to thank you for being a good girl, Krysten. And I also just want to make sure we're still good."

She stopped in front of him. She smiled as she looked up at him.

"Yeah, we're good, honey," she said. "And for the record, the only guy I'm still 'gah-gah' over is you."

She stood on her toes and gave him a quick kiss. Then, she ran off into the bedroom.

"That's nice," he said. "Let's keep it that way."

"So do you think your mother really took care of the Lindsay situation?" she called from the bedroom.

"We can only hope," he said. "For tonight, I just want to forget about the whole thing and focus on us."

"Me too."

A minute later, she came out of the bedroom. "We've been eating out a lot this week," she observed. "Are you sure you can afford it?"

"That's what credit cards are for," he said. "Getting through life's many little tragedies."

"That's very true," she agreed. "Though I would hardly call Lindsay a 'little' tragedy. She's more of a typhoon."

"You may be right," he said. "Let's just hope the typhoon is over."

"Amen to that," she said while grabbing her purse. "Are we ready to go?"

"I've been ready for half an hour."

"Don't get smart, wise guy," she said. "Remember, we're going to see that guy that I'm all 'gah-gah' over tonight."

"He doesn't even know you're alive."

"Then I guess I'm stuck with you."

"Must be a living hell."

"I've learned to live with disappointment," she poked. She kissed him again.

He opened the door.

"And I turned down Lindsay for this," he said.

"Daniel!"

"Okay, okay," he gave in with a smile. "You win. I'm sorry. I'm sorry! Let's go, my little 'gah-gah girl'."

He locked the door behind them as they left.

* * * * * *

"Well, this is an ugly scene," he observed. "It looks like your boy has a flair for the sick and grizzly."

"That's one disturbed little nut case," his partner agreed.

"So, now you see what we're dealing with, gentlemen," Paczecki said.

"And this isn't his first?"

"No," Paczecki said. "Handwriting experts have confirmed that the same person wrote the notes that were found at both scenes."

"So first he kills a prostitute," he said. "Then he kills a 51-year-old senator and his 20-year-old mistress. And he leaves these Jesus-freak notes at each of the murder scenes. Is that right?"

"These murders must be premeditated," his partner added. "Why else would he carry around paper and a pen?"

"He might keep stuff like that in his car," Grogan pointed out.

"What kind of a nut carries pens and paper in their car?" Van Leer asked.

"What kind of nut goes killing people, cutting out their hearts and leaving notes?" Grogan asked.

There was a moment of silence.

"It's okay, Patrick," his partner said. "Some people carry pens and paper in their car. It's not that strange."

"It's possible this guy knew both the hooker and the senator," Paczecki suggested. "Maybe he knew the hooker and the intern. But, I doubt those people travel in the same circles. Frankly, I think it's more likely that the hooker was more of an impulse kill. He saw her, got turned on and found that as some sort of reason to kill her. Then, he probably saw Zanella and Cosgrove out somewhere, and once again that set him off."

"You think these are all impulse kills?" he asked. "It does make sense."

"We've talked to our resident psychiatric expert a few times," Paczecki said. "He seems to think that it's a reasonable assumption that this guy has been victimized and traumatized and is trying to cope with severe distress and anxiety in a way that could well respond negatively to impulsive stimuli."

"And of course," he added. "Religion is a convenient excuse to justify himself."

"Sure," Paczecki nodded. "But religion may well have played a role in his problem."

"What the hell does that mean?" Van Leer asked.

"Nobody knows yet," Paczecki said. "This guy has some reasoning behind his actions. It's too early to tell what he wants. With just two crime scenes, it's hard to make a connection. And it's hard to pin this guy down to what he's up to."

"Well, speaking as a Catholic," Van Leer said. "I have no patience with these whackos that think religion is an excuse to go around killing people. I strongly believe what I was taught as a kid. But, God doesn't tell people to go around killing people! Not like this! Not because they do stupid shit like this! That's why God created Heaven and Hell. Sure, people sin! But that's why we have cops! That's why I became a cop!"

"Calm down, Van Leer," Paczecki said. "Believe me. I know how you feel. Kyle and I are both Catholics. We both believe in our faith, and we know people like Lindquist and Zanella sin. And God doesn't like sin. But that doesn't justify what this man is doing. We know this man is not a reflection of any real religion. And we know

God didn't call for any of this. This has nothing to do with God, or The Devil, or any religion or whatever. This is only about one really screwed up guy. He's giving the concept of religion a bad name. And it's our job to find him and stop him."

"Stan's right, Patrick," he said. "We can't take this personally. We all have to get on the same team. And I think it would be best if we all got on a first-name basis."

"Fine with me," Paczecki said.

"And all we have to go on so far," Spapper said. "Is that he's a white male, A positive blood with a size 11 shoe."

"Yup," Paczecki said. "He left a few bloody footprints on the carpet right there."

"And he also took a .38 Special registered to Audrey Lindquist from his first victim," Grogan added.

"The prostitute," Van Leer said.

"That's right."

"And did you say you were going to help out that other hooker?" Van Leer asked. "The one who killed her pimp?"

"He wasn't her pimp," Grogan corrected. "He was trying to force his way in and take the girls over. No doubt taking advantage of the Paradox headlines in the paper."

"So, why are you helping the hooker?" Van Leer asked.

"I'm not doing that much," Grogan said. "I'm just going to have a quick word with the DA. Maybe the judge, if it gets that far."

"Why?"

"Why not?" Grogan said. "She's basically a good girl. It was simply a case of self defense."

"A good girl?" Van Leer scoffed. "She's a hooker. She carries a gun. She shoots people. She's a murderer!"

"It was self defense!"

"That's enough, boys," Spapper said. "Let's get back to the case."

Grogan leaned over to his partner.

"I'm glad they gave us this extra help," he whispered. "This case is getting longer by the minute."

"Ssshhh," Paczecki cautioned as he watched the State detectives inspect the crime scene.

"I'm glad this case has nothing to do with religion," Grogan continued. "Because right now The Devil is making me want to punch that one guy right in the face."

"I know," Paczecki whispered back. "But 'love thy neighbor' instead, okay? For my sake?"

* * * * * *

Later that evening, the rain had all but stopped. There was still a light, cool drizzle that left a damp, misty haze over the deep, eerie darkness.

Toward the back of the tall, brick building, was a narrow, isolated alley. The only two small lights suspended from walls did little to illuminate the dreary, spooky atmosphere of the litter-ridden passage. A cheap, makeshift plywood platform just outside a screen door served as a smoking area for patrons near a crowded, back alley parking lot.

Four people were talking and laughing on the platform. When the last person threw his cigarette butt in one of the spittoons, they all went back in through the screen door.

The man held the door open for the two young women who stepped out onto the platform. Both women tried to shelter themselves from the drizzle under an inadequate overhang. They each took a cigarette from packs in their purses.

They shared a lighter and each took a drag.

"I don't believe you're leaving me, Vicky," she said. "I don't believe you're going to bail on girls' night so you can take off with some guy you just met in a place like this."

"You're the one who wanted to come here, Lindsay," she said. "Frankly, I don't believe you chose this place. Aren't you afraid Ethan will come looking for you here?"

"No," she said. "We never used to come here. Ethan never wanted to come to a place like Waivers. He always thought it was a cheap pickup joint."

"It kind of *is* a cheap pickup joint."

"So, why are you taking off with that guy?" she pressed. "I didn't know you were turning into that kind of girl."

"I'm not!" Vicky insisted. "I'm not going to sleep with him. We're just going someplace quiet so we can talk and get to know each other."

"Sure. Whatever you say."

"Lindsay!" Vicky defended with a smile. "You know me better than that."

"But this is supposed to be girls' night out."

"You'll be alright," Vicky said. "We came in your car."

"Yeah," she admitted. "But, I figured if I got wasted, you could drive us home."

"Are you planning on getting wasted?"

"No," she said. "I just needed a night out. All week long I've had no luck with Danny. Ethan has been driving me up the wall. He won't stop calling my cell phone or harassing me at work. I have that date tomorrow night with Betty Stark's religious friend. I just needed a girls' night. And now, you're bailing on me."

"That reminds me," Vicky said. "I have to get back inside before Tom disappears. Will you be alright?"

"I guess."

"You're not worried that Ethan will come looking for you here?" Vicky asked. "He knows you like this place."

"No," she said. "We never used to come here, so he'll never think of this place. Plus, he thinks I'm cheating on him, so he wouldn't think I need a cheap pickup joint. Is your friend parked out front or in the back?"

"I don't know."

"I still don't believe the owners let people park in the back here," she said. "It doesn't seem like a safe place to park."

"You come out here to smoke, don't you?"

"Yeah, but that's different."

"Listen," Vicky said as she tossed her cigarette in a spittoon. "I gotta go. Tom won't wait for me forever. You have your key to my place?"

"Yeah," she said. "Go on. Good night, honey. And keep your zipper up."

"Lindsay!" Vicky gasped with feigned shock. "Okay. Good night."

She hurried back in through the screen door.

Lindsay stood alone on the platform. She couldn't believe there weren't more people out here. It wasn't as busy in Waivers as she would have expected on a Friday night. It was warm, but the dampness gave her a chill.

She looked up into the darkness. The one lamp she could see gave off a scant light. It almost seemed like there was a halo around the bulb. A halo with a faint wisp of a rainbow around it.

She took a drag from her cigarette. Then she heard a voice.

"Hello, Lindsay."

She looked up. "Ethan!" she gasped.

"I had a feeling I'd find you here," he said as he stepped toward her.

"Stay away from me, Ethan," she said. "I told you we're through."

"We're not through," he said. "Until I say we're through."

"Oh God," she said. "You're drunk. Stay back!"

"You don't get to tell me what to do," he snarled. "I don't believe what you put me through this week. Where the hell have you been, you little tramp?"

"Don't, Ethan!" she said shakily as she backed away. "Don't touch me!"

"I'll touch you if I want," he demanded as he grabbed her upper arms. He shook her. "Where were you, bitch? How dare you try to leave me? What the hell is wrong with you? If you try that again, I'm going to pound you to a pulp!"

"Ow!" she sobbed. "Let go, Ethan! You're hurting me!"

"So what?" he growled. "You deserve it for what you fucking did to me, you whore!"

He let go as he slapped her hard across the face. She cried out as the force of his hand knocked her back against the wall. She bounced off the wall and fell off the platform and into a puddle.

"Ow, Ethan! Please stop!"

She had dropped her purse on the platform. Ethan snatched up her purse and started to rummage through it.

"Ethan!" she complained. "What are you doing? You have no right!"

She gasped as he dumped her purse out on the platform.

"Ethan! What the hell?"

He shuffled through the clutter and grabbed what he was looking for.

"Ethan!" she gasped. "My keys! What are you doing? Give me those back!"

"I'm keeping these!" he warned. "You ain't going nowhere, bitch!"

"You can't do that to me!" she averred. "Give me my keys!"

"I shouldn't have to do this!" he corrected sharply. "But you can't be trusted, you dumb little shit! If you stayed home where you belong, I could treat you like an adult. But since you insist on acting like a worthless little whore who likes to run away, I'll keep these 'til you grow the hell up!"

"Give me those!" she said as she got out of the puddle. "Look at that! You dumped my whole purse out, you ass! It's all over the place!"

"Then, pick it up!" he demanded. "*Pick it up*!"

She was crying as she crawled around on the platform on her hands and knees. She idly threw things back into her purse.

"Here's what's going to happen," he informed her. "I got your keys. I saw your car in the lot out back. You're going to go back to your car and wait for me. I'll drive you home where you belong. I'll pick up my car tomorrow after we've decided what to do about you being a dumb bitch who doesn't know who she belongs to. You got that?"

She was too busy crying and restocking her purse to respond.

He grabbed her roughly by the hair. He jerked her head up so she was looking at him.

"Ow! Ethan! Stop!

"I said, 'You got that', bitch?"

"Please stop, Ethan," she sobbed.

He still held her hair tightly as he gave her another hard slap. She was trapped on her knees. She cried openly as she finally said, "Yes, okay."

He finally let go of her hair. "Now get back to your car," he warned. "You'd better be there when I get there. I'll only be a minute. I got to take a whiz. Now, go!"

She stood up with her purse. She practically ran to her car in the back parking lot. She knew she had no choice. Her face hurt. Her hip hurt from when she had fallen off the platform. She was absolutely terrified.

Ethan didn't want to waste time going inside. He stepped behind the dumpster. It's a good thing he was alone.

When he was done, he stepped out from behind the dumpster. He was about to go to the parking lot.

However, he saw a man. Or rather, it was the silhouette of a man. In the dim lighting of the alley, he saw little more than just a faceless shadow.

"What are you looking at?" he asked in a threatening voice.

The silhouette didn't reply. It just stood still.

"Hey!" he shouted. "I'm talking to you! What are you, deaf?"

The silhouette still remained silent and still.

"Say something!" he warned. "What's the matter with you?"

Then, he gasped. In this insufficient light, it was suddenly obvious that the shadow-man was holding a gun.

With a new sense of fear, he took a step backward. "Hey," he said. "What is this? What's your problem, pal?"

The shadow-man took a step toward him.

He took another step back. "Why don't you put that thing away?" he suggested. "There's no need for any of this."

He began to tremble as the shadow-man pointed the gun squarely at the middle of his chest.

"Come on!" he coaxed nervously. "Joke's over! Cut it out! Who are you? Are you that guy Lindsay keeps talking about? What his name? Danny Stark?"

There was a silencer on the gun. It hardly made a sound as the silhouette fired two shots. His target stumbled back against the brick wall as the bullets sunk deep into the ribs near his heart.

He dropped the keys in his hand. He slid down into another shallow puddle. He was in pain. His chest was bleeding.

Even from his vulnerable position, he still couldn't see a face in that silhouette as it stood over him. He looked up from the puddle. The one light from the building next door made it look as if the silhouette had a halo.

There was no face. But there was a halo.

The damp drizzle kept everything in a haze. And as he looked up from the puddle, something else made him gasp. He didn't know if it was the haze, the blood or the pain.

Maybe it was the alcohol.

But somehow, it appeared as though horns had grown out of the silhouette's head! Just like The Devil! It sent a cold chill up his spine.

"Oh my God!" he cried. "Who are you? The Devil? Satan? Lucifer?"

The shadow-man still said nothing. He just aimed the gun right at his target's face.

"No, Lucifer! Please!" he begged. "Don't kill me, Satan! Please! I don't want to die! Please! Spare me, Lucifer! Please spare my life!"

He cried as he begged.

The shadow-man still said nothing. He just aimed the gun. He pulled the trigger.

Fifteen minutes later, Lindsay was still sitting in her car. She was still trembling with fear. Her face still hurt.

She couldn't believe Vicky had left the passenger door open. But at this point, she was grateful. She was glad to be out of that aggravating drizzle.

She was still terrified. But she was curious as to what was keeping Ethan. He shouldn't have been gone this long. She had heard a few cars coming or going. Still, it had been exceedingly quiet in this back lot.

A growing part of her wanted to go back into the bar. But, she had better not! Ethan had her car keys. There was no escaping him now. And she didn't want to risk making him any angrier.

She was so frightened! But how long would Ethan be?

Maybe he was so drunk he passed out. She knew she wouldn't be so lucky. Still, she decided to go looking. She cautiously got out of the car. She looked around.

"Ethan?" she called out.

There was no response.

She slowly made her way between rows of cars. She kept watching as she neared the alley where she had been smoking. She knew she should start looking there.

It didn't take long to reach the alley. She looked down the narrow, dirty passage. The dumpster and the platform were visible in the dim light. There was even some trash.

But, there was no sign of Ethan.

She called his name again. There was still no reply.

The ground was still damp. The rain was nearly over. There were smears on the ground that oddly seemed unfamiliar. She had just been down this alley and hadn't noticed these smears.

Could they be blood?

She didn't know. She didn't really need to find out. She cautiously ventured into the alley.

"Ethan?"

There was still no reply. No one was on the platform. It's strange how often this evening that platform was empty. Fewer people must be smoking these days.

She continued to look around as she neared the platform. A small, shiny object caught her eye on the ground over by the dumpster. She walked over and looked down.

"My keys!" she sighed with a smile. "But how…?"

She recognized them by the small fuzzy puppy on the key ring. She looked around.

Strange! Still no sign of Ethan. Oh well. Thank God for little favors.

She bent down and picked up the keys. Those spooky spatters and smears seemed to start here near the wall.

Could be blood. Didn't know. Didn't care.

She stood and glanced around. The coast was clear. She ran down the alley as quickly as possible.

She sped through the lot between cars. She reached her car with no sign of any other life. She made one last scan of the area. There was nobody in sight.

With a sigh of relief, she hopped in her car. She put the key in the ignition. The motor whirred but wouldn't catch.

"Come on!" she begged. "Please start!"

She turned the key again. Still no luck!

"Damn it!" she swore. "Please don't do this to me now! Please!"

She tried one more time. The car finally started.

She said a silent thank you. Then, she drove back to Vicky's place as fast as she could. She didn't feel safe until she was inside the apartment with the door locked.

Even then, she was still trembling.

* * * * * *

As the rain was drawing to a close in the dark of night, an attractive young couple sat at a table in a middle class restaurant.

"I can't tell you how good it is to see you, Stephanie," he said. "It's been murder going without seeing you. I've hardly even been allowed to talk to you since that sick little scene with your husband. I don't have to remind you how scary that was. And even when I've talked to you on the phone, you haven't sounded good. Are you alright?"

"I'm fine, Mark," she said. "But I'll admit I've missed you too."

"So, you still haven't told me," he said. "What did Trey do after I left?"

"It doesn't matter now."

"What does that mean?" he asked with concern. "Did he hurt you?"

"No," she said as if it were true. "We had sex, alright? Is that what you wanted to hear?"

"You had sex with him?" he asked with surprise. "Really? Did he force you?"

"What is it with you?" she questioned. "What would even make you ask such a thing?"

"I saw how he looked when he shot at me and chased me out of there," he reminded. "He was a raving maniac. What would make you have sex with a raving maniac?"

"He's my husband."

"This conversation is going nowhere," he sighed. "And it's not how I want to spend the brief time I have to spend with you. How did you get away from Trey tonight?"

"He's gone out of town overnight on business," she muttered. "Or so he says. Of course, he gave me the third degree before he left. Where am I going? What will I do? He said if I try to contact you, he'll go insane. I half expected him to whip out a chastity belt before he was done. He wouldn't leave me alone for a minute right after he caught us, but it didn't take a week for him to go right back to normal."

"It's the same with Cassandra," he said. "I think she's taking inventory at her boutique this evening."

"I just talked to her for the first time in a while," she said. "She's real hurt by this. It tore my heart out."

"We didn't plan this, Stephanie."

"That doesn't make it hurt any less," she said. "She told me she's done with you. She told me I could have you. She wants a divorce."

"She said the same thing to me."

"You know she doesn't mean it," she informed him. "Well, she may go through with the divorce, but she doesn't want me to have you."

"I don't want the divorce either," he said. "I wish there was a nice, clean, painless way out of this. I don't want anyone to get hurt. Not even Trey. Maybe we should both just go through with a divorce. Maybe it would clear the way..."

"This is not how I want it to be, Mark."

"I know," he agreed. "But what are we supposed to do? I can't just pretend I don't still feel something for you. I mean, I love my wife. But every moment I'm away from you is like a sentence to Hell. Even as I sit here now, it's nearly impossible to keep my hands off you."

He took her hand.

"I understand, honey," she said as she squeezed his fingers gently in hers. "But, we have to be strong. We have to think of the greater good. Oh God! This is like quitting a bad drug habit or something."

"Maybe we can start slowly," he suggested. "Like using the patch to quit cigarettes. Just so long as I don't have to quit touching you cold turkey."

He leaned over and kissed her.

"You're not making this easy," she said. "And, I don't think they have a patch for this."

"Too bad we couldn't invent one," he said. "We'd make a fortune."

He kissed her again. This kiss was longer and more intimate.

"I should've known it was a mistake to just come out and see you face-to-face," she said. "I always convince myself before seeing you that I'm going to be strong in my resolve. But then when I see you, I just melt. And you don't even try to cooperate."

"Well, I have the same problem," he admitted. "I want to be good. But when I see you, I can't help myself. I just want to..."

This was a very long and passionate kiss.

"You know we shouldn't do this," she said.

"We'll be kicking ourselves tomorrow," he said before another long kiss.

"I haven't finished my food yet," she said.

"That's why they invented doggy bags."

There was another kiss.

"Damn it, Mark," she said. "I'm still hungry."

"I know how you feel," he said. "But what I'm hungry for won't show up on the bill from the restaurant."

She pulled away before they kissed again.

"No!" she averred. "I'm at least going to finish eating first."

"Alright," he sighed. "You have a point. I have to pay for this food. We might as well enjoy it."

"Thank you," she said. "At least one of us has to exercise a little restraint. We're supposed to be trying to end this thing."

"I know you're right," he admitted. "And, I'd like to save my marriage. I do love my wife. But how are we supposed to end this? You and I do have something special, Stephanie. You know that. And what's going to change? You said yourself that even after Trey caught us, it didn't take him a week to bury himself in work again. And your sister is never going to stop devoting her whole life to that store of hers."

"That doesn't give us a free hand to do whatever we want," she said.

"So what do you suggest?"

"I don't know," she said. "I don't want to think about it right now."

"Me either," he said. "I don't have all night. I'm not sure how long Cassandra will be at the boutique. Can we go to your place?"

"That's not a good idea."

"I thought you said Trey was out of town."

"That's what he said," she explained. "But frankly, I don't trust him. He was supposed to be gone all day last Monday when he caught us. I never saw him like that. I don't want to go through anything like that again."

"I thought you said he didn't hurt you."

"Sure," she said. "But he's been a lunatic all week. God knows what he'll be like if he catches us again. He shocked me with how crazy he got on Monday. You can never tell how crazy people can get until you see it up close. And this city is full of crazy people. They're everywhere. It could be the person next to you. Have you heard about that maniac the papers are calling Paradox? He thinks he's killing people in the name of God. Last week, he killed a hooker. And this week he killed a married senator who was screwing some young intern who was half his age."

"Yeah, but that's not Trey," he scoffed. "What are the chances? One in a zillion? Trey's not even religious, is he?"

"He is a little," she said. "I don't think he's that bad. But I bet even those who are close to Paradox have no idea who he is."

"Oh, stop being paranoid," he said. "There are millions of people in this city. You will never run into that psychopath Paradox. And Trey is definitely *not* a serial killer!"

"I know," she said. "I'm just saying you can never tell how crazy people are until you find out the hard way."

"Are you sure Trey didn't hurt you?"

"Yes!" she insisted. "Now will you drop the subject, please?"

"So what do we do tonight then?" he asked. "Go to a motel?"

"I hate going to motels."

"So what should we do then?"

"I don't know," she complained. "It's all so complicated. I want to end this mess, but I don't know what to do."

He leaned over and kissed her.

"Let me simplify things for you," he offered. "At least for tonight. We'll go to a motel for now. We'll worry about tomorrow when it happens."

She just looked at him. She didn't speak. She was weakening again.

He kissed her again. It was a longer, more passionate kiss.

"What do you say, honey?" he coaxed. "The Quarter Moon Motel?"

"I hate that place!"

"I know, sweetie," he said before the next kiss. "But you love their hot tub."

"This is absolutely the last time, Mark!"

"Of course it is."

She felt so guilty as she kissed him again. It almost made her sick to feel this compulsion…knowing she would surrender and follow him into that motel room.

But even as she kissed him, she knew it would not be the last time.

* * * * * *

It was very late. It had been a long night. He'd been through so much. He was tired. He didn't have much blood on his clothes.

Good thing.

He'd had to use a burlap bag. It was a stroke of luck that he'd accidentally left one in the trunk of his car. Weighing down the bag was the hard part.

Well that, and finding a time when no cars were on the bridge. He didn't want any witnesses when he threw the weighted body into the river.

But that was all over now. He just wanted to get some sleep.

He grabbed some bottled water from the refrigerator. He plopped himself down in a big chair in the living room. Late night television was so pointless and puerile. It was bound to put him to sleep.

He left the sound low, so the inaudible drone would help him doze off. He closed his eyes.

Then, he heard a noise. People were talking. He opened his eyes. The sounds were coming from the dining room. He jumped out of the chair and ran to the source of the voices.

As he stood at the entrance to the dining room, he couldn't believe what he saw. Two people were seated across from each other at the main table. There was a chessboard set up between them. They had just started a game.

"Senator Zanella!" he gasped with shock.

The senator looked up impatiently from his game. "Ssshhh," he said to the intruder. "I have to concentrate. This girl is a good Chess player."

"B-but...you're d-dead!"

"Yes," said the senator. "And thanks for that. But I still need to focus on this game."

The girl moved her queen's knight. "You ruined one of my favorite outfits, you know," she pointed out. "I paid a fortune for this thing."

He gawked at the blouse she had worn that night. It was sliced with blood stains splattered and spilled just as it had been when he placed her corpse in the bed.

"You!" he stammered. "You're both…how did you get in here?"

"There are no locked doors when you're dead," the senator explained. "Now will you please be quiet?"

He moved a pawn.

"But, this is my house!"

"Yes," the intern said. "But this is more peaceful than my place. The police are tearing it apart. We were murdered there, you know."

"Yes," he nodded from the doorway. "But, why here? Why Chess?"

"It's the ultimate game of conquest," she explained. "Good vs. evil. We have to see who wins."

She took the senator's pawn with her bishop.

He was very confused. "Who wins?" he asked. "I don't understand."

"I'm God," she said.

"I'm Satan," said the senator.

"God?" he asked in shock. "Satan?"

"Yes," the senator replied impatiently. "Satan. The Devil. Lucifer. Beelzebub. I'm sure you've heard of me."

"She's not God!" he declared. "And you're not The Devil!"

"You're right," the senator smiled. "You caught us. We're not the real deal. The real God and Satan are vacationing together in Cancun. The Devil has a thing for Mexican chicks."

"Stop this blasphemy this instant!" he demanded. "You're making this all up! You're trying to confuse me!"

"That's what Lucifer does, my child," the senator imparted.

"You're not Lucifer!" he insisted. "You're not even here!"

The senator's eyes grew dark and sinister as he asked, "Would you like a demonstration?"

He didn't know what to say. He was still scared.

After a few moments of silence, the dining room curtains erupted in flames. Angry fires engulfed the curtains with a malicious roar.

The man in the doorway was startled. He let out a scream of sudden panic and fear.

"Spontaneous combustion," the senator explained. "Everyone's favorite."

"Will you both stop talking please?" she asked. "It's your move, Lucifer."

"Stop this!" he cried. "My curtains!"

"Don't worry," the senator said. "I won't burn your house down. Not yet, anyway. We just want to finish our game in peace."

"But…my curtains!"

"I believe Satan told you we have a game to finish," she said impatiently. "And you have some unfinished business of your own. I still haven't forgiven you, young man."

"Stop it!" he shouted. "You are not God! He is not Satan! This is blasphemy!"

"No, this is Chess," she corrected. "And you still have a lot of work to do."

The senator moved his rook out. "Leave the guy alone," he said. "He's fine."

"He still has a lot of work to do," she insisted.

The curtains were still burning.

"So he sins," the senator said. "It's no big deal. He's only human."

The intern took the senator's rook with her queen.

"Oh," the senator grunted. "I didn't see that. He keeps talking. He's ruining my concentration."

"I said he still has a lot of work to do," she repeated.

The curtains were a raging inferno.

"No! Stop it!"

"This game isn't over yet," the senator declared. "We're only just beginning."

"You still have a long way to go, young man," she stated with authority. "You still have a very long way to go!"

"No-o-o-o!"

He squeezed his eyes shut. He covered his ears with his hands. He was trembling.

After a few seconds, he opened his eyes. Everything was quiet. Everything was still. No one was sitting at the dining room table.

There was no chessboard.

The curtains were not on fire. In fact, they looked perfect.

He just stood in the dining room doorway. He was still trembling and very confused.

CHAPTER 8

NASTY HABITS

The weather was clearing beautifully for Saturday morning. Dark, gray clouds were being ushered out toward the east. A gorgeous blue sky exhibited a declining populace of puffy white clouds scurrying past a bright, warm yellow sun which rose over the increasing bustle of the urban scenery.

She was still a little shaken and depressed. She sat in front of the television with a cup of coffee in her hand. Saturday morning cartoons still amused her.

Her friend finally took a seat on the sofa with a coffee cup of her own.

"Morning, honey," she beamed. "How was your night?"

"Not as good as yours, I imagine," she muttered. "So where did you end up going last night?"

"Tom and I went to Natasha's Café and Bistro over on Bentley," she said. "I'd never been there before. It was a nice place. You should try it out sometime."

"So, did you two hit it off?"

"Yeah," she smiled. "Tom's a great guy. He works for a big brokerage firm downtown. He's taking me out again tonight."

"Did you two…?"

"Lindsay!" she interrupted. "Of course not! You know me better than that!"

"Just asking."

"What did you do after I left?" she asked. "Anything exciting?"

"No."

"Oh God, Lindsay!" she suddenly gasped. "What happened to your face?"

"Does it show?"

"Well, it's not too bad," she commented. "Just a couple of small purple bruises. What happened? Did you get drunk and fall down or something?"

"No," Lindsay shook her head sadly. "I ran into Ethan last night."

"Ethan?" she inquired with growing concern. "He did that to you?"

"It was right after you left," Lindsay explained. "Only a minute or two. I hadn't even finished my cigarette yet. He just appeared right out there on the smoker's platform. I never thought he'd look for me at Waivers. He was so trashed."

"Oh my God," she said. "What did he do?"

"He was pissed," she explained. "He started yelling and cursing. I told him to go away 'cause we're through. He knocked me off the platform."

"Oh! Honey!"

"He grabbed my purse," Lindsay continued. "He dumped it out on the platform so he could grab my keys so I couldn't go anywhere."

"Are you kidding me?"

"I was crawling around in the rain on the platform," she went on. "I was putting my stuff back in my purse. I probably ruined my good jeans. He hit me again and told me to wait for him in my car."

"What did you do?"

"I waited in my car for a while," she replied. "By the way, Vicky, thanks for leaving the passenger door unlocked again."

"Sorry."

"Anyway," she said. "Ethan never showed up. I figured he was so drunk that he passed out by the dumpster or something. But I went to the alley to see."

"You didn't go back into the bar?"

"The last place I saw Ethan was in the alley," she explained. "He still had my keys. I couldn't go anywhere without getting my keys back. But when I went to the alley, Ethan was gone. But my keys were on the ground."

"Really? I wonder what happened."

"Me too," she said. "But I didn't take the time to worry about it right then. I just figured, thank God for small miracles. I grabbed my keys and got out of there as fast as I could. I just came here."

"Here?" Vicky said. "Ethan didn't follow you, did he? I don't want any problems over here."

"I don't think so," she said. "Like I told you, I don't know what happened. Ethan just disappeared. I think we're safe. I'm just going to be careful where I go from now on."

"I told you that last night," Vicky reminded. "So, now what are you going to do?"

"I don't think I have to worry about Ethan," she said. "I'll just have to watch where I go. But, I'm worried about tonight. I can't go out on a first date with this new guy if I look like the bride of Frankenstein."

"Don't worry," Vicky said. "It's not that bad. A little make-up ought to cover it."

"Do you really think so?"

"Yeah," she assured her. "It won't take much. You'll be fine."

"I hope you're right," she said. "I was thinking of cancelling. I'd hate to do that on a first date, but I can't let him see me like this. Sure, I'm only seeing him to make Danny jealous. But that plan won't work if this Jeremy guy thinks I'm hideous-looking right from Day One."

"You've got nothing to worry about," Vicky reiterated. "Except for that making Danny jealous thing. I still think you shouldn't hurt this guy. It's wrong. Plus, you never know how guys are going to react. Just look at what happened with Ethan last night."

"I know," she said. "But I have to do something to get Danny back."

"Why don't you let Danny go?" Vicky suggested. "Why don't you give this new guy an honest chance?"

"I love Danny."

"Will you just give it a rest, please?"

"I have to follow my heart."

"Following your heart got you beaten up on the smokers' platform outside of Waivers," Vicky reminded. "It landed you here in my apartment. And you've got Danny's mother trying to buy you off and set you up.

Please don't hurt this guy. The dry cleaners are holding my best funeral dress for ransom until I come up with $13.75."

"God, Vicky," she said. "You're always so melodramatic."

"I'm just looking out for you," Vicky said. "You can't always have a miracle pop out of thin air like whatever it was that saved you last night."

* * * * * *

"I'm glad we've reached the point where we can investigate this case on our own," he said. "Those city cops get on my nerves. Especially the young one. Frankly, I don't think they could find a murderer if they saw him standing over the body while holding a smoking gun."

"Take it easy, Patrick," he said. "We don't have much to go on either. We don't even know where the senator went on the night he was killed. Since he was sneaking around having an extramarital affair with an intern who was half his age, he was being discreet. Nobody knows where he was. We've sent out press releases and put out a few TV spots asking the public to let us know if they saw him that night. But until someone comes through with some leads, we're as 'in the dark' as those other cops."

"I know," Van Leer said. "I'm just frustrated. Their resident psychiatrist, Dr. Thorndyke was a big help. He's as obtuse as our shrink. 'The killer is confused and traumatized…taught to link religion to his own self hatred.' It's the same bullshit our Dr. Finkleman would spout off."

"It's meant to help us get into the mind of the killer."

"It doesn't help us pinpoint who he is," Van Leer said. "The only help we need right now is the kind that will help us get our hands on the murderer."

"What the doctor told us is very insightful," he said. "It teaches us what to look for while we're sifting through suspects. For instance, he told us this man has probably become delusional. There's a good chance he's already hallucinating, thinking he's talking directly with God. He may be paranoid to the point of thinking The Devil is out to get him."

"Oh, big deal!" Van Leer scoffed. "I could've told you that. And I didn't need a fancy degree from Harvard to figure it out."

"You need to calm down, Patrick," he said. "We could learn a lot from that doctor."

"Oh, horse puckey!" Van Leer argued. "We'll catch this whack job when we connect that senator to the prostitute. There has to be a link. I'm not even saying they know each other. Hell! The senator seemed to be doing alright for himself without hookers. But someone knew them both. There's a connection there, and we'll find it… with or without some shrink's mindless psychobabble."

"How did I ever draw you as a partner?"

"Hey," Van Leer defended. "You could've done a lot worse. You're lucky you didn't get stuck working with that Grogan. Do you believe that guy? He's going to go talk to the DA on behalf of a hooker that murdered some pimp. What's up with that?"

"Don't let it bother you," he said. "Just stick to the case."

"We've got nothing to work with."

"Now you know how the city cops feel."

"They had a whole extra week to work on it," Van Leer said.

"And absolutely nothing has surfaced yet," he reminded. "So they had a whole extra week to get frustrated. They've talked to a few people who knew Miss Cosgrove and the senator. There are more people to talk to. But, this is going nowhere. I don't think this was done by someone who really knew them. That was Paczecki's impression. And I would tend to agree with him at this point. Of course, we'll look into it ourselves. But, for all of your griping, those city boys are no idiots."

"I know, Ray," Van Leer sighed. "You're right. I'm sorry. You know I'm usually not a bad guy. But this case just gets me riled."

"Just take it easy and act professional," he advised. "Remember we're all on the same team."

* * * * * *

The mood in their small living room hung heavy in the air. He sat in front of the television and watched her run back and forth through the apartment.

"So you're not going to say anything?" he asked.

"What is there to say?"

"I don't know," he suggested. "Yell at me. Throw something. Cry. Anything."

"I don't feel like it, Mark," she said. "I'm sorry if that disappoints you. I'm just not in the mood."

"Listen, Cassandra," he said. "I'm sorry. I don't know how else to say it. I'm very, very sorry. I don't mean to hurt you. I don't want a divorce. Believe it or not, I still love you very much."

"We've already had this conversation a number of times, Mark," she reminded. "And no matter how many times you say you're sorry or that you love me, you keep going out every time my back is turned and you screw my sister. If that's your idea of love, I can do without it."

"It's not that simple, Cassandra."

"I can live without that too," she said. "The fact that loving someone doesn't make it simple. You love someone, but you can't 'just simply' stop fucking her sister! I can *seriously* do without that!"

"Will you stop running back and forth and talk to me?"

"I *am* talking to you, Mark," she corrected. "My lips are moving. Words are coming out. If that's not talking, what is it?"

"Sarcasm isn't going to help any."

"But sleeping with Stephanie *does* help?" she inquired. "I can't even take a night to take inventory at my boutique. I can't even come home at 10:30 at night without finding you gone. You're nowhere to be seen. Thank you for being honest, at least. It's nice to know you confessed right away when you came home. I'm glad you at least didn't insult my intelligence with a bunch of lies."

"I came clean right away to cut down on the arguing," he said. "I wanted you to know that I want to be honest. And I really do want to save our marriage."

"Being honest is a good start," she said. "But it's not enough by itself. You have to stop cheating on me too."

"I'm trying, Cassandra."

"No!" she shouted. "You're not trying! If you were trying, you wouldn't have been in a cheap motel with my sister last night while I was taking inventory at my store!"

"Good," he said. "You're finally yelling. Let it all out. I know I deserve it."

"I'm not going to yell anymore," she said. "I'm past all that. No more yelling or crying or eating my heart out or blaming myself for the fact that you're an asshole. If you want Stephanie, fine! I hope you two will be very happy together. As soon as the divorce comes through, you two can do whatever you want! I don't care! Until then, I'll be at my mother's."

She came out of the bedroom again.

"Will you please put that suitcase down?" he asked.

"I don't think so," she said. "It is kind of heavy, but I don't expect you to help me with it. I only ask one favor of you, Mark."

"And what's that?"

"Could you get the door for your wife?" she asked. "Can you at least do that for me?"

"Cassandra, please don't go."

"Fine!" she snipped. "I'll get the door myself!"

As she marched to the door holding her large suitcase with both hands, he jumped to his feet.

"Alright! Alright!" he said. "I'll get the door for you. But, I really wish you would stay and talk."

He opened the door. She turned to face him from the doorway.

"It's been a wonderful marriage, Mark," she declared with a hint of sarcasm. "It's been lovely knowing you. I'll be back later to get more of my things. But for the moment, I can honestly say that I hope you just drop dead!"

"That's not a very productive attitude," he said. "Maybe you can be more mature when you cool off."

She turned and stomped out the door.

"Don't count on it," she said as she walked away.

* * * * * *

"Alcazar!" the guard called as he opened the cell door. "You have a visitor."

She looked up from her cot with expectation. She smiled as she jumped to her feet.

"Hi, Kyle," she said. "This is a pleasant surprise. Thanks for coming to see me."

"How are you, Tanya?" he asked.

"I've had better days."

"I just dropped by to tell you I talked to the DA," he informed her. "It wasn't too bad. He told me that given Delaney's record, it's easy to believe you were acting in self defense. He almost wants to drop the whole thing. Of course, it still has to go to the grand jury. The man died. It still has to be investigated. It would help if Delaney had hit you or something."

"He did hit me!" she argued. "He hit Becky too. Why do you think I shot him?"

"Did you tell this to your lawyer?"

"Becky and I both did."

"They never saw any marks on you at the time, did they?" he asked.

"I heal fast."

"Look, Tanya," he said. "The DA is still looking into it. But he was still trying to find some way of getting you some help so we can get you off the streets. Wouldn't you like that?"

"I'm doing alright."

"Wouldn't you like to get out of this mess you're in?" he asked. "Maybe get a real job and maybe a real life?"

"Don't play Priest with me, Kyle," she said. "I'm not going to give you my whole life story. Just know that my whole life sucked. It's been hell! No DA or parole officer or cop or anyone in the courts is going to help me. And I don't want nobody's help. I've made it on my own this long, and I'll still be here when that DA is dead and buried."

"Well, how long do you figure you'll be a prostitute?"

"As long as it works for me," she said. "And don't get all judgmental on me, Kyle. Sure, I've thought about getting out. But it's not that easy. This isn't just some nasty habit like forgetting to recycle. It's my life. It's what I've always done. What do I put on my job resume? Do I say I've been a hooker since I was sixteen? Who do I list as my references? The last five johns I screwed?"

"You could list me as a reference," he offered.

"That's awfully sweet of you, Kyle," she said with a softening tone. "But get off your pulpit already. I'll be fine. Okay?"

"Just trying to help."

"I know. And thank you."

After a pause, she added, "Any luck finding that killer?"

"It's been difficult," he explained. "We've talked to people around here who knew Miss Cosgrove and the senator. Nobody had anything we could use. Since they were keeping their affair a secret, it's been hard pinning down where they were last seen. We sent out some press bulletins and stuff in the papers and some TV spots. We just now got a call from a waitress who works at a restaurant called The Robin's Egg. It's a ritzy place uptown."

"I think I've heard of it."

"Apparently," he continued. "Zanella and Cosgrove had a late dinner there the night they were killed. It's the last place they were seen alive. Me and Stan are going up there tonight to ask some questions. Hopefully, something will turn up."

"I hope it works out."

"Thanks."

After another pause, he said, "Well, I guess that's all, unless you have something to add."

"Actually," she said. "I'm glad you came over. There was something I wanted to tell you about the night Audrey was murdered."

"And what's that?"

"Well, you have a lot of time to think and remember things when you're in jail," she said. "And I remembered that the last guy who picked up Audrey was in a Cadillac."

"I think we already established that," he reminded.

"No, you don't understand," she went on. "Audrey and I both approached that car, but she got there first, so I let her go. But at first, she almost backed away. She said, 'oh, it's you.' And she said something like, 'The last time I saw you, you were driving an old rust bucket.' She almost didn't go with the guy."

"And?"

"I didn't think much of it at the time," she said. "But now I remember something that happened a few days earlier. Audrey approached a guy that stopped for a red light. He was driving an old piece of junk. The guy started yelling from the car. He was calling us names like harlots and fornicators and saying we'd all go to Hell, telling us to repent. We told him to go fuck himself and he sped off. Do you think it might be the same guy?"

"Could be," he said. "Did you get a good look at him?"

"Not really," she said. "He was wearing shades. White guy in his twenties. Dark, neat hair…looked religious."

"What kind of car was he driving?"

"A brown Chevy four-door sedan," she said. "I don't remember the model. It was kind of beat-up with a big dent in the back passenger's side door. I think the backing of the back seat was even ripped. Late '80s or early '90s. Does that help at all?"

"Possibly," he said. "Did you get the license plate?"

"Sorry."

"Would Becky have seen more?"

"I doubt it," she said. "She was farther away than I was. Is Becky out of jail yet?"

"I don't know," he said. "I'll look into it for you."

"Thanks," she said. "If she is, it'll be hard catching up with her again. I don't think you'll find her on the corner of 23rd and Fairdale again."

"You're right," he agreed. "She probably will have to find a different street corner. Oh well. Thanks for the tip, Tanya. That little tidbit could come in handy."

"Thanks for your help too, Kyle," she said. She gave him a hug and a quick, grateful kiss. "You're a doll."

"You're welcome, honey," he smiled. "And, listen. I meant what I said. If you need any help getting out of this whole street corner thing..."

"Just go be a cop, will you, Kyle?" she interrupted sweetly. "Go find that scumbag that murdered Audrey."

"I'm working on it."

* * * * * *

That night was a beautiful, warm night. The air was as clear as you could have hoped for. The darkness was deep, rich and true.

A young couple sat in a quiet booth in an elegant club. The music was a gentle backdrop to the intimate ambience of the establishment.

"This is a nice little place," he observed. "I'm glad you suggested it."

"I'm glad you like it."

"So did you have a good time tonight?"

"I have to admit," she smiled. "I enjoyed it more than I was expecting."

"Why? What were you expecting?"

"I don't know," she shrugged. "Just the fact that Betty Stark set us up was a little intimidating. Frankly, I didn't know what to think."

"So you know Betty set us up?"

"It was kind of obvious, Jeremy," she said. "She's not much of an actor."

"Don't you like Betty?"

"She's okay," she said. "But this set-up thing is ridiculous. I don't know why she did it, but it could've been worse."

"I'm glad you approve, sort of."

"Well, it's only a first date," she pointed out. "It's a bit too early to tell. How about you? Did you enjoy yourself?"

"Yes," he said. "But, I must admit this is the strangest first date I've ever had."

"How do you mean?"

"Well," he ventured cautiously. "Usually, the girl wants the man to choose where to go, and pick her up in his car and give her the royal treatment. But you did everything backwards. You told me where to meet you for drinks. Then I had to follow you in my car to a restaurant of your choosing. Then I had to follow you here. And again, you picked out this place. It's bizarre."

"I'm sorry," she said. "Did I put you off?"

"No, it's okay, Lindsay," he said. "I'm just not used to that behavior. You did everything but pay for the food... or anything."

"Well, I am a traditionalist about some things," she teased.

"Like paying."

"Exactly."

"I'm sorry," she said. "I guess I'm still a bit squeamish. I'm just coming off a bad break-up. I'm still a little gun shy."

"Is it still too soon for you?"

"Not really," she shrugged. "I'm not sure. The guy was a bit of a control freak. I guess I just didn't want to give up too much control too soon."

"Wow," he commented. "He must have really done a number on you. How bad was he?"

"I'm just glad I got away from him."

"How did you get away?" he asked. "I know a lot of control freaks don't like to give up girls if they want to control them."

"I'd rather not talk about it."

"Of course," he said. "Okay. I'm sorry. I didn't mean to pry. I was just hoping he didn't have anything to do with those bruises on your face."

"Oh my God!" she gasped as she touched her cheek. "Can you still see bruises? I thought I covered them with make-up."

"It worked in the beginning," he informed her. "I didn't see them at first. I guess you need a touch-up."

"I'm so embarrassed!" she said. "I didn't want you to see those. Especially on a first date. I could just die!"

"Don't let it bother you," he said. "It's not bad. I almost didn't see them at all. You're still a very beautiful woman, Lindsay."

"Thank you."

"I was a jerk for even mentioning it," he said. "It's just when you mentioned your ex was a control freak, I…"

"Let's just drop the subject all together, shall we?"

"Fine," he said. "You seem to be getting a little jittery. Are you alright?"

"Sorry," she said. "I'm just bugging for a cigarette."

"Again?" he said. "Do you always smoke this much?"

"Not always," she said. "Only when I'm nervous."

"What is there to be nervous about?"

"I don't know," she said. "First date, bruises, just some other personal things."

"Well, don't worry about the date," he assured her. "You're doing fine."

"I hope my smoking doesn't bother you," she said. "I know how non-smokers can be. I know it's a nasty habit. I should quit, but there's always some turmoil going on in my life that makes it difficult. I guess I always have excuses. I suppose 'excuses' are just another nasty habit of mine."

"For a girl like you, I could get used to it," he said. "The smoking, not the excuses. Perhaps I can help you quit. I just hope you can put up with my not drinking."

"That's right," she recalled. "You've been drinking orange juice all night. It makes a refreshing change. You get too much Vitamin C instead of too drunk like my last guy. That's the kind of change I could live with. I could do without drinking myself."

"I could help you kick that nasty habit too," he offered.

"Okay, just slow down, pal," she teased. "I don't want to change too much too quickly. I happen to like a lot of things about myself. I have a lot of good qualities."

"I can see that," he said. "Alright. We'll only deal with one improvement at a time. And if there's anything you don't want to improve, I'll learn to deal with it. And believe me. I see a lot of things in you that don't need any improving."

"Thank you."

There was a short pause.

"Well, I suppose it's getting late," he said. "I should get home. Tomorrow is Sunday. I have to go to church."

"And I'm still dying for a cigarette."

"Do you go to church?"

"No," she said. "I guess I'm a heathen."

"That's another thing we can work on."

"Slow down," she said. "Don't work on me just yet. I only met you just yesterday. Remember I have a problem with control freaks."

"You're right," he said. "We only just met. I'm sorry."

"That's alright."

They stood. They shared a quick, casual hug and kiss.

"Mmmm," he said. "Thanks for the cherry-flavored lip gloss."

"Do you like it?"

"It's like kissing a cherry-flavored ashtray," he commented.

"I forgot," she laughed. "You non-smokers are so touchy. I'm sorry. I'll try to do better next time."

"Don't worry about it," he said. "I love cherry-flavored ashtrays. But if I have to kiss an ashtray, next time I'd prefer watermelon."

"I'll keep that in mind," she laughed. "Good night, Jeremy. And thank you. I had a great time. Call me next week. We'll set something up."

"Good night, Lindsay," he said. "You're welcome. I look forward to seeing you again."

She left with a sweet smile.

She walked out into the dark parking lot. It was still warm. There were people in the streets, and noise and neon lights.

It was a different world than the intimate club inside.

When she reached her car, she glanced around nervously. She was still a little edgy about Ethan. She hadn't heard from him all day. Part of her was relieved. However, she couldn't shake the feeling that something was wrong.

The way he disappeared the previous night was curious…and a bit unsettling.

She didn't see anything in the parking lot. She got in her car and started the engine. She pulled out of the lot and into the busy city streets.

Her mind began to wander. It had been a decent evening. Jeremy seemed like a nice man. Of course, she'd done everything she could to steer them to a place where Danny might have seen them.

But, Danny never materialized. Oh well.

It was only a first date. There would be others.

Still, she pondered how to turn this thing into a way to make Danny jealous.

CHAPTER 9

AGGRESSIVE

A few nights passed nearly without incident. His father tried to talk to him once. The dead prostitute appeared before him one evening as he made dinner. But for the most part, he had gone through the beginning of the week without any unearthly sightings.

However, there was something about Tuesday night.

He came home earlier than usual. He was tired. He'd been busy. Perhaps, that's why the spirits had left him alone.

He was cooking dinner. It was a late dinner for him. But he was a good cook. He had a few pans working on the electric stove.

Suddenly, one of the burners erupted in flames. He jumped back in shock. The fire shot around the pan and high up into the air. He was able to reach around and turn off the burner. But, the fire continued to rage.

He removed the pan. It was scalding hot. He threw it into the sink, splattering an entrée fit for a king all over the sink and counter.

The fire was still stretching and leaping up into the smoky atmosphere.

He used a few dishtowels in a cautious but desperate attempt to extinguish the blaze.

The towels were blackening, but they were dampening the malicious fire.

He grabbed another couple of things without thinking. He used everything he could get his hands on to put out the flames. He cried out as he burned himself once or twice.

But, the fire finally died.

Even with the air vent already on full, there was too much smoke in the room. He'd ruined a number of good towels. There was no way to save his dinner. There would be a lot to clean up.

At least a disaster had been averted.

Still, he swore under his breath.

Then, he heard voices in the dining room.

He looked in through the doorway. He sighed to himself, "Oh no! Not again! That probably explains the fire."

The senator and his young girlfriend were playing Chess again. The game hadn't gone very far. But this time, his father was standing behind the senator. And the prostitute was standing behind the girl.

Without looking up, the senator said, "Well, well. It's about time you joined us. We've been waiting."

"I h-had a…"

"I know," the senator interrupted. He still wouldn't look up from the game. "The fire. As I recall, you like pyrotechnics. I had to use them to get your attention last time too."

"You…" he stammered. "You could've burned my house down!"

"Then stop making it necessary to use the dramatics to get your attention!" the senator admonished.

"Please just leave me alone," he said. "Why are you doing this to me?"

"Will you be quiet?" the girl said sharply. "We have to concentrate on this game! It's bad enough we had to start over again! Satan keeps cheating!"

"Sorry," the senator said. "It's in my nature."

"I had to get this prostitute to watch you," the girl said. "It's so ridiculous. I know we're friends and all, Lucifer. But loving you is a challenge."

"Hey," the senator defended. "I had to get this clown behind me to watch you too. You think just because you're God you're beyond reproach."

"Stop it!" he shouted. "You are not Satan! And she is not God! You tried to blaspheme last time you were here! I won't have it!"

"God does not blaspheme!" the girl corrected sharply.

"You shouldn't make Her angry," the hooker instructed. "She makes bad things happen when She gets mad."

"Stop it!"

"I gave you my heart the last time I saw you," the hooker reminded. "Do you still have it?"

Suddenly, his breast pocket felt wet. A warm liquid seemed to be running down his shirtfront.

He gasped. He looked down to see the deep red blood stain spreading down his chest. The stain stretched down over his belly. A pulsating, heart-sized lump was in his pocket.

"No!" he screamed in fear.

"Don't make so much noise, son," his father cautioned. "Try to act mature. There's an important game going on."

"It's your move, Lucifer," the girl said.

"Nice move, God," the senator said. "But, you're falling right into my trap."

"No!" he screamed. "This has to stop!"

Suddenly, the girl looked up from her game. There was a dark anger in her eyes.

"You unworthy sinner!" she growled. "You have so much to atone for! Every time you take one step forward, you take three steps back! Satan will love to get his hands on you in Hell!"

"I'm looking forward to it," the senator told him. "I have a special place for you."

"No!" he shouted. "You can't! I've tried to do my best!"

"You have so much to do," the girl informed him.

"Why, just look how much you lusted after me," the hooker reminded.

"You were always a bad boy," his father pointed out.

"You have so much to do for me," said the girl. "So much! You will have to be more aggressive in your efforts to atone for your sins."

"You are not God!" he insisted. "You can't be!"

The entire house began to shake with a loud rumble.

"So much work!" the girl reiterated with authority.

"So much work," the prostitute repeated.

The house was shaking as if a massive earthquake was underway. Even the chess pieces were bouncing around and falling off the board.

"You have so much to do to atone for your sins," his father said.

"So much work!" the girl demanded.

The house continued to quake loudly.

"No-o-o-o!"

Everything suddenly went silent. There was nobody sitting at the dining room table. There was no chessboard and no prostitute. Even the house was dormant.

He was alone. He was confused. Everything was still. His shirt was spotless.

He was still quivering.

Suddenly, he turned back into the kitchen. The towels were still on the burner. The food in the other pan was now burned to a crisp. The odor was repulsive. The entrée was still splattered across the sink and the counter.

But, there was no sign that the fire had ever been real.

He wanted to be furious. But he was still too scared.

* * * * * *

The following morning, she was sitting at the kitchen table. She was dressed for work. It was still early. The sun was still struggling to climb over the high-rise horizon of the wakening city.

As he walked into the room, she asked, "What are you doing up this early, Michael?"

"I couldn't sleep last night," he mumbled. "Rough night last night."

"What's the matter?"

"I don't know," he said. "I've been a bit jumpy lately. I'm out of sorts. I'm sure it'll work itself out. Are you on your way to your store?"

"In a few minutes," she said. "I'm taking my time today."

"Why?" he asked. "Are you alright?"

"I suppose," she sighed. "I filed for divorce a few days ago. I guess I still can't believe I'm actually going to have to do this."

"So, you're going through with it, huh?"

"What choice do I have?" she asked. "If Mark isn't going to stop seeing our sister, I couldn't possibly stay married to him."

He sat down with his own coffee cup. "I don't blame you," he agreed. "I'm just sorry you have to go through all this, Cassandra. I'd still like to kill the little bastard for you."

"Thanks, Michael," she said. "But, don't trouble yourself. He's not worth it. Believe it or not, I'm starting to get used to it. I'm not even mad at Stephanie anymore."

"How could you not be?" he asked. "I still can't believe she'd do that to you!"

"I don't know," she sighed. "Maybe it was my fault. Maybe I shouldn't have devoted all my time to the store. After all, Mark is my husband. He deserves a certain amount of time and attention from me."

"Don't do that to yourself, sis," he said. "This wasn't your fault. *They* did this to you! And if either one of them cared for you, they wouldn't have!"

"Thanks, Michael," she smiled. "It's nice to know I have your support."

"Hey," he added. "You're the victim here, Cassandra. And you shouldn't be victimized by people who love you."

"Wow," she observed. "You really feel strongly about this, don't you?"

"Well, you're my sister," he reminded. "And of course, so is Stephanie. But still, I just hate seeing my own family do this to each other."

"I didn't know you were so family oriented."

"I'm not usually," he said. "But family has to pull together during times of crisis."

"And this rates as a crisis?"

"Don't you think so?"

"Yes. I guess I do."

"Well, that's the important thing," he said. "I just want you to know you have my full support."

"Thank you, Michael," she said. "That's very comforting."

"That's what family is for."

* * * * * *

He was running late when his cell phone rang. He made no effort to hide his aggravation as he answered, "Hello?"

"Hi, Danny," said the caller. "It's me."

"Lindsay?" he said with the same level of aggravation. "What is it now? I'm late for work!"

"Hey," she defended. "I've hardly called you at all these past few days."

"And believe me," he said. "I appreciate it. But you shouldn't be calling at all."

Her eyes narrowed as she heard a female voice on Danny's end ask, "Is that Lindsay again? I'm getting tired of this!"

"Calm down," she heard Danny say. "I'll handle it."

"You can tell Krysten to relax, Danny," she declared with confidence. "The main reason I called was to let you know I've found someone else."

"You have?"

His happiness was an unexpected surprise. "Well, sort of," she stammered. "I mean, not really. We've talked a few times. We went out last Saturday. First date."

"That's wonderful," he said. "Congratulations!"

"Well, I…"

She could sense an anger rising in her as she heard Danny say, "Hey, Krysten! Lindsay has a new guy! She went out with him last weekend!"

The anger grew more intense when she heard Krysten say, "Great! Wish her all the best for me!"

"Did you hear that, Lindsay?" he said. "Even Krysten is happy for you. She wishes you all the best."

"Yes, well…" she began. "It was only one date."

"That's how it starts," he imparted.

"I didn't want to rush into anything," she stuttered. "We've talked a few times on the phone. But I want to take it slow. We have another date set up for tomorrow night."

"That's excellent," he smiled. "I hope it works out."

"Well, I..." she went on. "Maybe you and Krysten would like to double-date."

"I don't think so," he said. "You two should get to know each other."

"Well, where are you two going to be tomorrow?" she pressed awkwardly. "Maybe we'll run into each other..."

"No, no, no," he said. "You just go out and have a good time. Once again, that's great news, Lindsay. Congratulations. Gotta go. 'Bye."

"But, Danny..."

Her stomach churned as it became obvious that he'd hung up. She slowly hung up as well.

"Was that Danny again?" her friend asked. "This is really getting pathetic, Lindsay!"

"Love is not pathetic, Vicky!"

"Yeah, but *you* are," Vicky argued. "When are you going to let this go? You said your date with Jeremy went well. You've talked to him on the phone a few times. You have a date with him tomorrow. Why don't you give him a chance? He might even turn out to be better than Danny."

"Nobody's better than my Danny!"

"When are you going to get it through your thick skull that he's moved on?" Vicky asked.

"He hasn't moved on," she insisted. "I told you about that kiss."

"That was a week and a half ago, at least!" Vicky reminded impatiently. "You have to stop living in the past! Anyway, I'm surprised you tried a full frontal attack:

telling Danny outright about Jeremy. I thought you were going to be more subtle."

"I couldn't think of anything subtle," she said. "I'm intentionally taking it slow with Jeremy so I don't lead him on too quickly. I don't want to be cruel if I don't have to be. That makes it difficult to be subtle. Anyway, you saw how the full frontal attack worked. Danny actually sounded happy for me! He's bluffing! It was just because Krysten was in the room with him!"

"Lindsay," Vicky declared. "You're losing touch with reality. You're beginning to sound like Ethan."

"I am not!"

"By the way," Vicky asked. "Whatever happened to Ethan?"

"I have no idea," she said. "I haven't seen or heard from him since that night he hit me on the smokers' platform outside of Waivers. Not even a phone call."

"Doesn't that worry you?"

"Why should it?" she asked. "I'm glad to be rid of the asshole. Maybe he finally grew up and decided to stop stalking me."

"Isn't that what you should do with Danny?"

"Nonsense!" she scoffed. "Me and Danny were meant to be together. And he was just bluffing about being happy for me. I just know it! Since the full frontal attack didn't work, I'll have to get more aggressive in my tactics. I know he'll be jealous if he actually sees me and Jeremy together. I'm absolutely certain! Danny would go nuts!"

"Lindsay," Vicky warned. "Don't go overboard. Control yourself."

"Don't worry," she said slyly. "I'm always in control."

"Even assuming that's true, which is a stretch," Vicky said. "What are you planning?"

"Never you mind," she assured. "I know what I'm doing."

* * * * * *

"Caught up on your paperwork yet, Stan?"

"Shut up, Kyle."

"My, my," he grinned. "That's a fine attitude for so early on a Wednesday morning."

"It's way too early on a Wednesday morning," Paczecki grumbled. "We still have an important case hanging over our heads. We're still spinning our wheels and going nowhere. And instead of being allowed to go out and try to stop a serial killer, I have to get stuck at my desk filling out forms."

"I know how you feel," he said. "I almost feel like I'm in a race with The State Police to solve this case, and we're losing."

"So why are you joking around?"

"Just trying to lighten the load," he said. "Do you think Spapper and Van Leer are having any better luck than we are?"

"I doubt it," Paczecki said. "If they were, they'd be obligated to share whatever they learned with us. God, this case is killing me! We've talked to everybody we could find at The Robin's Egg. We've even talked with customers who paid that night by credit card. There are a few people I'm still watching. A few of the staff members make me a bit nervous. But overall, I still have an empty feeling in my gut. I still think we're missing something."

"Me too," he agreed. "If it had been a cash customer, there's no way to pin him down. We've checked security tapes and everything. It was impossible to identify some of the people on the tape. Nothing on it looked immediately suspicious. But even the owner we talked to admitted there are gaps in that tape. There are certain small spots their cameras don't cover. Of course, a customer would probably never be aware enough to dodge all the cameras. But a staff member might…"

"We saw all the staff members on film," Paczecki pointed out. "Besides, it's not like we're expecting to see the actual murders on tape. We're just looking for suspicious activity. That could be anything."

"Or we could find nothing," he said.

"I know," Paczecki grunted. "It's tearing me apart! There's got to be something! There's got to be a link!"

"With only two murder scenes," he pointed out. "There's still not enough to make a full determination. Joe Zanella was a well-known senator. Almost anyone would know what he looks like. And Marissa Cosgrove was obviously not his wife. Anybody could see that. The Robin's Egg is not necessarily going to lead us to Paradox. For all we know, he could pick his next victim in some greasy spoon diner. Let's face it, he didn't find Audrey in any fancy restaurant."

"You've got a point."

"And for all we know," he added. "Paradox didn't even find Zanella at The Robin's Egg. He could've been trailing the senator all night. Perhaps he was just waiting at the apartment for them to return."

"Either of those scenarios would require a hell of a lot of patience," Paczecki said.

"And intelligence," he said. "But our friend seems to be blessed with both of those qualities."

"That's true enough," Paczecki said. "But even though it would've been easy enough to find out where the senator was staying, they weren't killed at his place. They were killed at Miss Cosgrove's apartment."

"I'm just saying we can't nail ourselves to The Robin's Egg angle," he imparted. "Maybe we should look into who could've been aware of the fact that Zanella was paying Cosgrove's rent."

"We looked into that already!"

"Not very well," he said. "We were a little too quick to jump into believing the murderer followed them home."

"Maybe you're right," Paczecki sighed. "Maybe we should go back to that apartment building and ask around again. It wouldn't hurt. And I don't want to just sit on my butt 'til that guy kills somebody else! We've got to find the link between Lindquist and Zanella!"

"What if there is none?"

"Oh, there is one," he argued. "And if we don't find it soon, someone else is going to die!"

* * * * * *

That evening was dark and peaceful. It was the middle of the week. The night life was active. But it lacked the passion and intensity of the weekend.

It was nearing 10:00. They were sitting in a nearly upscale tavern uptown. They had their own little table by the back door.

"I still don't think we should've come here," she said.

"Why not?"

"I keep telling you," she reminded impatiently. "My brother Michael works next door at The Robin's Egg. I'm trying to keep this thing discreet."

"We've been through this already, Stephanie," he said. "He's next door. He won't see us. We're being as discreet as we need to be. Besides, he knows what we're doing, so what's the problem?"

"He doesn't approve."

"He's not your mother," he said. "Besides, he's still next door."

"The owners of this place also own The Robin's Egg," she reiterated. "I told you that. Sometimes, they send people over here from next door if they're short of help. It's not hard to picture running into him tonight."

"Do you see him anywhere?"

"Not yet."

"So don't worry about it," he assured her. "Even if he sees you, what do you think he'll do? Kill you?"

"I just don't want to cause any more disharmony in the family," she explained. "I feel awful about everything that's happened, Mark. My sister's barely speaking to me. I'm the cause of her impending divorce…"

"So am I," he interrupted. "And that affects me more than it does you. I don't want this divorce either. But I don't know what to do. I love Cassandra very much.

But I'm in love with you too. What am I supposed to do about that?"

"You can't be in love with two people at the same time," she averred.

"A year ago, I would've agreed with you," he said. "But now, the answers aren't so clear. Everything's not so black and white. You know what I mean, Stephanie. Didn't you tell me you still love Trey?"

She nodded.

"See?" he pointed out. "It's a complicated issue. By the way, how did you get away from Trey tonight? Is he working again?"

"Yes," she said. "But that's all the more reason why I want to end this, Mark. We've been starting to repair things in our marriage. It's been hard, but I'm starting to get through to him. I'm almost getting him to believe that I want to fix things and be faithful. We made love once or twice. And I think he's coming around. He wants to believe me, and I want to give him something to believe in."

"And what does that mean to us?"

"We have to end this, Mark."

"You keep saying that," he told her. "We both keep saying it. But how do we do it? How am I supposed to be without you?"

"I don't know," she said. "Just do it."

"When you find out how," he said. "Let me know."

There was a brief pause.

"This is a nice place," he observed while glancing around. "Not as swanky as next door, but it's got a nice atmosphere. I've always wanted to check this place out.

I was wondering what to make of a place called Lumpy Bill's. I'm glad we came."

"I'm not," she muttered. "I've had this eerie feeling that someone is watching us all night. It's starting to give me the creeps."

"Oh, you're just being paranoid," he said. "Nobody's watching us."

"How do you know?"

"Who would want to watch us?" he questioned. "What is there to watch?"

"I don't know," she said. "What if Trey's really not out somewhere on business?"

"Do you really think he'd be that calculating?" he asked.

"Yes."

"Then, why are you here?"

"Because..."

He waited for her to finish after her voice trailed off. When she didn't continue, he answered, "You're here for the same reason I'm here."

He leaned over and kissed her. That familiar unsettled feeling returned to her gut. However, she allowed the kiss to carry her a bit too long.

Finally, she pulled away.

"Don't, Mark."

"What's the problem, Stephanie?" he asked. "Don't fight what we both feel."

"I told you I want to fix things with Trey."

"And I want to fix things with Cassandra," he said. "But, where are they? Are they here fixing things? No. Cassandra's at your mother's. She's perfectly happy leaving things broken. And Trey thinks business is more important than your marriage."

"He doesn't think that," she defended. "He just… he…"

"See?" he said. "*You* can't even justify his behavior."

"But…"

Again, she was faltering. He took the opportunity for another kiss. She let the kiss linger, even though she knew where this always led.

Finally, she pulled away.

"I think I'll just finish my drink and go home," she said.

"Why don't you come back to my place?" he offered. "We won't run into Cassandra. And we won't need a motel."

"One of us has to be strong," she explained. "And apparently, that's never going to be you."

"Don't talk like that, Stephanie."

"I mean it, Mark," she insisted. "I want this to stop. And I don't feel right tonight. I really have a feeling that something is wrong."

"Nobody's watching us," he argued. "I promise!"

She knew she shouldn't let this kiss happen. Once it started, she knew she was in trouble. He had already weakened her resolve.

She wanted to consider Trey. She wanted to think about Cassandra.

But at that moment, all there was…was this kiss.

All there was…was Mark.

They finished their drinks. She knew what she had to do. At least, for now.

She would just have to be determined to never see Mark again. That was the only way.

But, how would that be possible? He was part of the family. Even if Cassandra got the divorce, he would still be part of the family.

Wouldn't he?

She followed him out to the parking lot. The secluded parking lot behind the restaurant. They had parked there because she had said she didn't want Michael to see them together.

She still had that nervous feeling. She still had that feeling that they were being watched.

But she knew she was only being silly. Who would be watching them?

She allowed Mark to lead her through the dark, secluded parking lot, between rows of cars. Farther away from the lights of Lumpy Bill's.

No one seemed to be in the parking lot. So nobody could be watching them.

Right?

Mark had his arm around her shoulders. She felt glad to be with him. She felt guilty to be with him.

No one would be watching them. She didn't hear the sound of someone opening the trunk of his car.

She was happy to be with Mark. He made her feel the way Trey used to make her feel. Back before they were married.

She would go with Mark back to his place. Nobody would ever know.

No one would be watching them. Being watched? What a silly notion!

She didn't notice the car with the open trunk when Mark stopped her. They laughed. He took her in his arms. They kissed.

It was another one of those kisses…until…

Mark jerked suddenly. He bit her tongue. It hurt!

He seemed to go limp as he let go of her. She was curious. She was confused.

All of a sudden, he fell away and dropped to the ground. She looked down at him with fear and panic. He didn't move.

She didn't have time to react. She didn't see the brown Chevy four-door with the open trunk.

She barely had time to look up in time to see a dark shape.

Then, she felt a sharp, heavy thud on the top of her head. Waves of pain rippled through her brain.

For a brief moment, she saw stars.

Then, everything went black.

CHAPTER 10

ULTIMATE SIN

It was Thursday morning. That meant nothing to her. She sat in her mother's big, beautiful kitchen. She didn't bother to turn on the light.

The curtains were parted. Streams of sunlight poured in through the window. A fan almost seemed to spread the sunbeams around the room like the little dust particles that danced around before her eyes. It looked to her as if the sunbeams were spotlights and the dust particles were performing a stage show just for her.

She found it amusing. It temporarily distracted her.

Then, she took a gulp of the coffee that was growing cold in her cup. She looked at the chair beside her. It was the first chair she had knocked over at the Memorial Day picnic. When she had gotten into a fight with her sister.

And it was all over a man. Do you believe it? It was all over some guy she had been foolish enough to marry.

She had been foolish enough to think she was in love with him once. She had been foolish enough to think she would be with him for the rest of her life.

She had been so sure of it!

She had been foolish enough to believe that true love really existed.

She had been such a fool!

A comforting voice sounded behind her. "Good morning, Cassandra."

She didn't even turn around. "Hi, Mom," she muttered.

"You're still here?" Betty asked with concern. "It's almost 9:00. Aren't you going to your store today? You're incredibly late, aren't you?"

"I'm taking the morning off," she said. "I just need a break. I wanted to catch up on a little sleep. This working nonstop is starting to get to me."

"Are you alright, dear?"

"I'm fine, Mom," she said. "Just a bit tired. Everything is starting to catch up to me. It's been a rough couple of weeks."

"I know it has," Betty said. "But, you'll get through it. You're smart. You're tough. You're tenacious…"

"That's nice of you to say, Mom," she muttered. "But I'm not feeling particularly smart or tough at the moment."

"Oh? What's wrong?"

"This!" she said while pointing around the whole room with her open hand. "This whole thing of being here! I'm a married woman, and I'm staying at my mother's because I'm getting a divorce! I'm tired of working 24 hours a day, seven days a week and not having anything to show for it but a divorce decree and my old bedroom from high school at my mother's place! Technically, I know I don't even have a decree! I only filed the papers on Monday, but you know what I mean!"

"Oh, sweetheart," Betty said in a motherly tone. She took a seat at the kitchen table. "This is really getting to you, isn't it?"

"I thought I had it made," she explained. "My own business, the perfect marriage…at least I thought it was the perfect marriage. What happened?"

"No one knows how these things happen, Cassandra," Betty imparted. "They just happen. It's part of life."

"Was it my fault?"

Betty was caught off guard. "What?"

"Was it my fault?" she repeated. "The divorce? Should I have spent more time with Mark? Was it a stupid mistake to start my own business?"

"No," Betty assured her. "Of course not. You wanted to be in charge of your own life. You wanted to make your own way in the world."

"But, look where it got me."

"If Mark had a problem," Betty reasoned. "He should've reached out to you. He should've communicated his feelings to you."

"But, what if he tried?" she asked timidly. "What if he tried, and I just wasn't listening?"

"Don't do that to yourself, Cassandra," Betty advised. "Don't blame yourself because your husband chose to give in to temptation and ignore the path of righteousness."

"Mom," she complained. "Please don't bring religion into this."

"Why not?" Betty asked. "If you two had been following The Word of Our Lord, none of this would have happened."

"This is not the time, Mom."

"It's always the right time to follow The Lord," Betty insisted.

"But, this hurts, Mom," she said. "It hurts a lot!"

"And it's going to hurt for quite a while," Betty said. "Believe me. I know. When your father died, I thought my life was over. It hurt so much. It was the worse feeling in the world. But I lived through it. I gradually got stronger. And my family and my God helped me to persevere and survive."

"So the pain will go away eventually?" she asked. "I would've thought I'd have run out of tears by now. But I still cry every day."

Betty was silent for a moment. Then she said, "Maybe it's time I told you."

"Told me what?"

"I promised myself I wouldn't say anything to you kids," Betty confided. "Especially you girls. Perhaps I shouldn't…"

"What is it, Mom?"

"Well, I…" she hesitated.

"Spit it out, Mom. Come on. Please?"

"Okay," she said reluctantly. "I guess you're old enough. I suppose you deserve to know. Cassandra, your father cheated on me once."

"What?" Cassandra gasped. "Dad cheated on you? When? What happened?"

"Well, you know I used to be a nurse, right?" she reminded. "You probably don't remember those days. I lost my job shortly after Danny was born. You're father was a very ambitious lawyer in those days before he was hired by the DA's office. He was working all the time. He was a great lawyer and he made lots of money. He loved his family. He simply adored you kids. You and Stephanie were the light of his life."

"When did he start cheating?"

"Like I said," she continued. "I lost my job at Mercy Hospital shortly after Danny was born. Since your father was always working, I was alone all the time with you kids. And don't get me wrong. I loved you kids. I wouldn't have traded you for the world. But it was difficult juggling work and kids. I started drinking when you were a baby. And between the nonstop schedule of a nurse and a few health problems, I developed a problem with pain killers and uppers. I was fired for stealing from a drug cabinet at work. I was a mess."

"Mom!" Cassandra gasped. "You never told me any of this before. You were fired from the hospital?"

"Yes," she nodded. "That's the real reason I decided to be a stay-at-home mom. And without a job to keep me grounded and a husband who was always working, my problems became worse. We managed to have Michael, but things were very strained in our marriage. He got a job at the DA's office thanks to some political friends. And he started having an affair with some girl at work."

"Oh my God," Cassandra replied. "How long did it last?"

"Not long," she said. "I think they only slept together a few times. But it brought all our troubles out into the light of day."

"I can't believe it," she stammered. "Daddy cheated on you! Do any of the other kids know?"

"Only Michael," she answered. "He heard us arguing about it at the time. That was eight years ago. Michael was only thirteen. It really tore him apart. He was furious with your father. I don't think Michael ever forgave him. I made him promise not to tell any of the other children, especially you girls. I didn't want you to hate your father. But it was only after I saw how Michael reacted that I knew I had to make some changes. Your father and I both saw that we had to straighten ourselves out. Your father ended his affair, although it took a few tries. And I cleaned up my act. I quit the pills and the drinking, and I turned to The Lord to get me through all my troubles."

"So, that's what happened?"

"God helped me kick my addictions," she admitted. "And He helped me through the devastating agony of your father's infidelity."

"Oh, Mom," she exclaimed. "I'm so sorry! I didn't know!"

"That's alright, dear," she said. "I didn't want you to know. I don't want you to hate your father. He was a good man, Cassandra. He really was. And he loved you children so much. I wish you and Stephanie knew what you meant to him. But your father and I were only human. We both made a lot of mistakes. But we tried to correct the things we did wrong. I was so angry and hurt when I found out he cheated on me. I felt just like you do right now. But with God's help, I pulled myself up and saved my life and my marriage."

"I don't know what to say."

"There's nothing you *can* say."

"And Michael knew the whole time," Cassandra said. "The poor kid. That must have been hard. No wonder he's so angry with Stephanie. Maybe that's why he's so..."

Her voice trailed off.

"Maybe that's why he's so what, dear?" her mother asked.

"Oh, nothing," Cassandra said. "Never mind. So why are you telling me this now?"

"I want you to realize that I understand what you're going through," she said. "God has a plan for everything. We may not know what that plan is, but God will always take care of things. Of course, God took your father from me four years ago. I'm not sure what His wisdom was in that, but I'm sure He knew what He was doing. It's a shame, too. I don't think Michael ever forgave your father. And it must be so hard for him having lost his dad when there were so much bad feelings between them. A boy shouldn't lose his father until they can make things right between them."

"And they never found Dad's killer," Cassandra said sadly.

"That's true," she said. "They think they knew who it was, but they never caught up with him. I suppose in some way, that must have fit into God's plan too."

"You don't suppose Michael could have...?" Cassandra began. She couldn't finish the thought.

"What?" she asked. "Kill your father? Michael? Don't be ridiculous. Your brother was in school at the time. I just wanted you to know that I'd considered divorcing my husband at one time. But, I took my marriage vows seriously. I stayed with him and we worked things out. And God worked His plan as He saw fit."

"Are you saying I shouldn't divorce Mark?" Cassandra asked.

"You promised in church before God that you would stay married 'til death do you part," she reminded.

"Do you really think Mark and I can work it out?"

"Of course you can," she assured her. "With The Lord's help."

"And you think God will take care of things?"

"As I always tell you, darling," she smiled. "God always takes care of everything."

* * * * * *

The traffic was fairly heavy for a Thursday morning. He kept his eye on the road. And there was an all too familiar heavy ache in the pit of his stomach as they approached their destination.

They stopped for a red light. He looked over at the passenger's side.

"Anyway, Kyle," he asked. "What's going on with that prostitute friend of yours? Did you follow up on that?"

"Who? Tanya?" Grogan said. "Yeah. They have her scheduled to appear before a grand jury next Wednesday. It looks like she's got a pretty good case for self defense. I talked to her and her lawyer. He's a pretty sharp guy. His name is Chang. He's got photos of Tanya and Rebecca. Apparently, they were both bruised by Delaney when he started his crap with the girls."

"So, the little pimp actually hit those girls?" he asked. He started driving when the light turned green.

"Yup," Grogan nodded. "And nobody at the station bothered to notice when they hauled the girls in. I guess nobody cared to. I asked Tanya about it a few days ago. She gave me some wise-ass answer in return. I suspect she was just getting defensive. It must be a sensitive topic for her."

"You talked to the hooker and her lawyer?" he poked. "Not to mention you talked to the DA before. How tangled up in this mess are you going to get? That's a little bit involved for some girl you just know from the station, isn't it?"

"Hey," Grogan parried. "I told you before I'm a Catholic. It's called Christian charity. Look into it. I'm just showing my concern for a friend and a fellow human being."

"Christian charity?" he prodded. "Are you sure you're not getting any fringe benefits from this deal, pal?"

"Let it go, Stan," he said with faltering patience. "Nothing's going on. She's just a friend from the station. She doesn't have anyone else to look out for her, so I'm just giving her a hand. It's no big deal."

"Okay, Mr. Christian Charity," he persisted. "Have it your way. It's no big deal."

"Watch the road, Stan," Grogan said. "That looks like our stop up ahead."

There were flashing lights and a crowd a few blocks ahead of them. A couple of black and white patrol cars completed the somber picture.

"This guy always finds the best neighborhoods to dump bodies, doesn't he?" Grogan grumbled. "I mean, look at this place. Don't the people who live here have enough problems without some serial killer using it as his garbage dump?"

"Hush," he cautioned. "And straighten your tie. It's time to act professional."

He parked the car as close as he could. They got out and made their way through the crowd.

As he neared the yellow crime scene tape, he smiled, "Well, well. Kilgallon and Weinberg. Long time, no see. How did you get the privilege of working another one of Paradox's little masterpieces?"

"We were the first ones on the scene again," Kilgallon said.

"Lucky you," Grogan muttered.

The detectives stepped over the crime scene tape.

"Alright," he muttered. "Let's do this. Walk with me, Weinberg. Break it down for me. What do we have here?"

They strolled casually over to the bodies.

"It does look like Paradox again, sir," Weinberg said. "Same brutality, the whole nine yards. It's a young couple this time. He's 27, she's 29. The man's name is Mark Genovese. The woman's name is Stephanie Wagner."

They looked down with disgust.

"Oh!" Grogan gasped. "This guy never lets up, does he? Each scene is worse than the last! And what's this thing he has for hearts?"

"What else can you tell me, Weinberg?"

"Ligature marks on the wrists of the victim's suggest they were taken here from somewhere else," Weinberg informed him. "We figure Paradox picked them up somewhere and took them here to kill them."

"Sounds like a fair assessment," he agreed.

"The girl was easy to ID," Weinberg continued. "Her maiden name is Stark. She's the daughter of the late

Andrew Stark. He worked as an attorney for the DA's office for about twelve or thirteen years before he got killed about four years ago. His widow, Elizabeth still lives at the same address on Amherst on the northern end of town."

"Andrew was killed, huh?" he asked. "Who killed him?"

"It's presumed he was killed by a Eugene Rousseau," Weinberg explained. "Stark got him convicted of armed robbery and second degree murder. Somehow, Rousseau escaped as he was being transported upstate a year later for some appeal or something. They never caught him. It's assumed he fled to Canada."

"So, it's not too likely this is connected to Rousseau," he conjectured.

"Not likely," Weinberg agreed.

"We still need to find a connection between a prostitute, a state senator and the daughter of a murdered DA," he said.

"And someone's going to have to tell her mother," Grogan added. "It's going to be rough on her. She's already been through a lot, losing her husband like that and all. I hate to admit it, but that unpleasant task should probably fall in our lap."

"Yeah," he grunted.

Just then, they were joined by two state detectives.

"Good morning, Stan...Kyle," Spapper said. "Another victim of our little friend, is it? Oooh! That's a horrid sight! So, this is what a fresh murder scene looks like when Paradox wants to come out and play, eh? This guy really is a lunatic."

"Morning, Ray…Patrick," Grogan said. "It really makes you wish you'd listened to your mother when she told you to stay in school and get a 'respectable' job. Doesn't it?"

"This *is* a respectable job," Van Leer said. "Getting the scumbag who did this off the street is a vital service to humanity."

"He's got a point there," Paczecki agreed.

They all looked down at the bodies. Spapper bent down and held the note that was pinned to a bloody shred of clothing near what was left of Stephanie's chest. He kept the note still in the breeze so everyone could read:

I covet.
I am the Paradox that is All Mankind.
God holds a special place in Hell
For those who indulge
In the ultimate sin of the flesh!

"That chicken scratch looks familiar," Van Leer commented.

"We gotta stop this guy," Spapper said as he stood.

"Are you a religious man, Ray?" Grogan asked.

"I believe in God," Spapper replied. "My family was not fanatically religious when I was growing up. But we did go to Temple on a weekly basis."

"Temple?" Grogan asked. "So Spapper is a Jewish name, is it?"

"It is for me and my family," he said. "Why? Do you have a problem with that?"

"Not at all."

"God created us so we could all live together in harmony," Spapper explained. "There are hundreds of religions on this planet. God did not give us our religions so we could use them as an excuse to act like this. God would never condone anyone who partakes in this kind of activity."

He was pointing down at the victims.

"Very well put, Ray," Paczecki nodded.

"They've placed the time of death between 10:00 and 2:00 last night," Weinberg threw in.

"Thanks, pal," Spapper said.

"So, where do you want to begin?" Van Leer asked.

"Well, these two weren't married," Grogan said. "Not to each other, anyway. Judging from that note, I'm guessing Paradox is aware of the fact that at least one of them is…or was married to someone else. Since the girl's mother is the widow of someone who worked as a DA, I figure someone ought to let the mother know what happened to her kid. Maybe we can get a fix on who knew these two were having an affair, if they even were having one. And perhaps we can find out who would've wanted these two dead, and if there's a connection between these murders, Zanella's murders and the dead prostitute."

"Have you inspected the crime scene yet?" Spapper asked.

"No," Paczecki said. "We only got here a few minutes before you. Officer Weinberg was still filling us in on what they know when you got here. If you like, he can fill you in and you can look around here. Grogan and I can go talk to the girl's mother. She deserves to know her daughter's dead. Maybe we'll get some clues while we're there."

"The girl's father was a DA, huh?" Spapper said while rubbing his chin. "Perhaps we're the ones who ought to talk to the mother. After all, we are The State Police."

"But, we've been on this case longer," Paczecki argued. "Besides, Kilgallon and Weinberg haven't even told you what they've ascertained yet."

"Alright," Spapper said. "Either place is a good way to start. Tell you what. We'll stay here, catch up, look around and see what we can dig up. Maybe someone in one of these buildings saw something last night. You start with the girl's mother. We'll keep in touch and compare notes around lunchtime. Okay?"

"Fine," Paczecki nodded.

As they walked back to their car, Paczecki asked the other officer, "Kilgallon? Do you have an exact address for that Elizabeth Stark?"

"Let's see," Kilgallon said as he looked in his note pad. "I've got her down as living at 1249 Amherst Street on the northern end of town. That's a nice neighborhood."

"No doubt," Paczecki said. "Thanks, my friend. Let's go, Kyle."

"Right behind you."

They crossed over the crime scene tape and made their way through the onlookers. They got into their car. Paczecki started the engine. He pulled away from the curb and steered their way north.

"Why do things like this always draw a crowd?" Grogan muttered. "There are a lot of sick people in the world. Don't these people have lives? Or jobs?"

"Maybe if they had lives, they wouldn't depend so much on their morbid curiosities," Paczecki theorized.

An uncomfortable minute of silence passed as they drove.

"You know, Kyle," he added cautiously. "That girl? Alcazar? She's just a hooker."

"She's a human being, Stan!" Grogan argued. "It's too easy for too many people to forget that fact! Including you!"

Another awkward pause lapsed.

"Now will you just drop it?" Grogan added. "Jesus Christ! I swear you think about her more than I do!"

Paczecki let most of the rest of the ride pass in silence. He figured it was the best way to go.

As they turned on to Amherst, Paczecki finally said, "Well, this is our third set of victims from Paradox. Enough of a pattern should be emerging that we actually have a chance of catching this bastard."

"With three Catholics and a Jew on the case," Grogan smiled. "What chance does he have?"

"I hear you."

The tension in their silence was easing.

"I'm sorry I snapped at you before, Stan," Grogan said. "It's not you. It's not even about Tanya Alcazar. It's about this case! It just drives me nuts that people like this use religion as an excuse for violence and animosity. I've been a devout Catholic all my life. But, I've always tried to be tolerant of other people. The main message in all the major religions I've been exposed to is that people are supposed to be nice to each other. Why is there always some whacko who wants to turn it around into something like this?"

"I don't know," he answered. "I guess violence is just in our nature. Some people just need to rationalize it in different ways."

"That's exactly what these religions are supposed to prevent…not cause," Grogan declared. "Our religion says that we're supposed to be nice to people. That means everybody."

"And that includes Tanya Alcazar?" he conjectured.

"Of course it does."

"Thanks for the reminder."

"You just had to bring her into this conversation, didn't you?" Grogan complained.

"Sorry," he said as he pulled up to the curb. "1249 Amherst. This is the place. Are you ready, Kyle?"

"Let's do this."

They got out of their car. They walked with a deliberately somber, professional poise toward the front door. They flashed their badges as the door opened. An attractive young woman in her twenties with long chestnut brown hair and beautiful brown eyes stood in the doorway.

It took them by surprise.

"Good morning, ma'am," he said. "I'm Detective Paczecki. This is my partner, Detective Grogan with the City Police. We were looking for a Mrs. Elizabeth Stark. Is she at home?"

"She went out for a while," she said. "I'm her daughter, Cassandra Genovese. Can I help you?"

"Any relation to Mark Genovese?" Grogan asked.

"He's my husband."

The detectives shared a glance.

"May we come in, ma'am?" Paczecki asked. "We need to talk to you."

"Ah...sure." She allowed them to enter and led them to the living room. "What's the matter? Is anything wrong?"

"Stephanie Wagner is your sister?" Grogan asked.

"Yes. Why?"

"Perhaps you should sit down, ma'am," he suggested.

The fear of disaster that had started in the pit of her stomach was rapidly spreading. Her whole body grew tense as she took a seat.

"What's going on?" she asked with concern. "What's this all about?"

"Uh...ma'am," he hesitated. "We regret to inform you that Mark Genovese and Stephanie Wagner were found murdered in an alley downtown."

Her beautiful brown eyes were already wide with nervous anticipation. Her face went pale. For a moment she couldn't breathe. What the detective had told her almost didn't register in her brain.

Then, the shock hit her like a lightning bolt from Heaven.

"Oh my God!" she muttered. "I don't believe it! He finally did it! Trey finally did it! The son of a bitch!"

She collapsed on the sofa in a wave of tears.

The detectives allowed a sympathetic period to pass as she cried into a cushion. But, her initial response caught their interest.

After a minute or two, he offered, "Ma'am? I'm very sorry for your loss."

She may have managed a 'thank you' between tears.

"But, did you mention a Trey?" he continued. "Who's Trey?"

She sat up. She wiped her eyes as she tried to control her weeping.

"Trey Wagner," she sniffed. "Stephanie's husband."

The detectives shared another glance.

"You think he did it?" he asked.

"Well, didn't he?"

"Why don't you tell us?"

She was still having a hard time controlling her crying. She kept grabbing tissues from a box on the coffee table.

"Are you implying that Stephanie and Mark were having an affair?" Grogan asked. "And that you and Trey both knew about it?"

"The whole family knew," she sniffed. "That's why I've been staying with my mother the past few days. I just filed for divorce."

"How long have you known about the affair?" he asked.

"Since Memorial Day weekend," she sniffed. "About two weeks."

"And Trey's known about it that long?" he asked.

"Yes."

"I assume he didn't take it well."

"No."

"Would you care to elaborate?" he asked.

"Well, Steph and I got into a fist fight about it here on Memorial Day Sunday," she explained. "I'd found out the night before. I suspected for a while, but I didn't think my sister would do that to me."

"So, you'd suspected they were having an affair even before the holiday?" Grogan asked. "What made you suspicious?"

"I'd heard they were spending time together," she said. "Trey and I both work a lot. We're never home."

"What do you do?"

"I own my own boutique," she explained. "Cassandra's Collectables on Lafayette Street downtown. It's fun, but it takes up a lot of time. And it's hard work."

"And what does Trey do for a living?"

"He's got some fancy job with a PR firm on Fifth Ave.," she said. "I think it's called Yuegler and Dubois, Inc. I think he has to do a lot of traveling, dealing with rich, important clients. I don't really know much about it. He makes a fortune, though."

"Tell me more about Trey," he said. "How did he react when he found out that his wife was having a fling with your husband."

"I guess it came to a head on Monday," she said. "Memorial Day. He came home early and caught them together. He took a couple of shots at Mark with a gun."

"Trey has a gun?"

"It was a surprise to me," she nodded. "To Stephanie too. She said she didn't even know Trey had a gun."

"She didn't even know he had one?" he asked. "And this was Memorial Day Monday? Do you know what kind it was?"

"No," she explained. "Steph didn't know. She wouldn't know anything about guns. Neither would I. But, I don't think Trey was trying to kill Mark at the time. According to Steph, he only took two shots. He chased Mark out of the house and threatened to kill him if he ever caught them together again."

"He threatened to kill him?"

She nodded.

"And what did he say to your sister?"

"Well…" she hesitated. "That didn't go so well. Stephanie told me that after Mark was gone, Trey started acting like a lunatic. He was waving the gun around in her face, calling her names, threatening her, scaring her half to death…"

"I'll bet," Grogan said. He knew there was more. "And then?"

"He told her that she needed to be reminded of who she was supposed to sleep with," she reluctantly continued. "So, he dragged her into the bedroom by her hair…and he…forced her to have sex with him."

"So after chasing Mark out," he recapped. "He's threatening Stephanie, scaring her, then he drags her into the bedroom by her hair and forces her at gunpoint to have sex with him?"

"Pretty much."

"Did anyone report this to the police?" he asked.

"No," she said. "She blamed herself for the whole incident. After all, it was her husband. He was just mad because he found her cheating on him."

"Rape is still rape."

"Stephanie didn't look at it like that," she said. "It was her husband. And it was her fault."

"I see," he decided to drop the issue. "Is Trey a religious man?"

"A little, I guess. I don't really know. Why?"

"Has he ever been to a fancy restaurant uptown called The Robin's Egg?" he asked.

"A few times at least," she said. "I don't know how often, though. My baby brother Michael works there as a waiter."

"Michael Stark!" he gasped with sudden recollection. "Of course! He's your brother. I do believe we've met him before."

"You met my brother Michael?" she asked with a confused expression. "When?"

"Mrs. Genovese," he began. "Do you watch the news or read the papers at all?"

"Yes."

"Are you familiar with the killer the papers are calling Paradox?" he went on.

"Yes…what are you saying?"

She was obviously getting tense again.

He spoke with extreme caution. "We believe your husband and your sister are the latest victims of Paradox," he said.

"No!" she gasped in shock. "Not Mark! Not Stephanie! I can't believe…but that would mean that Trey…Oh God! I can't…No!"

She collapsed into a wave of tears on the sofa again.

They allowed her to have a minute or two to adjust.

However, she wasn't done crying yet when he asked, "Do you know where Trey was last night?"

"He must've been out of town," she sniffed. "Or else Trey and Stephanie wouldn't have gotten together."

"Is that how they operated?" Grogan asked. "Is it possible that Trey might have pretended to leave town so he could catch them?"

"Yes," she managed to say. "That's what he did the day he shot at Mark."

"It is?" Grogan asked. "That's how he caught them?"

"I believe so."

"Where does Trey live?"

"834 Wabash," she managed to say. "They had their own little house not far from here."

"Would he be home now?"

"I doubt it," she sniffed. "He'd probably be at work, assuming he got back from wherever he was last night."

"You told us Michael knew about the affair?" he reminded. "How did he take it when he found out?"

"Not well," she managed to say. "He was very disappointed in Stephanie."

"Where does Michael live?"

"Here with Mom and me," she said. "But he's not home now either."

"Does Trey have any other family?"

"Just his mother," she said. "That's all I know of, anyway. His dad died when he was ten or eleven. Car crash, I think. He looks in on his mother every once in a while. She's old and sickly. I don't know much about her. I only met her a few times."

"So, you don't know what's physically wrong with her?" he asked.

"No."

"Is she a religious woman?"

"I don't know," she said. "I told you I don't know anything about her. I don't even know where she lives. Some apartment downtown, I think. She doesn't have much money, and Trey doesn't do too much to take care of her. She a very unpleasant woman. I can tell you that. The few times I saw her, all she did was bitch. Especially at Trey."

"I see."

"What kind of car does Trey drive?" Grogan asked.

"A blue Porsche," she said. "Only a year or two old. He was doing alright for himself."

"How about your sister?" Grogan continued. "What did she drive?"

"A little green Hyundai," she said. "Ugly little thing, but she bought it with her own money. She's been working part-time as a receptionist for some office complex downtown. I think their called The Heritage Doctors Group or something. They're over on Madison."

"Does Trey's mother drive?" Grogan persisted.

"If she does," she said. "Her car can't be much to look at. I told you she has no money. And Trey never took good care of her."

"I'm sorry, Mrs. Genovese," Grogan added. "But I just have to ask. The day that Trey shot at Mark, nobody called the cops? Not even Mark?"

"I can't tell you why Mark didn't call the cops," she managed to say between tears. "I don't really know. We never discussed it. That day was a sore subject for us. Maybe it was the embarrassment of getting caught. But Mark didn't know what Trey did to Stephanie afterward. She never told him. And she made me promise not to tell him either. She called Mark later that day and told him she was fine. I guess Mark just figured it was best to let it drop and just forget about that day. It seemed to be in everyone's best interest. Nobody ever suspected that two weeks later, Trey would..."

She began sobbing all over again.

"Alright," he said. "I think we've taken up enough of your time. Again, I'm sorry for your loss, Mrs. Genovese."

"Do you really think Paradox killed my sister and my husband?" she asked. "Could Trey really be a serial killer?"

"It's too early to say anything about Trey, ma'am," he said. "We'll keep you informed. But, Paradox is the one who murdered Mark and Stephanie. And, Paradox definitely knew that Stephanie and Mark were having an extramarital affair. Again, we're sorry."

"Thank you," she said as she led them to the door.

She was crying again before she closed the door behind them as they left.

As they walked to their car, Grogan said, "Poor girl. That's got to be harsh."

"Yeah," he grunted. "That news would be hard on anybody."

"We're going to have to talk to Michael Stark again too," Grogan said.

"It looks that way."

"I don't believe you didn't even ask her if anyone else knew about her husband's affair," Grogan stated.

"I just couldn't," he sighed. "The girl was so broken up. And who could blame her. Losing a sister and a husband together in such a ghastly way."

"I see what you mean."

"We have enough to work with on the Trey Wagner angle for now," he said.

Grogan waited until they were in the car before he asked, "You really think Wagner is Paradox. Don't you?"

"I'm not entirely sure yet," he said as he started the car. "Could be. It looks good so far. Mrs. Genovese seems to think Wagner killed these last two victims. And she has every good reason to think so. The connections to The Robin's Egg are beginning to add up. And I doubt Michael would kill his own sister. Not the way we saw in that alley. Trey has a more likely motive, and a lot of interesting aspects I want to explore. Wagner is definitely our first real suspect. I'll tell you this about Trey Wagner: I want to talk to that boy as soon as I can get my hands on him!"

He drove off into traffic. They quickly sped back into the city.

Book Three

Yearn

CHAPTER 11

TAUNT ME NO LONGER

Early that evening, she was getting ready to go out. She was putting on her makeup in the bathroom mirror.

Her friend knocked on the door. "Lindsay!" she called through the door. "Are you going to be in there all night?"

"No," Lindsay called back. "I'll be out in a minute."

"Well, hurry up," she said. "You've been in there for over an hour."

"Take it easy," Lindsay replied. "I'm almost done."

She had it down to a science. It was practically like an art form.

You can't rush art.

She finished what she was doing. Everything had to be perfect. When she achieved the standard she required, she finally unlocked the bathroom door.

As she stepped out into the hall, her friend said, "God, Lindsay! It's about time! What were you doing in there? Composing a symphony?"

"Yes, I guess I was," Lindsay said. "Do you like how it turned out?"

She posed as her friend inspected the outcome of her efforts.

"Not bad," she commented. "Definitely second date material. That top might be a little slutty, though."

"Do you think so?" Lindsay asked. "Should I change?"

"No," she said. "Go with it. Drive the guy nuts. Why not?"

"I don't want to drive him *too* nuts," Lindsay said. "Remember. I'm only going out with him to make Danny jealous."

"Are you still on that Danny kick?" her friend asked with a look of revulsion. "Lindsay! When are you going to stop this obsession of yours. Let go of Danny already, and give this new guy a chance."

"I can't, Vicky," she said. "I'll always love Danny. I'm devoted to him. I'm completely committed to him."

"Well, if you're not committed," Vicky said. "You ought to be. This is totally out of control. You need to move on. There are already too many psychos in this city. Have you seen the headlines in the paper this evening?"

"No."

"Well, check it out."

She pointed at the newspaper on the coffee table for Lindsay to read.

PARADOX MURDER SPREE CONTINUES

"That nut is still out killing people?" she shrugged. "Oh well. That has little bearing on my life. I've got a date tonight and I'm running late."

"Doesn't the very thought of mass murderers bother you?" Vicky asked.

"Maybe a little," she allowed. "But, there are millions of people in this city. What are the chances that I'll ever run into one nut case like that? What are the chances that I'll even know anybody who runs into a nut case like that?"

"Who knows?" Vicky said. "For all we know, it could be the guy who lives across the hall from us."

"Fat chance!" she scoffed. "Does the paper say who the latest victim was?"

"No," Vicky said. "They're keeping it quiet until the families are notified."

"Families?" she asked. "Plural? How many people did he kill this time?"

"The paper says a couple."

"Oh," she said. "Well, it's probably another senator or hooker or something. I don't know anyone like that. Listen, Vicky. This has been fun. But, I really have to get ready. Jeremy will be picking me up in a few minutes."

She looked at the clock on the wall.

"In fact, he's a little late already."

"Jeremy's picking you up here?" Vicky asked. "How did you let that happen?"

"He insisted," she said. "And I have to admit, it's only fair. He put up with a lot from me on our first date. I can't get carried away. I can't let my true intentions become too obvious."

"You can't get carried away?" Vicky laughed. "I'm sorry, sweetheart! That ship has sailed."

"Very funny."

"Oh, talking about getting carried away," Vicky added. "Have you ever heard from Ethan in the past few days?"

"No," she said. "And I can't tell you how relieved I am. Why would you even bring his name up?"

"Aren't you in the least bit concerned?" Vicky asked. "He traps you at Waivers, tells you to wait for him in the car, then he disappears and you never hear from him again? How can you not be worried? What if something horrible happened to him?"

"What if it did?" she replied. "It wouldn't hurt my feelings any. It would be one less problem in my life. Anyway, don't worry about it. I'm sure nothing happened. I'm not lucky enough to have him just die."

"Lindsay!" she gasped. "That's a terrible thing to say!"

"How can you say that?" she asked. "After what he did to me, a quick death would be too good for him."

"I still think it's kind of strange that he just vanished without a word," Vicky said. "Shouldn't we at least drive by Waivers and see if his car's still in the parking lot?"

"Vicky, you fool," she laughed. "That was like a week ago. No matter what Ethan's problem is, if he left his car in the lot at Waivers for any reason, the owners would've had it towed the very next day without asking any questions."

"I guess you're right."

"Of course I'm right," she said. "Now will you forget about Ethan? That's what I'm trying to do. My focus right now should be on Danny."

"How about focusing on Jeremy?"

"Him too," she said. "I'm going to see if I can get him to take me to The Robin's Egg tonight. I figure if Danny's brother Michael sees that I'm really with another guy, he'll tell Danny, and then we'll see how 'not jealous' Danny really is."

"Lindsay," Vicky said. "That's just sad, even for you. This obsession of yours has to stop. Just give this Jeremy guy a real chance. Please?"

"I know what I'm doing, Vicky."

"No," she shook her head. "That plan you just described makes it sound like you belong in a straightjacket in a rubber room in the nearest mental hospital we can find."

"Vicky, you're just being…"

She was interrupted by the doorbell.

"Oh," she smiled. "That must be Jeremy! Gotta go! Wish me luck, Vicky!"

"Break a leg, kid."

Lindsay attempted to look like she hadn't been rushing to the door when she opened it with a smile.

Hours later, she was sitting across from Jeremy at a small table in an intimate little club uptown.

"So, do you like this place?" he asked.

"Oh, yes," she admitted. "I have to say it's a delightful little place. What's it called?"

"The Midnight Fountain," he said. "I'm glad you like it. And I'm sorry I wasn't as cooperative as I was on our first date. I'm just used to being 'the man' when I go out with a girl. I like having some say in what we do and where we go."

"I don't blame you," she said. "I'm sorry I put you through that before. As I mentioned earlier, I'm a little afraid of control freaks."

"I can understand that," he said. "And I see that your face healed nicely. You didn't need much makeup tonight, but you still look much healthier…and more naturally beautiful."

"Thank you," she said with a shy downward glance.

"I take it you haven't run into whoever bruised you before?" he queried.

"No," she said. "And frankly, I'd rather not talk about it."

"Of course," he said. "I'm sorry. And I'm sorry I didn't take you to The Robin's Egg either. I know it's a nice place. I just wasn't in the mood. I had other plans."

"That's okay," she said. "I know you wanted to be 'the man'. But, I think we've done enough apologizing to each other. I'm sick of hearing the word 'sorry' being kicked back and forth between the both of us."

"You're right," he said. "Sorry…oh! I mean, I shouldn't have said that! Strike that! I take it back. I'm not the least bit sorry."

"That's more like it," she smiled. "I see you haven't lost your taste for orange juice."

"And I'm not sorry about that either," he said. "I told you I don't drink."

"And yet, I'm still enjoying myself."

"Why do you say that?" he asked. "Do you usually need to be with drunks in order to have a good time?"

"No."

"Do you like being with drunks who hit you?" he asked in a slightly daunting tone.

"No," she answered defensively. "What is this? What makes you think I would ever like to be with drunks who hit me?"

"Our last date," he said with a softening tone. "I can't imagine you got those bruises from someone who was sober."

"I thought we were going to drop that subject," she averred.

"You're right," he said. "I'm sorry. I'm very sorry I brought it up. We were just talking about 'no more apologies', and now I have to apologize for my behavior again. I don't know what got into me. I'm not a total prude about drinking, but excessive indulgence is an issue I feel strongly about."

"That's alright," she assured him. "Just take it easy, Jeremy. I don't drink that much. But I could probably take a lesson from you in controlling my urge to imbibe."

"I'll admit," he said. "You haven't drunk that much at all tonight. Or even the last time I saw you. You've been very good so far."

"See?" she said. "You have nothing to worry about."

"Now, if we could just do something about your smoking," he said.

"I believe we had this discussion last time," she pointed out. "Don't try to fix me too much all at once. I told you about control freaks."

"You're right again, of course," he admitted. "But, I won't apologize for trying to save your life."

"Okay," she smiled. "I guess I can accept that. But, speaking of smoking…"

"You need another one?"

"I can't help it," she said. "It's been over two hours."

"More like twenty minutes."

"Really?" she asked. "Maybe I do need help. But not tonight."

"Yes," he sighed. "Well, I suppose it's getting kind of late."

"And I have to go to work tomorrow."

"Tell you what," he suggested. "I have to wash up. Why don't you go out and have a cigarette? I'll be out in a few minutes."

"That sounds good."

She went outside. It was a beautiful dark night. It was warm. She leaned against the hood of Jeremy's car. It certainly was a clunker.

She lit a cigarette and took a drag. She slowly blew a cloud of smoke into the air.

She had to admit to herself that she was having a certain amount of fun with Jeremy. He wasn't such a bad guy. But, he had a bit off an attitude about drinking and smoking. Those issues would cause trouble in the near future.

It's not as if she drank all that much. But his righteous attitude would be hard to put up with for too long.

She took another drag.

She couldn't put her finger on it, but there was something about Jeremy that made her a bit nervous. Something wasn't quite right.

And she realized she was going to have to hurry. She was going to have to think of a way to use Jeremy to make Danny jealous...

...before this thing with Jeremy began to turn sour.

* * * * * *

Later that night, he was nodding out on the sofa. The television was on. He wasn't paying much attention to the show.

Everything was quiet.

Then, he was awakened by a noise in the dining room. He heard voices.

His heart leapt up into his throat. That familiar tightening in his gut started again. This was becoming all too customary. He knew what to expect.

He knew who would be waiting for him. He didn't want to face his unwelcome company.

The voices grew louder as he froze on the sofa. He dreaded the thought of getting up to encounter these treacherous interlopers.

Then, a girl appeared in the doorway. Her skin was more pallid than it had been when she was alive. Her eyes were so vacant. Her body was cut, torn and bloody.

Even her blonde hair was messy. Just as it looked as she lay dead in the alley.

"Stephanie!" he gasped.

"Won't you join us?" she invited. "We're having a party."

"A party?"

"We're celebrating being dead," she explained. "It was the senator's idea."

"It was?"

"Sorry there's no cake," she apologized. "The dead don't eat. And there's no music. The dead don't dance."

"Please just leave me alone."

"Well, if you won't come and join us," she said. "I guess we'll just have to come here and join you."

"Please don't!"

She walked in and sat beside him on the sofa. He tried to slide to one side. He didn't want her to touch him. Her clothes were shredded. She was bleeding all over everything.

He was trembling. She was sitting a little too close to him. They were only a few inches apart.

She turned to look at him with those vacant eyes.

Then, the senator stepped into the doorway. "Is this where the party is now?" he asked. "Nice choice. It's a better atmosphere."

He took a seat in an armchair.

Then, the prostitute stepped into the doorway. She said nothing. She just took a seat beside Stephanie on the sofa.

Then, his father stepped into the room. He was the only guest who wasn't cut up and bloody. "Hello, son," he said as he took a seat in the other chair.

Lastly, they were joined by the senator's young lover. She was perfectly willing to sit in the senator's lap.

She was the first to speak. "Hello again," she said.

"Hello," he muttered in a shaky voice.

"We're having a dead party," she said. "And you're the guest of honor because you killed us all."

"You told me to kill…" he began. "I mean God told me to kill you."

"It's alright, my son," she said. "You can call me God. After all, I *am* God!"

"You are not God!" he demanded.

"And you may call me Satan," the senator said. "Or Lucifer. Whichever you prefer."

"Stop this!" he shouted. "You are not God! And he is not Satan! God would never be sitting in The Devil's lap!"

"You ran out of chairs," she explained. "But, don't worry. I won't hold that against you. It's not a sin to be under-furnished for a party."

"What party?" he argued. "This isn't happening! You're not really here!"

"I'm really here," she argued. "God is everywhere."

"I'm really here," the senator said. "Or else God wouldn't be sitting in my lap."

"I'm really here," said the prostitute.

"And I'm really here too," Stephanie said. "And I would like it if you would honestly, truly join our dead party."

"Stop it!" he shouted. "All of you! You're trying to trick me! You're trying to fool me and confuse me! I won't listen!"

"You should listen to the people you kill, son," his father said.

"I've tried to teach you to walk the path of righteousness," she said.

"Don't listen to her," the senator said. "You're doing fine."

"I tried to teach you to live without sin," she continued.

"A little sin every once in a while never hurt anyone," the senator said.

"You should listen to the people you kill, son."

"STOP!" he shouted as he covered his ears. "I won't have this! You have been tormenting me for too long! Quit it! I've done my best to lead a virtuous life!"

"You are a wretched sinner," the prostitute said.

"No!"

"If you were dead like us," Stephanie suggested. "You could join our dead party."

She touched his arm. Her skin was cold and clammy. She smeared blood on his arm as her fingertips glided down to his wrist. He jerked his arm away from her.

"Don't touch me!" he cried.

"What's the matter, lover?" asked the prostitute from her seat. "Don't you like to be touched? I know you do."

"Don't speak to me, you depraved little harlot!" he scolded. "I never touched you!"

"But, lover," she reminded. "You shouldn't lie before God. You touched me, then you killed me! You killed me because you lusted after me. Remember?"

"That's why you had to redeem yourself," said the girl in the senator's lap. "Because you are a foul, unclean sinner."

"Don't listen to her," the senator said. "Personally, I love sinners."

"I gave you my heart, lover," the prostitute said sweetly. "Are you taking care of it?"

He gasped. However, he refused to look downward.

Even though he could suddenly feel the heart-sized organ pulsating in his shirt pocket. Even though he could sense the warm, gooey liquid flowing from his chest and spreading rapidly down across his clothing.

He refused to look.

"Take my heart, you wretched sinner," the prostitute said.

"Touch me," said Stephanie. "Take my hand and join us. Embrace your true nature."

"Listen to those you have killed, son," his father said.

"I am Satan," the senator said. "I have a special place for you back home."

The girl in the senator's lap said, "You are such a foul sinner. When will you follow the path of righteousness?"

"Take my heart."

"Embrace your true nature."

"Listen to us, my son."

"...the path of righteousness..."

He could feel the pulse in his pocket. His hand was hot and sticky. He raised his hand. It was covered with the blood that had spread downward from the heart in his pocket. He screamed.

"Touch me. Embrace your true nature."

"...foul sinner!"

"Take my heart...."

"Enough!" he shouted at the top of his lungs. He covered his ears with his bloody hands. "I will not listen to another word! You have tormented me for far too long!"

Everyone fell quiet.

He pointed at the senator. "You are not Lucifer!" he demanded. "And she is not God! You are all the sinners, not me! I killed each and every one of you because you were all depraved sinners! You deserved to die! All of you! God commanded it! You died and God's true will was done! Leave me! All of you! Taunt me no longer, you wicked, unholy demons from Hell! I will not listen to your heresy any longer!"

Everyone was silent for a moment or two.

Then all the demons suddenly vanished.

He glanced around nervously. His breathing was labored. He couldn't bring himself to move or speak. He was quivering.

There was nothing in his pocket. There was no blood on his shirt or his hands.

And he was left alone in the quiet, empty room.

* * * * * *

He walked to the kitchen window. He looked up at the stars. There were so many stars. Just the ones in his view must have numbered twenty or thirty. And to think of how many millions of stars there were out there…the ones he would never see.

It staggered the imagination.

The sky was still a ruthless, pitiless black. A dull grayish moon hovered low over the urban horizon like a bug trapped in a web.

The moon couldn't move. Nor could it escape. The city would hold it prisoner until its death at sunrise.

He sat back down at the table. He relished the darkness around him. It went well with the pain and sorrow that weighed heavily on his thoughts.

Suddenly, the light flipped on. It startled him. He looked up.

"Michael?" she said from the kitchen doorway. "What are you doing up? It's 3:00 in the morning."

"Hi, Mom," he said. "I know. But, I'm used to being up this late."

"But you didn't go to work tonight."

"Yeah," he sighed. "But, I still couldn't sleep. I'm just so depressed."

"I know, son," she said. "We all are. Would you like some coffee or something?"

"No, thanks," he said. "I got some lemonade. I'm not even thirsty. I just needed to have a glass of something in front of me."

"Why?" she asked. "You couldn't even see it in the dark. Why didn't you turn the lights on?"

"I dunno."

She poured herself a glass of lemonade. Then, she sat by her son.

"This has been hard on everybody," she said. "Who would have ever expected something like this could happen?"

"And the cops think it's that serial killer they've been looking for," he said. "Personally, I still think it's Trey."

"We can't jump to conclusions, dear," she said. "If the police think it's that psycho killer in the papers, they have their reasons. Remember that man said they found a note. And what they told us about the bodies…I just can't fathom. You wouldn't even let me go with you to see the bodies…my own daughter…"

"Me and Danny went down and saw the bodies," he said. "The cop suggested it. And it's a good thing too,

Mom. You don't want to see what we saw. Believe me. You don't want to see it."

"But, she's my daughter."

"That's exactly why you don't want to see what that butcher did to her, Mom," he said. "I don't even think the guy at the mortuary can make her presentable for the funeral. We might be better off just leaving the casket closed..."

"But, Mr. Viola at the funeral home is an old family friend," she said. "And he does an excellent job. Remember when he did your Aunt Charlotte? And your father?"

"This is different, Mom," he insisted. "Aunt Charlotte got hit by a car. And Dad just took two bullets. Believe me. You don't want to see what happened to Stephanie."

"It doesn't seem right," she announced. "Keeping a mother from seeing her own daughter..."

"Mom?"

"Yes, Michael?"

"Do you really think Trey could've done it?" he asked. "Do you really think Trey might be Paradox?"

"It's hard to imagine," she said. "I'll admit Trey isn't the man I would've picked for your sister. He's not a gentle soul. But, he makes a lot of money."

"Money isn't everything."

"I suppose you're right."

"You still haven't answered my question," he said. "Do you think Trey is Paradox?"

She was silent for a minute. Then, she muttered, "I don't know."

"When you think about it," he pointed out. "It makes sense. That was not just a regular murder. And whoever killed Steph must've know about her infidelity."

"Stop it, Michael," she said. Tears filled her tired eyes. "I don't want to even think about it!"

"Alright, Mom," he said. "I'm sorry. All I know is... if Trey did that to Stephanie, I'll kill him!"

"Michael!"

"I mean it," he said. "I'll tear him limb from limb!"

He stopped when his mother began to cry. He put his arm around her.

"Sorry again, Mom," he said. "I'm just upset."

He held her for a minute until the crying subsided.

"I guess I should be happy you loved your sister so much," she sniffed.

"I did," he said. "That's one of the things I was considering before you came in just now. For the last few days of her life, I wasn't very nice to Stephanie. I blamed her for causing disharmony in the family and hurting Cassandra. I may have even called her a slut once or twice."

"Michael! You didn't!"

"That's one of the reasons I'm so upset," he said. "She left us when I was still mad. My last words to her in this lifetime were not very nice."

"Well, I'm sure she knew how you felt about her," she said.

"Yeah," he said. "She knew that I felt she was a slut!"

"She knew you were just upset when you said that."

"It was the same with Dad," he said. "I don't think I ever forgave him for what he did to you. We hardly spoke those last few years. He knew how disappointed and betrayed I felt. And whatever he did, I never allowed myself to forgive or forget."

"Sons idolize their fathers," she reasoned. "When you found out he wasn't perfect, I suppose it kind of burst your bubble."

"For years, I couldn't even look him in the face," he said. "And now, I've done the same with Stephanie. She wasn't perfect, so I scorned her. And then she left us before I could make things right. I let my anger get the best of me. I act out. Then, people die before I can apologize. First, Dad. Now, Stephanie. People always die before I get a chance to make things right."

He began to weep. This time, his mother held him and offered words of comfort.

"Your father and Stephanie both knew you loved them, Michael…"

They shared a good cry. After which, Betty told her son, "Don't feel guilty about your father or Stephanie. I promise, Michael. They both knew how you really felt."

"Thanks, Mom."

"Perhaps you should go and get some sleep," she suggested. "Tomorrow's going to be a busy day."

"Okay," he said. "Good night."

He went up to his bedroom. He stayed very still in bed. He tried to sleep. But, he just couldn't close his eyes. The darkness was a reminder of everything he'd done wrong.

Suddenly, a faint glow appeared near the foot of his bed. He sat up and stared in disbelief. There seemed to be a face in the ghostly emanation.

"Oh God!" he gasped. "No! Stephanie! It can't be!"

"Forgive me, Michael," she said in a distant voice. "Please forgive me."

"No, Stephanie," he said. "It's you who should forgive me!"

"I married Trey because we never had a father," she explained. "Dad was never there, but Trey was. Trey was there, Michael."

"Don't Stephanie! It's alright!" he said. "I'm the one who's sorry."

"Then, after we got married," she continued as if she couldn't hear him. "Trey was always working. So Trey was never there. That's how it began with Mark. Mark was there, Michael…Mark was the only one who was there…"

"It's okay, Steph!"

The light began to fade.

"Don't go, Steph!" he begged. "Please don't go! I'm sorry, Steph! I'm sorry!"

It was too late. The light was gone. He was left with nothing but darkness.

Darkness and fear…and he was left to wonder if what he had just seen had been real.

Had his sense of guilt gotten the better of him?

He sat alone in the darkness. And he started to weep again.

"Paradox or not," he vowed to himself. "If Trey did this to Stephanie, his corpse is going to look ten times worse than hers when I'm through with him!"

CHAPTER 12

INSANITY

She was happy it was Friday. It was the end of the work week.

However, it was gray and gloomy outside. Rain spattered against the windows in a constant reminder that an umbrella would be needed.

She had just enough time to finish her coffee and have a cigarette before she had to leave for the day. The television was showing the news. The weatherman came on.

That was good, she thought. She was only watching to see how long the rain would last.

"How was your date last night, Lindsay?" her friend interrupted.

"Not bad," she said. "Jeremy's not a bad guy. But, I know it could never last too long. He's a bit too religious. And he sounds off about my drinking and smoking a little too often."

"It's that bad, is it?"

"It's not terrible," she commented. "I could have fun with him for a while. But, it'll never be anything permanent. He snapped at me once, though. That caught me off guard."

"What did he say?"

"It was something about the bruises I had last week," she explained. "And how I wouldn't have gotten hurt if I spent more time with people who don't drink."

"Hmm," her friend said with a curious expression. "That's bizarre."

"I told him a little about Ethan," she admitted. "But not much. I suppose it's easy for him to imagine what happened."

"That was still an odd thing for him to say," her friend remarked.

"I have another date with him tomorrow night," she said. "It should be fun. But he wouldn't take me to The Robin's Egg last night. He wanted to be 'the man'. I have a feeling that if I'm going to use him to get at Danny, I'm going to have to step up my efforts. I can't afford subtlety anymore."

"You're *still* obsessing about Danny?"

"Why would that surprise you, Vicky?" she asked. "I told you things weren't really working out with Jeremy."

"Then, don't go out with him anymore," Vicky advised. "Move on! Find someone else and forget about Danny!"

"You don't understand, Vicky," she said. "You don't understand the scope and depth of true love, because you never had true love for yourself! There's something special between me and Danny that will last forever!"

"No, Lindsay!" Vicky argued. "You're the one who doesn't understand! Stalking an ex-lover is not true love! It's insanity! I'm talking full-blown dementia! People get arrested for what you're doing! And don't talk to me about true love..."

They both stopped. Their eyes grew wide.

"Wait a minute!" Lindsay gasped. "What did the news guy say?"

They both turned their attention to the television. The anchorman was telling the story of how the identity of the latest victims of Paradox had finally been revealed.

"Oh my God!" Lindsay sputtered. "I don't believe it! Poor Danny! I have to go to him!"

"You can't be serious, Lindsay!"

"What?" she asked. "At a time of family crisis like this, Danny needs me!"

"Danny doesn't need a stalker right now," Vicky said. "He's got enough problems. Leave him alone."

"Stop calling me a stalker," she insisted. "I'm not a stalker. I'm the one who loves him the most. He needs me for support."

"He already has a girlfriend."

"That tramp?" she scoffed. "I told you about her! She can't be there for him like I can! I'm the one he needs now."

"Don't do it, Lindsay," she said. "Leave Danny alone!"

"But, Vicky..."

"I mean it, Lindsay," she pressed. "Promise me! Promise me you won't harass Danny!"

She opened her mouth to speak.

"Promise me, Lindsay!"

She was silent for a moment. Then, she secretly slid her hand behind her back. She crossed her fingers. "Okay," she said. "I promise."

"Do you mean it?"

"I promise! I promise!"

"Okay," Vicky said. "I have to go to work. Remember you promised to be good."

"God! You're such a nag! Alright already!"

Vicky left the room.

Lindsay wore a sly grin as she took her hand from behind her back. She finally uncrossed her fingers.

* * * * * *

Raindrops were steadily flicking against the windows. And four depressed young adults sat in the living room.

"I feel guilty just sitting here," he said. "There's so much to do."

"Take it easy, Danny," his brother said. "The day is young. It's hard for anyone to get motivated. Mr. Viola hasn't even set a date for the funeral yet."

"Thanks for the reminder, Michael," he said. "I'm sure the girls need to be told all over again how difficult it's going to be for the mortuary to put all of Stephanie back together again so she'll look almost human for the funeral."

"I didn't mean it like that!"

"Boys!" Krysten stepped in. "Please don't fight. Nobody needs that right now. We're all upset. Please don't make it worse."

"Alright," he muttered. "Sorry, Michael."

"I still don't understand why you won't let us see her," Cassandra said. "She's my sister too. And Mark is my husband!"

"Believe me," he insisted. "You don't want to see them. You're upset enough. Seeing them will only make it worse. Even Michael almost lost his lunch when he caught a glimpse of those bodies."

"So did you, tough guy," Michael protested.

"That's enough, boys," Krysten spoke up. "Everyone's sad. Animosity won't solve anything."

There was a moment of silence.

"You wouldn't think it would be legal to keep a woman from seeing her dead husband," Cassandra muttered.

"No one absolutely forced you," Danny reminded. "The cops didn't need you for positive identification. Michael and I took care of that. Plus, both of them were carrying driver's licenses. Mr. Viola at the mortuary didn't like the idea of keeping you from seeing the bodies. We convinced him. And it wasn't hard to do after he saw what we were dealing with."

"Really, Cassie," Michael added. "We're only doing it for your protection. You know they're dead. Seeing those corpses isn't going to do anything but make you feel worse."

"He was my husband!" she argued with tears in her eyes. "I need closure!"

"That's what funerals are for," Michael reminded.

"I'm sick of people telling me what to do," she said, nearly crying. "Just hours before I found out, Mom was trying to convince me not to divorce him. She was going on about "til death do us part', and telling me that God will take care of everything!"

She looked up and saw Betty standing in the doorway.

"Well, I guess death has parted us now, huh, Mom?" she ranted. "Is this what you meant when you told me to leave it in God's hands? Is this how your God takes care of everything?"

Betty stood stunned for a moment. An anger washed over her face. Everyone expected her to explode. Then she began to weep. She turned and ran out of the room.

"What the hell, Cassandra," Danny scolded. "How could you talk to Mom like that? She just lost her daughter! This is even harder on her than any of us!"

"Really, Cassie," Michael agreed. "You crossed the line there."

"To hell with both of you!" she cried openly. "Sure, Mom lost a daughter! And I can't begin to know what that feels like! But I lost a sister *and* a husband! Mark didn't mean shit to any of you! But he was my husband and I loved him! Mom only lost one person in all of this! I lost two! My grief is twice as deep as hers!"

"This isn't a contest, Cassandra," Danny said.

Krysten jumped to her feet. "Maybe I should go check on Betty," she offered.

"No," Danny said as he rose. "I should go. I'll do it. Stay here and see if you can keep the peace with these two."

Krysten sat back down. Cassandra was still crying.

Danny walked to his mother's bedroom. She was lying on her bed with her back to him. She was shaking, and obviously sobbing in her pillow.

"She didn't mean it, Mom," he said from the doorway. "She's just upset."

She just kept shaking as she sobbed.

"This has been exceptionally hard on her," he said. "She was fighting with both of them when this happened. She feels a lot of guilt about how it all turned out."

"We all feel sad," she sniffed without moving. "We all have guilt. Our family was not in the best shape when this happened."

"I know," he admitted. "But, dwelling on the past isn't going to change anything. Cassie loves you. She didn't mean what she said. She just needs to lash out. She'll come around. You'll see."

"I know that," she sniffed. "Cassandra was always a deep and caring person. Compassion was always one of her virtues."

She paused.

"But, what she said about God!" she declared. "How could she?"

"It was all in the heat of the moment," he reasoned. "I'm sure she'll get over it. And I'm sure God will understand. I've heard that compassion is one of His virtues too."

"No, you don't understand, Danny," she said as she rolled over to face him. "I've thought the same thing! I've blamed God and doubted His wisdom! I've scoffed at his fairness and his sense of justice! In my heart, I have mocked my God!"

"Well..." he began with a touch of shock. "It's the same as it is with Cassandra. You were upset. God will understand."

"But, it's not the first time," she told him. "The first time was when your father died. It seems that whenever someone in the family dies, instead of turning to The Lord like I should, I turn my back on Him! I mock Him!"

"Nobody's perfect, Mom," he struggled for an appropriate answer. "Everyone has moments of doubt. It's only natural. As long as we don't stray for long and we fall back in line, God can forgive the occasional indiscretion."

"Do you really think so?"

"Of course."

"I'm glad," she said. "And Cassandra?"

"She'll come around too," he assured her. "To you. And to God."

She smiled as she sat up on the edge of the bed. "Come here," she said.

He walked over and sat beside his mother. She gave him a big hug.

"You're a good son, Daniel."

"You're not too bad yourself, Mom," he smiled as he held her.

Afterward, he stood. "So, you'll be okay?" he asked.

"I will be," she said. "I just need to be alone for a while."

"Okay," he said as he walked to the door. "Take it easy. Get some rest. We have things covered out there."

"I love you, son."

"Love you too, Mom."

He went back and joined the others.

"She'll be okay," he announced. "But she needs some 'alone time'. You really need to talk to her though, Cassandra."

She wasn't ready to talk yet. She just nodded as she sniffled.

A cell phone began to ring. Everybody reached for their phone. It was Danny's.

He quickly answered, "Hello?"

"Hi, Danny," said the caller. "It's me. I just heard about what happened. I can't tell you how sorry I am!"

"Oh," he said with a twinge of disappointment. "Thanks, Lindsay."

"Stephanie was such a sweet girl," she said. "It's such a shame! Is there anything I can do, sweetheart?"

"No, Lindsay," he said. "You don't need to do anything. We're fine."

Krysten suddenly looked up. She jumped out of her seat. "Is that Lindsay on the phone?" she grumbled. "I don't believe she has the nerve! Give me that phone!"

"Calm down, Krysten," he said. "I can handle it."

"You've been saying you can handle it for two whole weeks!" she snipped. "She's still calling! She's still harassing you! She's still on your back every minute! And you refuse to tell her to just go away!"

"I tell her to stop calling all the time," he argued.

"Well, it's time to make it stick, so there are no more misunderstandings," she snipped. "Give me the phone!"

She snatched the cell phone from his hand. "Lindsay!" she barked. "I've had enough of this bullshit! There have been two major deaths in this family! Danny lost a sister and a brother-in-law! And the cops think his other brother-in-law is a serial killer! This is not the time for you to be causing any more of your crap!"

"I'm not causing any crap," Lindsay argued. "I'm genuinely concerned for Danny! And I want to help him!"

"He doesn't need your help," she insisted. "He has *me* now!"

"You forget, Krysten," Lindsay pushed. "This is my family too! I was with Danny for over two years! I've known these people a lot longer than you have!"

"You made the decision to abandon this family over a year ago!" she scornfully reminded. "This isn't your family anymore! This family is just history to you now!"

"I will always be a part of Danny's life!" Lindsay insisted. "The sooner you get used to that, the sooner you'll stop getting those bags under your eyes, you little troll!"

"Don't start hurling insults, you drunken slut!" she seethed. "I'm telling you for the last time! Stay away from us or I'll go over there and skin you alive!"

She hung up the phone. She handed it back to Danny.

"That was unnecessary, Krysten," Danny scolded.

"No it wasn't," she argued. "It was long overdue. And believe me, Daniel. If that little whore calls or bothers us again, I will keep my promise to kill her!"

She stormed out of the room.

"Just what this family needs," Michael muttered. "Another cat fight over a guy."

He glared at Danny as he stood.

"Hey," Danny defended. "It wasn't my fault. I've told Lindsay a thousand times to stop calling me. Anyway, I thought she told me she has a boyfriend or something."

"Just don't let that little bitch ruin our sister's funeral," Michael scowled.

The look on his younger brother's face told Danny that it was best not to respond.

Michael marched angrily out to the kitchen.

Danny looked over at Cassandra. She didn't even glance up. She was in her own little world of misery.

It only made Danny feel worse.

Meanwhile, Lindsay hung up her cell phone. She was driving to work in the rain. She didn't like Krysten's intrusion into her call to the man she loved.

Her blood was boiling. She considered calling back immediately.

Then she decided, no. It was too soon. Tempers were a bit high. For the moment, she would just keep driving.

But, her mind was racing with ideas about how to proceed.

* * * * * *

They sat impatiently in the reception room facing the secretary.

"I'll tell you," he grumbled. "I'm not going to sit here long waiting for this Bozo. We're detectives with The State Police homicide division, for Christ's sake!"

"Calm down, Patrick," Spapper said. "We'll give him a minute or two out of courtesy before we make a fuss."

"I don't like these people," he continued. "This case still doesn't make sense. Wagner doesn't fit the profile. Serial killers are usually single."

"Well, Wagner is obviously disturbed."

"I would've thought we were way off with this guy," he said. "But he had a motive to kill these last two victims. Still, it doesn't add up that he would include his wife and her lover in a murder spree that seems to spring from some religious source or something."

"We still don't know all the facts," Spapper reminded. "It's a good thing his mother-in-law had a key to his place. When we got that search warrant, we got to look through his house."

"We didn't find anything suspicious," he said. "That makes me even more positive that we're on the wrong track."

"Those bullet holes showed us bullets from a .38 Special," Spapper said. "That helps to prove Cassandra's story. And a .38 Special is a definite good sign that we're on the right track. I'll admit that something still smells fishy. But Wagner's disappearance and this company's refusal to cooperate with those city cops makes me awfully suspicious."

"You're right," he agreed. "This case just keeps getting stranger and stranger by the minute."

"Hello, gentlemen," said a polite, condescending voice. "My name is Sheldon Yuegler. How may I assist you today?"

They rose to their feet. They instinctively reached for their badges. "Hello, Mr. Yuegler," he said. "I'm Detective Spapper with The State Police. This is my partner, Detective Van Leer. May we speak with you privately for a moment?"

"Certainly," Yuegler said. "I think I know what this is about. Cindy, will you hold my calls please? And see that we're not disturbed."

"Yes sir."

"And would you gentlemen like some coffee?"

"No thank you, sir," Spapper said. "This is official police business."

"Of course," Yuegler said. "Right this way, gentlemen. Excuse us, Cindy."

"Yes sir."

As they stepped into his office, Van Leer leaned over to his partner and whispered, "This guy is so sickeningly sweet and condescending, it makes my teeth hurt."

Yuegler closed the door behind them. He offered them a seat.

"Now, what can I do for you, gentlemen?"

"Does Trey Wagner work for your company?" Spapper asked.

"Yes he does," he said. "I talked to another set of detectives about all this only yesterday."

"We know," Spapper said. "Apparently, you weren't very cooperative. They were going to launch a major investigation into the operations of your entire company. And indeed, they do have the right to do that. But we told them to let us try to talk to you first. You see, they're city detectives. We're with The State Police. We're hoping you'll be a bit more talkative with us."

"Mr. Wagner's wife and her brother-in-law were murdered two nights ago," Van Leer explained. "We want to talk to Mr. Wagner about it, but he hasn't been seen since his wife was found viciously murdered in an alley. Can you see why that makes us wonder about his whereabouts?"

"I certainly can," he nodded. "But, I can assure you our Mr. Wagner didn't kill anyone. He was out of town on business."

"Where?"

"I'm sorry, sir," he said. "But I can not give out that information."

"You don't seem to realize," Spapper said. "Wagner is suspected of being the serial killer known to the press as Paradox. That case involves not only his wife...it involves a noted state senator. And there are others! Wagner is in a lot of trouble if he can't tell us where he was during certain murders."

"I'm not worried," he said. "Because I know for a fact that Mr. Wagner didn't kill anyone."

"Are you aware," Spapper asked. "That harboring a fugitive and impeding a State police investigation are serious offenses? Not only could you go to jail, but a major full-scale investigation of your business can be initiated. We could close this place down if any improprieties are discovered."

"I had this exact conversation with those detectives I spoke with yesterday," he said. "This is a multi-million dollar business. We are basically a PR firm. We have a lot of very rich clients. Some of them are famous. Our clients pay us large sums of money to help them with their public image...and often we have to take care of problems. Problems that our clients would like to keep private. Our complete discretion is one of the main services we provide. It's why we charge so much money. If our discretion is compromised, or if our clients feel we can't be trusted, we stand to lose a lot of clients. We stand to lose a fortune. We will essentially be run out of business. Mr. Wagner is what you might call a problem solver. He gets called on, sometimes without much warning to go places where our clients have problems that need to be solved...with a great deal of discretion. Revealing where he was and who he was with would make a certain rich client very unhappy. Can you understand my dilemma?"

"I sure can," Spapper nodded. "Here's another dilemma for you. If Wagner can't provide an alibi for the nights when his wife and Senator Zanella were murdered, he will be charged with being a serial killer. We'll lock him in the slammer and throw away the key. Then, we'll launch a major investigation into this company and tear it apart client by client. And you won't have to worry about whether the company goes bankrupt, because the state penitentiary will be feeding you for a mighty long time. How's that for a dilemma?"

"Gentlemen," he smiled. "Be reasonable. My livelihood is at stake."

"Listen, Mr. Yuegler," Spapper said. "We don't care about your client. We couldn't care less if the king of France wears women's underwear. I don't give a shit if the biggest star in Hollywood watches child porn. We don't care! That's not why we're here! We need to verify where Trey Wagner was when certain people got murdered!"

"And you *have* verified it," he said. "I assured you he wasn't in town on the nights in question. I told the other policemen specific dates as well."

"But you weren't with him," Spapper argued. "We need witnesses. You couldn't even show us airline tickets."

"Our clients often provide private transportation," he informed them. "I told you that discretion is a top priority…"

They were interrupted by a knock on the door.

"I'm sorry, Mr. Yuegler," Cindy said through the door. "I know you didn't wish to be disturbed. But, Trey Wagner's back."

He noticed how the detectives' ears perked up.

"Thank you, Cindy," he sighed. "Send him in."

The tall, well-groomed young man with dark hair entered the room.

"How did everything go, Trey?"

"Very well, Mr. Yuegler," he answered. "It's all been taken care of."

"Excellent," he said. "Trey Wagner, these are detectives with The State Police. I assume they would like to speak to you."

They displayed their badges.

"What about?"

"Is there somewhere we can go to get some privacy?" Spapper asked.

"I prefer to remain present, if you don't mind," Yuegler said.

"I have nothing to hide from my boss," Wagner assured them.

"As you wish," Spapper said. "Where were you two nights ago between the hours of 11:00 and 3:00?"

"Out of town on business."

"We got that answer from Yuegler," Spapper said. "I need something more specific. I'm going to need you to prove it."

"Why? What's this all about?"

"Come on now, Mr. Wagner," Van Leer said. "Are you going to pretend that you aren't even aware that your wife and Mark Genovese were found murdered in an alley yesterday morning?"

"My wife?" Wagner went pale. "Murdered? But when? How? Who…?"

"Why don't you tell us, Mr. Wagner?" Van Leer pressed.

"What's that supposed to mean?"

"It's no secret, Mr. Wagner," Spapper said. "That you knew your wife was having an affair with her brother-in-law Mark Genovese. And isn't it true that you caught them together in your house? You took two shots at Genovese with a .38 Special and threatened to kill him if you caught them together again. Isn't that true?"

"I was upset at the time," he said. "I was in shock."

"Where is the gun, Mr. Wagner?" Spapper asked.

"In my coat pocket."

"Take it out very slowly," Spapper cautioned. "Slow and easy, Mr. Wagner. Don't make any sudden moves."

The detectives stayed poised for action as they watched Trey slowly extract his gun from his pocket.

"Place it carefully on the table and step away," Spapper ordered.

"What is all this?"

"Just do it!"

He placed the gun on the table as instructed.

"I'll hold this for the moment," Van Leer said as he took the gun. "Is this registered?"

"Well," he hesitated. "I have to admit it isn't. I have a friend who owns a pawn shop. He sold it to me cheap about a month or so ago because he needed to unload it. I don't know why."

"So, for all we know," Van Leer said. "This gun could be hot."

"Could be," he shrugged. "I didn't bother to ask."

"Do you even have a permit to carry a gun?" Spapper inquired.

"No."

"Then, why do you need to carry a gun that isn't registered without a permit?" Spapper pursued.

"In this business," he answered. "You can never tell when it might come in handy."

"I'm starting to wonder how legitimate this business is," Spapper observed.

"I assure you gentlemen," Yuegler said. "Everything about my business enterprise is completely on the up-and-up. I didn't know Mr. Wagner was carrying a firearm."

"Any other weapons on you, Mr. Wagner?" Van Leer asked.

"No."

"Let's just make sure, shall we?" Van Leer asked.

He quickly frisked the suspect as Trey asked, "What the hell's going on here? Give me a break, guys. I just found out my wife got murdered. Give me a minute to absorb and process!"

"Two weeks ago," Spapper explained. "A prostitute named Audrey Lindquist became the first victim of the killer the press have been calling Paradox. Are you familiar with the case?"

"I've seen something about it in the papers."

"A .38 Special much like this one was taken from Ms. Lindquist by the killer," Spapper continued. "About a week later, a noted state senator and his mistress were the next Paradox victims. You were out of town that night. And your boss refuses to offer any proof of your whereabouts, although he swears you were on business."

"Wait a minute…" Trey began.

"Then two nights ago," Spapper interrupted. "You were supposedly 'out of town' again when your wife and her lover...who you knew about...were found murdered in an alley by someone using the same MO as Paradox. You have threatened your wife and her lover in the past. You have a gun matching the description of the gun taken from the prostitute...a gun that you can't account for... will your friend at the pawn shop vouch for the fact that he sold you the gun?"

"Under the circumstances," Trey admitted. "Probably not."

"So, you can't account for the gun," Spapper deduced. "Do you see where I'm going with this?"

"You have got to be kidding me!" Trey argued. "Are you trying to imply that I killed my wife? Are you trying to say that I'm Paradox?"

"Let's put it this way, Mr. Wagner," Spapper announced. "You are our first real suspect."

"This has got to be a joke!" Trey grumbled. "You can't be fucking serious! Tell them, Mr. Yuegler! Tell them how ridiculous this is!"

"Gentlemen," Yuegler piped in. "I can assure you that Trey was on legal and legitimate business for our company when these sad incidents occurred. He couldn't possibly have committed these crimes you accuse him of."

"You've been assuring us of all sorts of things all over the place," Spapper said. "We don't need your assurance. What we need is hard evidence."

"Hang on," Trey suddenly gasped. "You're saying my Stephanie was definitely killed by Paradox?"

"That's right," Spapper said.

"You mean she was all sliced to ribbons?" Trey sputtered. "The bastard even cut out her heart?"

"Right again."

"Oh my God!" Trey fell into a chair. With his elbows on Yuegler's desk, he started crying into his hands. "No! Not my Stephanie! What did that maniac do to you?"

"Very convincing, Mr. Wagner," Van Leer said. "If I was a member of The Motion Picture Academy, I'd nominate you for a little gold, bald statue."

"What?" he barked. "I just found out my wife was murdered, you son of a bitch!"

"It took you long enough to turn on the tears," Van Leer observed.

"I told you I needed time to process," he heaved through his sobs. "Besides, you've done nothing but accuse me of mass murder since I walked into the room. I just got into town after taking the red-eye flight from halfway across the country. I stop at my office to check in with my boss before going home for a shower and a nap. And two cops are here waiting to tell me my wife was viciously slaughtered, and then they blame me for being a psychopathic serial killer! What the hell? Give me a minute! How could you even think I would do such a thing to my wife? I love her!"

"Yes," Spapper nodded. "We know how much you loved your wife. And we know what you're capable of doing to her."

"What do you mean by that?"

"The day you caught your wife with Genovese," Spapper reminded. "The day you shot at your wife's lover. That's the day you raped your wife at gunpoint."

"What?" he growled. "Who told you that?"

"Apparently," Spapper answered. "Your wife confided in her sister Cassandra. She told her sister that after you chased Mark out of the house, you were waving the gun around in her face, you threatened to kill her, then you dragged her into the bedroom by her hair and forced her at gunpoint to have sex with you."

"Cassandra told you that?" he asked. "And you believed her? Don't you see? She's just making that up! She's upset about her sister! She wants an easy target… someone to pin it on. She's mad at me because she knows I was fighting with Stephanie about her affair with Mark. Her sister and her husband are dead, and I'm the easiest person to blame!"

"Are you saying you didn't rape your wife on Memorial Day?" Spapper asked.

"Of course not!" he spat. "I did shoot at Mark. And sure, Steph and I argued after he was gone. Then, we made up and had sex. It's as simple as that. Married people have sex, you know. That's part of life."

"Call me crazy," Van Leer said. "But, I find Cassandra's account of the story a lot easier to swallow."

"She wasn't even there!" he argued. "How could she possibly know? Besides, gentlemen…I ask you…how is it even possible for a man to rape his own wife? We're married, for God's sake!"

"It's easy for a man to rape his own wife," Van Leer said. "If he's sticking a gun in her face."

"Oh, this is ridiculous!" he scoffed. "She was my wife!"

"That attitude only makes it so easy to believe you're guilty," Van Leer commented.

"That doesn't even make sense!"

"So let's go over this again," Spapper said. "No one will vouch for your illegal possession of a gun that matches the description of the gun taken from Audrey Lindquist. Is that right?"

"The man has a job, a pawn shop and a family to consider," he reasoned. "We meant no harm. He just wanted to get rid of a gun, and I told him I could use one. How could we know something like this could happen?"

"And where were you on the Saturday night of Memorial Day weekend?" Spapper asked.

"I don't know," he grumbled. "Home with my wife, I suppose."

"No one called that night or anything?"

"I doubt it," he shrugged. "Not that I remember."

"So, your only witness for that night…your wife…is dead," Spapper pointed out.

"How convenient," Van Leer added.

"Now wait a second!"

"That's the night Audrey was murdered," Spapper continued. "On the nights when Senator Zanella and your wife were murdered…you were supposedly out of town on business both nights. Is that right?"

"Yes, but…"

"And are you going to offer any positive proof as to his whereabouts, Mr. Yuegler?" Spapper asked. "You've heard this conversation. Now is the time to speak up."

"I've tried to explain to you gentlemen," Yuegler said. "Our clients depend on our sense of discretion. They pay us a fortune to keep their identities and their problems confidential. If we betray their trust, we stand to lose rich, important clients and a lot of money. And if word gets out that we can't be trusted to keep quiet, we'll lose other important clients. Our whole multi-million dollar business would collapse!"

"I'll take that as a 'no', Mr. Yuegler," Spapper said. "So, you have no alibis for any of the nights in question, Mr. Wagner. And you have a motive for killing your wife and Mark Genovese. In fact, you have threatened them, and shown a propensity for violence."

"A propensity for violence?"

"You raped your wife."

"We've been through all that," he sighed with impatience. "I didn't rape her! How can a man…?"

"I'm satisfied," Van Leer interrupted.

"This is ludicrous!" he scoffed. "What possible motive would I have for killing those other people? A senator? Get real!"

"You read the papers," Spapper said. "Are you a religious man, Mr. Wagner?"

"Well, maybe a little, but…"

"That's good enough for me," Van Leer commented.

"I agree," Spapper nodded. "Cuff him, Patrick."

"Gladly."

Van Leer yanked Trey up to his feet. He pulled Wagner's hands behind his back and slapped the handcuffs on.

"Trey Wagner," Spapper announced. "You are under arrest for the murders of Stephanie Wagner, Mark Genovese, Joseph Zanella, Marissa Cosgrove and Audrey Lindquist."

"You're making a mistake!" Trey protested. "I'm innocent, I tell you!"

"You're also charged with possession of a gun without a license," Spapper continued. "And illegal possession of a firearm."

"This is insanity!" he shouted. "Let me go, you fools! I'm innocent! Mr. Yuegler! Call the clients! You know I didn't do anything! This is bullshit! Get me a lawyer! Do something!"

"Good idea, Mr. Yuegler," Van Leer said. "Get him a lawyer. Mr. Wagner, you have the right to remain silent. Anything you say can be used as evidence against you in a court of law."

He dragged Trey to the door of the office. He continued to read the suspect his rights.

"This is all a huge mistake!" Trey demanded.

"Don't worry, Trey," Yuegler said. "I'll get my best attorneys on it! We'll sue them for false arrest!"

"You go ahead and do that, Mr. Yuegler," Spapper dared him. "And maybe while we're at it, we'll launch a full probe into you and your little business here."

"You can't do that!"

"Oh no? Watch us!"

"Let me go!" Trey shouted. "I didn't kill anybody! I'm innocent!"

Trey continued to protest loudly as the detectives escorted him out of the building.

* * * * * *

It was nearing dinnertime. The rain had showered the streets all day. The overcast skies refused to allow any sunlight pass through. The dismal gray ceiling seemed to have become a permanent fixture over the city.

Roads were wet and slippery. Little rivers of runoff lined the curbs. The air felt damp and thick. It was the type of weather that could easily ruin a person's mood.

He stopped home for a rest. He had been driving around all day. There were always so many things to do. He couldn't imagine how anyone could get bored.

How could you…when life was so full?

He ran from his car to the front door to avoid the rain. Most of the time, he wasn't bothered by rain. He often found it refreshing.

Not this day, however. This day he found it cumbersome and aggravating.

He entered and hung his coat up so it would drip dry. He sat on his sofa and closed his eyes. Television was not the proper diversion when he was in such a mood.

He just sat as the gentle rain-on-window lullaby continued to sing him softly to sleep.

"Did you take out the garbage?"

The voice sounded familiar, but distant. In his drowsy state, he chose to ignore it.

"I'm talking to you, boy!" she said in a louder voice. "Did you take out the trash? You know today is trash day!"

He opened his eyes suddenly. He was startled and nervous. He glanced around.

She stood over him. Or at least, it seemed that way. The floral print on her dress reminded him of when he was a child.

Even her apron seemed eerie. He hadn't seen it in so many years. And she seemed so tall as he leaned back in his chair.

For a moment, he was shivering, almost cowering beneath her icy glare.

"What's the matter, boy?" Her words were almost more of an accusation than a question. "Are you deaf? I asked if you took out the trash. Don't you know that it's a sin to disrespect your parents?"

Her voice sounded intimidating at first. Scenes and quick flashes of childhood were suddenly racing through his head.

Memories…terrible, dreadful memories…

He had forgotten and suppressed for so long.

"Answer me, boy! God punishes those who don't behave…"

Then suddenly, she didn't seem so big. She was shorter than he was. Her face was lined and wrinkled. She had aged.

"Do I need to get that leather belt, boy? Or should I turn you over to your father? He knows what to do with little brats and sinners!"

"No!" he suddenly screamed.

She suddenly stopped talking. She was stunned. Her face wasn't as stern.

"Don't you dare say that man is my father!" he demanded. "I won't have it anymore! For years you made me call him Dad! You let me believe he was my real father! That man is not my father! Why did you lie to me, Mom?"

She was still stunned. She stared at him in disbelief.

"If you hadn't slipped up one day," he went on. "I would still believe that monster is my real father! He's not my father, Mom! Who is he? Why did you make me call him Dad? Who is my real father? Do you know? Do you care, you little whore?"

As he rose up from his chair, she began to look a bit scared.

"That man!" he growled. "You made me call him my father! Who was he? Who was my real father? Why was that man allowed in our house? Why was he allowed to do those terrible things to me? I'm not just talking about the beatings, Mother! I'm talking about everything that man did to me! You let him do those things, and he wasn't even my father!"

She took a step backward.

"You married that man and then you chose him over your own son!" he accused. "He was the sinner! Not me! You blamed me for his actions! You claimed that God has ways of punishing the wicked! You blamed me for his sins! You said I cut your bleeding heart out when I went against the will of God! You stood by and allowed that man to do those things! And then you blamed me! You were right about one thing, though. When I found out he wasn't my father, I did kill him! I had every right! And when you threatened to go to the cops, I did what you always accused me of! I cut out your heart!"

She took another step back as he approached.

"You were right, Mom!" he snarled. "I killed your husband! And when you chose him over me yet again, I cut your bleeding heart out! And then, I told everyone you moved to Canada because of Dad's death! I killed you once, Mom! And I'd gladly do it again! You were the sinners! Not me! Now once and for all, leave me alone!"

She vanished. And he was left by himself. He was angry. He was trembling with fury.

The rain was still falling.

And that evening, the newspapers boasted headlines such as:

PARADOX MURDER SUSPECT ARRESTED

CHAPTER 13

VENGEANCE

Did you ever have one of those dreams?

The kind of dream where you almost knew you were dreaming? Even though dreams occur while you are asleep? Even though they are subconscious exercises of the mind, you are having a dream where you are almost consciously aware of the fact that you are dreaming?

He almost knew. He was nearly aware. And yet, he couldn't wake up.

He knew why he was there. He remembered.

It had nothing to do with work. It was Allison.

She was the most beautiful waitress at the restaurant. She was the most beautiful woman he'd ever seen. He was so in love with her!

She didn't even know he was alive.

He wanted to talk to her. He wanted to ask her out. Was that so wrong? He had money. He had inherited a fine chunk of change from his uncle. Girls would have to be impressed with his financial status.

Right?

He was only still working as a chef because his mother told him a job builds character. And God does not look kindly towards shiftless lay-abouts.

So, why couldn't he approach Allison? Why couldn't he tell her how he felt?

Were his feelings unclean? Unholy? Was it really a sin to be in love?

Mom said it wasn't love. It was lust! His love was dirty and sinful.

That's what Mom said. But how could it be true? How could a love so pure be sinful?

His mind was in turmoil.

He wasn't even supposed to be working tonight. Nobody knew he was there. He stayed out of sight. He just watched her…the most beautiful woman in the world.

She looked fantastic in her waitress uniform! Why couldn't he tell her how he felt?

She walked by…so close he could almost touch her. And then she was gone.

And no one knew he was there.

Then…he saw someone else! Sitting at Table 8! What were they doing here?

It was his mother and…that man! That man he hated so much!

They knew he wasn't working here tonight. Why would they choose to eat here?

That man! It was only a few days earlier that she had slipped.

She had said, "It tears my heart out that you disrespect your father so much! He has done so much for you! For both of us! He took you in, adopted you, gave you his name and a home. That's right. You're not even his real son. You were born of my sin and degradation. It was that man who took me in and taught me the ways of The Lord. He taught me to change my direction and walk the path of righteousness. He tried to teach you as well. He tried to teach you to follow the ways of The Lord. But you spurned him, shunned him and chose the road to wickedness. It serves me right to have a son like you. You were born in sin, and you are a constant reminder of my folly. You are the evil incarnate that is the product of my wicked deeds. God punished me for my misdeeds by giving me a constant burden of evil. He was right for what He did. And you are the evil burden I must bear!"

Is that the way a boy should find out he'd been adopted? The way to find out his father was not really his father? The way to find out his whole life had been a lie?

And now, here they were: his mother and…that man!

"Tammy!" said the chef. "These are for Table 8. And here is the order for Table 12. Don't get the two Jambalayas mixed up. This one has shrimp in it and Table 8 is allergic to seafood."

"Right, Steve."

That's right, he thought. That man was allergic to seafood! He liked to order the Jambalaya without seafood. What a fool! It seemed like he was taking a chance.

That fool would take his life in his hands every time he ordered Jambalaya without shrimp in it! It would be so easy to make a mistake…or get trays mixed up.

Just like now. Tammy stepped away for a minute. Just for a second, really.

The trays were so close to him. It was like a gift from God.

Luckily, he'd always known the best discreet corners and places to go unseen.

Nobody could see him behind the vending machines near the pick-up station by the kitchen. He even had napkins, so there would be no fingerprints on the plates.

It would only take a second. Nobody would see him.

All he had to do was switch the plates. Just like that.

'Vengeance is mine sayeth The Lord.' Isn't that what The Bible said? And here, God was handing him a miracle. God's will. God's justice.

Vengeance for all that man has done. Revenge!

Tammy was a good waitress. She even asked again, "This is for Table 8, Steve?"

With a quick glance, Steve said, "That's right, Toots."

Tammy brought the food for Table 8. What a fool that man was for ordering the Jambalaya without seafood!

It was easy to position himself in a place behind some plants by the hall. He could watch the man take a few bites.

Everything seemed to almost go in slow motion.

The man's face began to turn red. He started choking and gagging as his cheeks began to swell. Mom went from looking concerned to a state of full panic.

The man fell to the floor. He began twitching as waiters and restaurant personnel came to his aid.

It was such a joy to watch! He wanted to stay and enjoy the fruits of his labor. But he knew he would have to be gone by the time the authorities arrived. He would have to be satisfied by just knowing that the little miracle God had handed him hadn't gone to waste!

God's will had been done. Justice had been served on a plate of Jambalaya.

And with the restaurant in a panic, it was easy to slip out the door without being noticed. It was so perfect! Only a fool would not have done it!

Allison would have to wait. This was so much more important.

It was foggy. It was murky. But, it was a memory.

And almost like falling off a building…falling… falling…

He was transported to another memory. One he would so rather choose to forget. A memory that had fallen back so deeply into his subconscious.

He would so rather choose to forget. He was in the kitchen.

He was washing dishes in the sink.

"You think you're so clever," she accused from behind.

He kept washing. He didn't even turn to face her.

"Don't you have anything to say, boy?" she asked.

"What do you want me to say, Mom?"

"Are you proud of yourself?" she queried. "Your father's in the ground. Dead and buried, and you got away with it."

"He's not my father!"

"Not this again," she said. "Genetics is just a formality. That man has been there for you your whole life. He saved me from a life of sin."

"In other words," he prodded. "You don't even know who my real father is."

"Don't start that again, boy!" she grumbled. "That man was all the father you needed. He cared for you. He took you in and gave you food, shelter and clothes. He tried to teach you to walk in the ways of The Lord…"

He spun around to face her as he shouted, "He molested me, Mom!"

"Don't say such things about your father!"

"He's not my father!" he growled. "And I'll say it because it's true! That man raped me many times over the years! He started touching me and doing inappropriate things when I was seven years old, Mom! You caught him doing it when I was eight! And instead of looking out for your son! Instead of protecting your child, you sided with that man! That stranger to this household! You blamed me for his filthy actions!"

"If he even touched you," she said. "Which I doubt, it was only because you seduced him, you wicked child."

"Seduced him?" he chided. "I was only eight years old! How does an eight-year-old child seduce his stepfather?"

"You were an evil child," she explained. "You were born of evil. You were the spawn of Satan. Your father only reprimanded you when you were bad! He only punished you when you turned your back on your Savior and embraced the ways of The Devil!"

"No!" he shouted. "I did not deserve what that man did to me! For ten long years that man abused me and you knew it! You knew about it and you turned the other way because you figured that if he left you, no one else would have you!"

"How dare you talk to me that way?" she scolded. "I am your mother! It tears my heart out when you act like an ungrateful brat! It hurts so deeply when you say those things about me and the man who was good enough to raise you as if you were his own son! You need to ask Jesus for forgiveness, you vile sinner!"

"Stop defending him!" he argued. "He was the vile sinner, not me! He raped, abused and beat me for over ten years and you let it happen! You were a sinner for allowing it to happen!"

"Don't accuse my dead husband of such things!" she denied. "You should never speak ill of the dead! It cuts my bleeding heart out when you show such a blatant disregard and disrespect for your elders! It's a blatant sin! It's in The Commandments that you should honor they mother and thy father!"

"Stop calling him my father!"

"Why does that bother you so much?" she inquired. "Why does the whole genetic thing make you crazy? I already told you. I was three months pregnant when I met Jason Blackwell. I had nobody. Jason helped me through a difficult time in my life. He taught me to find help in Jesus. We were married right after your first birthday. He's the only father you ever knew. Everything you have you owe to him."

"That doesn't give him the right to molest me," he countered. "For ten long years that man abused me! It only stopped when I fought back and beat the shit out of him! I had to fight back! God knows my mother would never protect me! Not only did you not help me, but you threw me out of the house afterwards! All I did was stand up for myself, and once again you chose that child molester over your own son!"

"He was not a child molester!"

"Yes he was!" he shouted. "Don't deny it! You caught him!"

"I caught him punishing an evil, ungrateful, misbehaving son!"

"I had to move out on my own and get a job in a restaurant to support myself," he angrily reminded. "I only started getting my inheritance from Uncle Rick a few years ago. And even then, it was only small monthly annuities."

"Is that why you killed your father?" she accused. "Is that why you killed him? So you could move back into this house? Get the fortune you knew he was going to leave you? Even after years of bad behavior and disrespect? You certainly moved back here quick enough after he was gone."

"What makes you think I killed him?"

"How else could something like that happen?" she asked. "Your father ordered that dish at that restaurant many times. They never made such a mistake before."

"There's always a first time for everything."

"That's the line of thinking that made it possible for you to get away with it," she said. "There was never much of an investigation. Everyone assumed it was an innocent accident. Just a mistake made by the restaurant employees."

"You didn't hold back any when it came time to sue the restaurant," he pointed out.

"They were ultimately responsible for what dish got served to whom," she said. "But that doesn't mean you weren't guilty."

"I wasn't even there that night," he said. "It wasn't my night to work."

"That's how you got away with it," she said. "I always suspected you were guilty. I don't know why you were there. I can't prove it by myself. But I know you were responsible. I just know you killed my husband!"

"You're crazy, Mom."

"Am I?" she questioned. "Maybe the cops wouldn't think so. Maybe the cops should take their time and investigate."

"They already ruled it as an accidental death."

"Perhaps they should reopen the case," she suggested. "Perhaps if I talked to the police, they would go back and look at the evidence. I wonder if the security tapes would show my evil son on the premises on the night when he didn't have to work."

"That's ridiculous," he scoffed. "What would I have been doing there? I didn't know you were going there that night. How would I have even had the opportunity to do such a thing?"

"I don't know," she said. "I just think the police should go back and look at a few things like the security tapes. What would you think of that?"

"Why should that bother me?"

"You tell me," she smiled. "All of a sudden, you look nervous, my son. Could it be I'm on the right track? Were you there that night, boy?"

"Of course not!"

"Then why are you so nervous?"

"I'm not nervous," he said. "I'm just mad. And I'm sick of this conversation."

"I don't blame you for being sick of this conversation, Jeremy," she grinned. "You know what really happened that day. I don't know how. But you knew. You were there. A mother knows these things. That was no accident. Was it, Jeremy?"

"How would I know?" he replied. "I wasn't there!"

"Maybe I really should talk to the police," she quietly taunted. "They would find something on those security tapes if they really looked. Wouldn't they, Jeremy?"

He turned away from her and leaned heavily on the kitchen counter.

"I don't know what they would find!" he simmered. "I wasn't there!"

"I think you do know," she pressed. "I think you know exactly what they would find. You wouldn't get your father's money then. Would you, boy? All you would get would be a life sentence in jail. That's where you really belong, isn't it?"

"Stop it! Shut up!"

"Even now you're disrespecting your mother," she goaded. "Maybe I should go to the police. It cuts my bleeding heart out to think my son is such a spiteful, evil, ungrateful sinner. I tried to teach you to follow Jesus. But you were born of evil, and evil is the only thing you know how to be!"

"Shut up!"

He opened the drawer by the sink. He pulled out a long knife. He spun around to face his mother.

"Jeremy!" she sputtered. "What are you doing? Put down that knife!"

"No!" he shouted as he raised the weapon. "I'm so sick of hearing you! All my life I had to listen to you rave about how I cut your bleeding heart out with every move I make! You want me to cut your bleeding heart out? Fine! You bitch!"

He buried the blade deep in her chest. It felt good to experience the blade's intrusion into her soft, warm flesh…and to see the blood gush out like a natural hot spring.

Her screams were like music to his ears. He kept stabbing and stabbing. Cutting. Slicing. Tearing flesh with the blade. He kept stabbing even after she stopped moving. He kept slicing even after the screams fell silent.

He didn't stop until he could reach into her chest and pull it out. He held the vital organ up in his hand. He stared at it and watched the blood run down his arm.

"You want me to cut your bleeding heart out, Mother?" he scoffed in a maniacal tone. "There! You finally got your wish, you bastard! *You're* the sinner! That's right! *You're* the sinner! Not me!"

He just stared at the heart in his hand.

Then, he woke up. He suddenly sat up in bed. He felt cold and clammy. He was shivering. The room around him was dark. He glanced over at his digital alarm clock.

It read 3:07. It was still the dead of night.

It had been a long time since he'd had that dream.

However, those memories could still be fresh and daunting. He could almost still feel the hot blood running down his arm.

* * * * * *

It was still raining on Saturday morning. The gray ceiling of clouds refused to budge. A steady shower continued to wash over the soaked urban streets.

Two detectives sat at their desks. One was doing paperwork as the other hung up the phone.

"Are we going back down into the city, Ray?"

"Not right away," Spapper said without looking up from his forms. "I have to catch up on some of this backlog."

"Well, I don't have to tell you who that was on the phone," he said. "They just dropped the murder charges on Wagner a few minutes ago."

"I figured as much."

"I'm not sorry we hauled him in though," he said. "Even as I was putting the cuffs on him I had my doubts. You wouldn't think this kind of psycho would be so foolish as to incorporate his own wife in his list of victims. Not with the note and the same MO and everything."

"Yeah," Spapper nodded. "I felt the same way. It was all a bit too clean, too neat and too easy. These cases never get solved this quickly. But we had to convince Wagner and Yuegler that we weren't screwing around about needing alibis for the nights of the Paradox murders. Lucky for them, a few of their clients came forward and provided the alibis that Wagner needed."

"Right," he chuckled. "It didn't help Wagner all that much. He still has illegal possession of a firearm, no gun license and carrying the gun across state lines hanging over him. He's still facing felony charges."

"I'll cry a river for him later."

"I still think you gave Yuegler too good a deal," he commented. "Offering not to investigate his slimy little company if he doesn't pursue his false arrest case. We should have thrown the book at him."

"What do we care?" Spapper shrugged. "It helped us get this whole mess cleared up quicker. All I promised is that we won't press the issue at this time. He'll get his just desserts in the end. Someone will catch up to him. Besides, we never could place Wagner at the scene of any of the murders. We did sort of 'jump the gun' a little."

"Like you said," he reminded. "We needed to get Yuegler and Wagner to take us serious. But now, we still don't have our killer. Our next step of course is to find out who else knew that Stephanie Wagner and Mark Genovese were having an affair. We really should've looked deeper into that question before this."

"Yeah," Spapper muttered. "We got a little too bogged down in chasing down the Trey Wagner angle."

"And now you're going to let those city cops question the Stark family first?" he asked.

"Well," he sighed. "They've been on the case longer. They're good cops. They've been good about sharing information with us. That family doesn't need to have all four of us converging on them all at once at a time like this in their lives. Besides, I have a mountain of paperwork to catch up on. And so do you. Especially after that shit with Wagner yesterday."

"Don't remind me."

"Come on, Patrick," he said. "Get started on those forms. If you catch up by noon, maybe I'll buy you lunch."

"Lunch at Palermo's?"

"Sure," Spapper shrugged. "If you like. Why not? And look on the bright side. At least we don't have to drive all the way over to the north side of town."

* * * * * *

She had a definite plan. Jeremy knew the Stark family. They were all friends. And since Jeremy was a religious man, he would want to help his friends in this time of sorrow. She had a date set with Jeremy that evening. Still, if she stopped by his house during the day, perhaps they could visit the Stark residence together. After all, Jeremy lived not too far from the Stark house.

Then, Danny would see her with Jeremy.

Then, we'd see how jealous Danny would be!

Plus, she would be there for the family. Helping them. Comforting them. Taking care of things. Getting back in their good graces. And Danny would see it all!

And that little slut he was with…even she wouldn't start any trouble during this time of family crisis.

It was the perfect plan. So simple. So innocent.

But, she knew it would work! Danny would be hers again by the end of the day!

* * * * * *

The room had a definite ambiance. It was formal and somber, yet tasteful. It was just the sort of setting for such an occasion. Still, no one wanted to be there.

No one ever did.

They stood before the carefully selected casket. Everyone felt the tension of the moment.

"Mom," he observed. "You're trembling. Are you going to be okay?"

"Yes, Danny," she sniffled. "I'm fine. I'm just nervous. I haven't seen her yet. This will be the first time. No mother should have to go through this."

"I did the best I could with what I had to work with," said the older gentleman in the tailored suit. "I can't tell you how much it broke my heart having to work on Stephanie. I've known her most of her life. And she was…"

He stopped himself from finishing the sentence.

"I'm sure you did a great job, Mr. Viola," Danny said. "I know you had a difficult task with her."

"Luckily, her clothes cover most of the damage," Viola said. "So, she looks pretty good now, all things considered."

"Okay, Mom," Danny said. "The wake is tomorrow. The funeral is Monday. Are you ready to take a look?"

"I'll never be ready," she said. "But I'm as close as I'll ever be."

"How about you, girls?" Danny asked. "Shall we take a look?"

Krysten braced herself. Then she offered a meek, "Yes."

Cassandra took a deep breath and nervously nodded her head.

Mr. Viola waited a moment. Then, he lifted the lid to the casket. The five mourners looked expectantly inside.

Everyone was afraid to speak.

Betty held a brave expression for nearly ten seconds. Then, she turned and marched briskly out of the room.

They couldn't see her. However, everyone could hear her crying.

Of course, that set off Cassandra. She exploded in tears as she stood there looking down at her sister.

Then, Krysten buried her face in Danny's shoulder. He held her tightly as she sobbed gently into his good shirt.

"You really did an excellent job, Mr. Viola," Michael said.

"Thank you," he said. "I did my best."

"It's fabulous," Michael reiterated. "Really. I wasn't expecting much after what I saw before you started. I don't know how you did it."

"That's enough now, Michael," Danny said softly. "But, I agree. Good job, Mr. Viola."

He nodded his appreciation.

"I think you can close it now," Michael said.

As he slowly lowered the lid, he said, "I'll give you all a moment to yourselves."

He turned and left the room.

"Should I go take care of Mom?" Michael asked.

"Let her go," Danny advised. "She'll come back when she's ready."

A few minutes later, she walked back into the room. Cassandra and Krysten had both stopped crying by then. The mood remained sullen.

"Thank you, Daniel," she said. "Thank you for not letting me see her before this. I don't think I would have handled it well."

"Me too, Danny," Cassandra said. "Thanks."

"That's okay."

"And Mom?" Cassandra added. "I really want to apologize for what I said the other day. About you and about God. It was wrong. I was upset. And I'm so sorry."

"That's alright, dear," she said. "I understand."

Mother and daughter held each other. And forgiveness was found among a few more tears.

When they finished their business with Mr. Viola, they opened their umbrellas and walked out into the drenched parking lot. Danny had announced that he and Krysten had things to do. They would be stopping by the house later in the day.

Everyone was about to get into their cars when a familiar Dodge pulled up near the spot where they had all parked. Two familiar gentlemen in suits stepped out into the rain.

"Detectives Paczecki and Grogan," Betty smiled. "It's a pleasure to see you. Any word on my daughter's murder?"

"May we get in out of the rain, everyone?" Paczecki asked. "We'd like to speak with you all, if you don't mind."

The Stark family members were all curious as they followed the detectives back into the building. Betty introduced them to Mr. Viola, Danny and Krysten. Then Mr. Viola allowed them some privacy in one of the rooms.

"This is a nice place, Mrs. Stark," Grogan said. "But, I'm surprised you chose a place so deep in the city. It seems to me there would be a thousand mortuaries closer to your house."

"Mr. Viola has been a family friend for a long time," she said.

"That explains it," Grogan said. "Mind you, we're not complaining. We just happened to see you as we were driving by. We were on our way to your place. This saves us quite a drive."

"I'm glad," she said. "So, what would you like to talk about?"

"They dropped the murder charges on Trey Wagner this morning," Paczecki said. "It appears his alibis checked out. Don't let it alarm you. We figured they would. Those State detectives only arrested him because Trey's boss wouldn't give up the names of his clients. We had to convince Trey and his company that we were serious about needing an alibi. Arresting Trey was a necessary evil."

"So Trey isn't Paradox?" Cassandra asked.

"No," Paczecki shook his head. "But he's still in jail at the moment. He still has some felony changes concerning that gun he had."

"One of the reasons Trey was arrested," Grogan explained. "Is because he had a .38 Special he couldn't account for. He had lame excuses for how he obtained it illegally. Paradox took a .38 Special from his first victim. A prostitute named Audrey Lindquist."

"So if Trey didn't kill my sister?" Danny asked. "Who did?"

"That's what we're here to discuss," Paczecki said. "It had to be someone who knew Stephanie and Mark. And it had to be someone who knew they were married, but not to each other...someone who knew about the affair."

"Who could have possibly known?" Betty asked. "It's not as if anyone broadcast it over the television airwaves or something."

"Oh come on, Mom," Michael said. "Everybody at your Memorial Day picnic knew. Remember the fight Stephanie and Cassandra had? It was a main topic of conversation during the whole picnic. And Mark wasn't there, but Trey was. Steph was introducing her husband to everyone."

"Who was at your picnic, Mrs. Stark?" Paczecki asked.

"She usually only invites the family," Michael said. "But this year she invited her whole church. There must've been over a hundred people there."

"So, there were over a hundred people from your church," Paczecki muttered. "And all very religious people, I take it. That's just marvelous. It could take a year to go through and interview that many people. Well, I guess I'm going to need the names and addresses of as many people as you can think of from the picnic. And of course, anyone else you can think of that would be of interest."

"Wait a minute!" Grogan interrupted. "Mrs. Stark, do you know anyone from your church or picnic who drives an old brown four-door Chevy sedan with a model year in the late '80s or early '90s?"

"Not off the top of my head," she said as she considered the question. "Of course there are a lot of people in my church. If I thought about it…hang on! Now that you mention it, I think Jeremy Blackwell drives an old beat-up Chevy Lumina. I think the model year is '92. It's brown and it's seen better days."

"Jeremy Blackwell?" Grogan asked. "He drives a 15-year-old Lumina? Is there a big dent in the back passenger's side door?"

"I don't recall specifically," she said. "But as I told you, the car is kind of beat-up."

"He was at your picnic?" Grogan pursued.

"Yes," she nodded. "He met Stephanie and Trey and Cassandra at the picnic."

"Is he a religious man?" Paczecki asked.

"Yes. Very religious!" she said. "I met him through church."

"That reminds me," Michael said. "Jeremy Blackwell? Now that I think of it, he was at The Robin's Egg the night the senator was killed."

"He was?" Grogan asked.

"Yeah," Michael nodded. "I didn't see him around midnight when the senator was there. But I saw him there around 8:00 or so earlier that evening."

"Are you sure?"

"Yup," Michael said. "It's easy to forget he's there. He pops in every once in a while. We don't make a big deal of it, and he doesn't make a fuss. But he stops by every once in a while because he's part owner of The Robin's Egg and Lumpy Bill's."

"What?" Paczecki blurted. "He's part owner of both restaurants? Your sister and Mark Genovese were last seen at Lumpy Bill's. Someone came forward and let us know. We knew the same people owned both restaurants. We talked to people at both places a number of times. Including the owners. And I don't remember anyone mentioning Blackwell."

"He's easy to forget," Michael explained. "The owners weren't paying their taxes and were having foreclosure problems. Jeremy came in and bailed them out with a loan. He's kind of like a silent partner now. He gets his share of the profits, but he doesn't get involved in any of the details. He's been known to show up at either place. He'll hang around, get dinner or whatever. But he stays out of everyone's way. I think the real owners are embarrassed about the whole thing, so they tend to forget he exists."

"They're embarrassed?" Paczecki said. "This is a murder investigation, not a popularity contest."

"No one ever really thinks of him," Michael clarified. "He doesn't really stick his nose into anyone's business. He shows up a few times a week. He hangs around a little. Well, maybe he 'lurks' around a little."

"Lurks?" Grogan asked.

"I don't know how to explain it," Michael said. "Sometimes you see him. Sometimes you don't. Sometimes he'll order dinner. Nobody ever charges him, because we all know he's part owner. But he's just an easy person to forget about. The owners don't really think of him as an owner, because he never takes part in any of the major decision-making. He's just easy to forget. He only bought into the place about eight months ago."

"You've known Jeremy for eight months, Michael?" Betty asked. "But I introduced you to him at my picnic. Why didn't you say something?"

"I only actually met him once back when he bought interest in The Robin's Egg," he said. "He didn't seem to recognize me at your picnic. I guess he doesn't pay much attention to the staff. And I probably look different in my waiter uniform. I just didn't want to make a big deal out of it. I didn't want to embarrass him…or get stuck talking to him. It just seemed best not to say anything. After all, he is sort of my boss."

"Let's get back on track," Paczecki interrupted. "So, Jeremy Blackwell has a financial interest in both The Robin's Egg and Lumpy Bill's. Michael saw him at The Robin's Egg earlier on the night Senator Zanella was killed. Blackwell is known to 'lurk' around these places every once in a while. He knew Stephanie and Mark were married, but not to each other. He's religious, and he drives an old, brown '92 Chevy Lumina sedan that's not in very good shape?"

"Yes," Betty said.

"Can you give us a description of him?" he asked.

"He's 29," Betty said nervously. "He's white, single, dark brown hair, well-groomed. He stands a little over 5'10", and weighs between 200-220. Why, detective? Are you suggesting that Jeremy Blackwell might be Paradox?"

"Well, if everything you just told us is true," Paczecki admitted. "I'd say he just jumped up to the top of our list of suspects."

"Oh dear," Betty muttered. "And to think I set him up with Lindsay Bainbridge."

"You set Lindsay up with Jeremy?" Danny asked. "That's her new boyfriend?"

"Well, I was just trying to get her to leave you and Krysten alone," Betty explained. "I didn't mean any harm. I hope he doesn't do anything to hurt her…or worse."

"We should be so lucky," Krysten muttered.

"Do you have an address on Blackwell?" Paczecki asked.

"He's staying in his mother's place while she's in Canada," Betty said. "It's over near our house on the northern edge of the city. I think he lives on Briarwood Lane. I don't know the exact house number."

Paczecki handed out a few of his cards. "If any of you can think of anything to add," he said. "Give me a call. And if you encounter Jeremy Blackwell, don't let on that we know who he is. And under no circumstances should you upset or excite him, and don't try to subdue him yourself. Paradox is a highly disturbed, sick and volatile individual. Probably even delusional. Almost anything could send him off the deep end."

"Did you say 'delusional', detective?" Krysten asked.

"Yes," Paczecki nodded. "Our psychiatrist gave us a profile that suggests Paradox is probably murdering people in the name of God because he thinks God is telling him to do it. He may think he sees and talks to God on a regular basis."

"He thinks God talks to him?" Cassandra asked.

"Most likely."

"So what should we do if we run into Jeremy?" Cassandra asked.

"Call us immediately."

"And you might want to warn your friend Lindsay Bainbridge to stay away from him too," Grogan added.

"Thank you, detectives," Betty said.

"Well, we should go look into this," Paczecki said. "Thanks for your time. You've been a big help. And I'm sorry we had to disturb you while you were…you know, here."

The detectives rushed out of the funeral home and into the rain.

As they got into their car, Paczecki shot his partner a sly glance. "An old, beat up brown Chevy sedan, huh?" he asked.

"See?" Grogan responded. "And you thought my talking to Tanya Alcazar was a waste of time."

"Once again," he admitted. "My partner the pervert cracks the case. Call in for auto records on Blackwell. And see if you can get an exact address. Then, call Spapper and see how long it will take him to drum up a search warrant. I have a good feeling about this. I think Blackwell could be the man we're looking for."

* * * * * *

It was approaching lunchtime. He was sick of the rain. He was sick of being haunted.

If you kill someone, aren't they supposed to stay dead?

He was already in a sore mood when he burst into his home on Briarwood Lane. He didn't even bother to close the front door. He saw his mother waiting for him as soon as he stormed into the house.

She sat on the sofa. Waiting for him.

"What are you doing here?" he asked as he entered the room.

"It's my house!"

"Not any more," he argued. "You left it to me in your will. You're dead!"

"The will hasn't been probated," she reminded. "Nothing's been settled. My will becomes null and void if you did anything to hasten my death. Or your father's. You know that. That was one of the reasons why you were so scared when I threatened to go to the police. You would lose all that money that I and your father left you."

"Stop calling him my father!" he shouted. "He was not my father, you worthless harlot! He was my stepfather! And he joined me in the car again today! I was driving around downtown and that little bastard just appeared in the passenger's seat! He's dead! I killed you both! Why can't you just stay dead!"

"Because God wants to punish you for what you've done," she sneered.

"God *has* punished me!" he exclaimed. "God has been punishing me all my life! Your vengeful God has been punishing me, even for things that were not my fault!"

He didn't see the young woman standing in the doorway by the front porch. She stood there in shock. She stood and stared as the man she was dating yelled at the sofa. But, there was no one else in the house. The man was essentially yelling at himself.

"I didn't deserve the punishment I received, Mom!" he ranted. "You and that man! That man that you made me call dad! He wasn't my father!"

"He was the only father you ever knew," his mother argued. "He saved both of us from a life of hell! He saved both of us from Hell!"

"He didn't save anyone but himself!" he shouted. "That man was a filthy child molester! He molested me for years! All those years he raped me, and you let him get away with it! You knew and you looked the other way!"

"All he did was punish an ungrateful child for his sins!" she asserted.

"No!" he screamed. "You can not justify what that unholy monster did to me! He was the sinner! He and you were the sinners for doing what you did to a child who trusted you! You put that monster above the welfare of your own son! You want me to admit it? Fine! I'll admit it! Yes! I killed him! I was there in that restaurant the night he died! I wasn't working at The Claremont that night, but I was there! God gave me the miracle I finally deserved. He allowed me to be in the right place at the right time! It was a miracle God gave me. I just happened to be in a place where I was able to switch plates so that man would get the Jambalaya with the shrimp in it! I knew he was allergic to seafood and I switched the plates! I enjoyed watching that monster gag and die!"

"How could you, son?" his mother grumbled. "How could you do that to your father?"

"Stop calling him my father!"

"It cuts my bleeding heart out to see what a wretched sinner you turned out to be," she commented sadly.

"And stop saying it cuts your bleeding heart out every time I stand up for myself," he demanded. "That man deserved to die like that! It was God's miracle that I was allowed to kill that man! And it was God's vengeance that made that monster die the way he did! And when his death was ruled as an accident, you confronted me! You blamed me! Just like you blamed me for the fact that the monster molested me! I ask you again! How can an eight-year-old boy seduce his stepfather?"

"You were born of evil," she reasoned sadistically. "And you will always be evil!"

"Stop saying I was born of evil!" he shouted. "You were the evil ones! Not me! I can't help how I was born! And no just and fair God would punish me for your sins!"

"Don't blaspheme in my house!" his mother scolded.

"You don't make the rules anymore, Mom!" he demanded. "You're dead! I killed you! That child molester's death was ruled an accident! You confronted me and threatened to go to the police, so I cut your bleeding heart out! Just like you accused me of doing every time I begged you to protect me from that monster you married! You're dead! And don't talk to me about money! I'm finally getting the inheritance Uncle Rick bequeathed to me that you and that monster tried to steal! I'm finally getting the money I deserve from the rapist you married after years of torment that you did nothing to stop! And I can't do anything with your money because I can't tell anyone you're dead! I have to tell everyone you're in Canada!"

"Canada?" she scoffed. "Why would you even dream up that I would go someplace like Canada?"

"What difference does it make?" he shouted. "My torment still won't end! You and that monster still won't leave me alone! I can't escape these wretched feelings of guilt! Even after what you two did to me, I still can't escape the guilt of killing my own mother! I try to please God! Every day I try to assuage my sins and redeem myself in the eyes of The Lord! I killed that loathsome prostitute and it wasn't enough! I killed that sinning senator and his fornicating whore who was half his age! That wretched man who flaunted his flagrant sins just because his wife lives in another city! Still, God was not satisfied! Even that sweet, wonderful Betty Stark! Such a righteous woman who tried to teach her children to walk in the ways of The Lord! When I saw her treacherous daughter flaunting her sin and infidelity in public… disgracing her mother and denouncing everything she was taught…I killed her too! Still, God won't forgive me and erase the guilt I suffer from the sin of killing my own mother! What will it take? What do I have to do to escape this guilt? Why can't I escape you monsters even after you die? What will it take to get your filthy blood off my hands?"

His mother said nothing. All was silent.

Then, he heard a noise by the front door. He spun around to see what it was.

"Lindsay!" he gasped.

"Jeremy!" she stammered in shock. "I…I have to go!"

She turned and ran out of the house.

"Lindsay! Wait!" he called.

He checked his jacket to make sure he had his gun. Then, he ran to the kitchen and grabbed the largest knife he could find. It was the same knife he always used. By the time he ran out to the driveway, Lindsay was trying to start her car.

The motor sputtered, but wouldn't catch. She was sobbing as she turned the key in the ignition again and again.

"Wait, Lindsay!" he shouted as he ran up to her car. "Give me a chance to explain!"

As he circled around to the driver's side, he heard her try the key again.

"Open the door, Lindsay!" he warned. "Let me talk to you!"

She turned the key again. This time, her car sprang to life.

"Stop the car, Lindsay!" he seethed. "Open the door!"

She reached for her stick shift. Jeremy used the butt of the gun to shatter the driver's side window. Lindsay screamed as she was showered by a spray of broken glass.

"I said open the damn door!" he snarled.

Lindsay shifted into drive and stepped on the gas as she felt his fingers on her throat.

She sped out of the driveway and into traffic without looking. Jeremy was forced to let go as the glass from the window gashed his arm.

"Damn it!" he grunted as he grabbed his bleeding arm. A quick look showed it was just a scratch. As an afterthought, it occurred to him that he just should have shot her through the window.

But, it was too late for hindsight.

He hopped into his brown Lumina and raced after his prey. He placed the gun and the knife on the passenger's seat. He looked up ahead for Lindsay's blue Jeep. It was easy to spot just a few cars ahead.

He had to catch her. He had to stop her. It didn't seem likely that he would be able to reason with her. But, he would have to try.

And if all else failed, he would just have to kill her!

Lindsay could see him in her rearview mirror. You couldn't miss that old, brown, beat-up piece of shit. He was a few cars back. Her nerves were a raw, tangled mess. She hadn't been this terrified since the last time she saw Ethan.

How did she always end up with these maniacs? How could she ever have been so unbelievably stupid as to leave Danny?

What in God's name was wrong with her?

She just kept driving. Saturday traffic was heavy. A steady rain assaulted her windshield. The roads were wet and slippery.

However, she couldn't afford a prudent speed. She was beginning to panic. Where could she go?

She needed Danny. He would know what to do. The Stark house was close to where she was. Danny was probably there because of...

But, she couldn't go there! She couldn't impose an insane serial killer on the Stark family at a time like this. Sure, Betty was the one who introduced her to Jeremy. But, Betty didn't know that Jeremy was Paradox!

Betty would never have done anything so cruel. Betty was a good Christian woman.

She had to drive somewhere...but where? Where is a police station?

Oh God! She had no idea! She couldn't think straight! It was all she could do to keep from bursting into tears.

She was trembling when she looked back in the mirror. It appeared that he had gotten a little closer. He was only two cars back now! Her heart leaped up into her throat.

She felt trapped. Why can't people drive faster in this town?

She had to lose him. With the squealing of tires, she quickly pulled off onto a different road. She wasn't sure where she was driving.

Instinctively, she steered roughly in the direction of Danny's apartment. She didn't know why. He probably wouldn't be home. Still, aiming for Danny's place just made her feel safer.

She had to swerve to miss a pedestrian. Her car slid. She almost hit a parked SUV.

Why did it have to be raining? Why did the roads have to be slippery?

Jeremy was still behind her. Panic was setting into every muscle in her body. She had to think of some way to escape. She didn't know how. Why couldn't she find a cop in this town?

She just headed south. She just steered roughly toward Danny's place.

* * * * * *

"It was nice of your mother to tell us to go home for a few hours," she said.

"Yeah," he sighed. "I want to be supportive, but there's only so much you can do. I told her we had some errands to run, but I just needed a break."

"Besides," she added. "You have to be allowed to grieve in your own way. That was the first time I saw

Stephanie like that. It was really hard to see her that way."

"Tell me about it!"

"Oh, Danny," she said as she wrapped her arms around him. "I'm so sorry you have to go through this."

"Thanks, Krysten," he said as he held her. "It's alright. I'll live through it. But I gotta tell you. I'd sell my soul for five minutes alone with Jeremy Blackwell!"

"Do you really think he's Paradox?"

"Those cops seem to think so," he said. "All the pieces seem to fit."

"How could anyone be so absolutely insane?" she asked. "What makes people do such things?"

"I don't know," he said. "It's a crazy world out there."

"So, what are we going to do?"

"Well, it's almost lunchtime," he informed her. "Would you like to go out somewhere for a bite to eat?"

"I'm not really hungry," she said. "But I guess we could go somewhere. Just to go. I don't feel like just sitting around the house."

"How about Bernard's?"

"Okay," she said. "Let me go get my purse."

Suddenly, his cell phone rang. He answered, "Hello?"

"Danny, it's me," the caller announced frantically. "Jeremy Blackwell is chasing me! He's going to kill me! Help me! Please!"

"What?"

"Jeremy Blackwell is Paradox!"

"I know," he stammered. "Or at least, I thought…I mean, the cops think…wait! How did you know? Wait! Krysten, come here!"

He put his speaker phone on as Krysten entered the room.

"I went to Jeremy's house to surprise him," the caller explained nervously. "Your mother set us up. I've been seeing him. But his door was open. He was talking to himself. Well, yelling to himself, actually. He thought he was arguing with his dead mother! But no one else was there!"

"His mother's dead?" he asked. "I thought his mother was living in Canada."

"She's dead!" she proclaimed. "Jeremy killed her! Her and his stepfather! He was ranting and raving and yelling about why he killed all those people! Jeremy is Paradox!"

"Okay," he said. "I believe you. Where are you?"

"Jeremy is chasing me," she whimpered. "I don't know where to go! I just started heading south down towards your place!"

"My place? Why?"

"I don't know," she blurted. "Danny, I'm terrified! Jeremy's going to kill me! He broke my window and I'm scared!"

"Where are you, Lindsay?"

"I just started driving," she whimpered. "I made some turns and twists to try and throw him off. But every time I think I'm safe, he shows up in my rearview mirror again! I'm getting lost and I'm running out of gas! I've been driving around like a lunatic for half an hour! You'd think I would've run into at least one cop by now!"

"We'll call the cops, Lindsay," he said. "But you need to tell us where you are."

"I'm on Spaulding headed south," she sniffled. "There's all these old, abandoned buildings and run-down…everything looks condemned! I just passed the corner of Gaines Ave."

"Spaulding and Gaines?" he said. "Damn! That *is* a bad neighborhood! You need to get out of there! Listen, you're just a few miles west of my place! Head east on the next turn you can find!"

"Okay, Danny," she whimpered. "I will! You've got to help me, Danny! Jeremy's going to kill me! I'm so frightened!"

"Everything will be okay, Lindsay," he assured her. "Stay on the line. I'll get Krysten to call the cops. We'll get you through this!"

"Thanks, Danny," she said. "You always…"

She stopped talking. Suddenly, she screamed. They heard the screeching of tires.

Then, the phone went dead.

"Lindsay?" he called. "Lindsay? Are you there?"

There was no answer.

"Damn it!" he grunted. "Something must have happened! I don't know if I should call her back or just wait for her to call."

"You're not really going to call her back, are you?" Krysten asked.

"Jesus, Krysten!" he scolded. "This is no time for jealous bullshit! This is a life or death situation! I'm going to try calling her again. Call those detectives we saw this morning. They'll know what to do."

She just looked at him for a moment as he dialed.

"Do it now, Krysten!"

She thought about Lindsay for a second. Then she reached into her purse. She was actually worried about Lindsay's safety as she took out her cell phone.

"She's not answering!" Danny declared nervously. "I hope she's okay!"

CHAPTER 14

COLD AND HEARTLESS

They pulled their car into the driveway. They parked right behind Paczecki's Dodge. Then, they quickly jumped out into the rain.

"Did you get the warrant?" Paczecki called from the front porch.

"No problem," he said as he joined them.

"It didn't take you long," Paczecki commented. "Good job, Ray."

"I know people," he said. "I have connections."

"Well, we're in luck," Grogan said. "The door's open and nobody seems to be home."

"He just left the door wide open like that?" he asked.

"Apparently," Paczecki said. "And we haven't heard a peep from inside."

"Well then, let's go have a look."

He took a cautious step inside. All four men had their guns drawn. They braced themselves for any unexpected problems.

"Jeremy Blackwell?" he called into the house. "This is the police."

There was no answer.

"Jeremy Blackwell?" he called again. "It's the police. We have a search warrant."

There was still no answer as all four men entered. They glanced around.

"Blackwell?" he tried one last time. When no one responded, he said, "Okay, men. We'll spread out and tear the place apart. And be careful everywhere you step. He might still be here. Remember. We're trying to nail Paradox! Patrick, you start upstairs. Kyle, you take the basement. Stan and I will start on the ground floor. Let's go."

They all went off into their assigned areas. They were only looking for a few minutes when a cell phone sounded.

"Detective Paczecki," he answered. "City Homicide."

Krysten told him everything she could about Jeremy's chase with Lindsay.

"And you say you last heard from her as she was heading south on Spaulding?" he asked. "Just past Gaines Ave.? That's a bad part of town."

"She sounded terrified on Danny's speaker phone," she said. "Now that she knows about Jeremy, I think he's going to kill her."

"We'll do our best to prevent that, Miss Salinger," he said. "Thanks for the call."

As he hung up, he called out, "Listen up, everybody! New information about Blackwell! He's been spotted chasing someone down Spaulding about half an hour south of here! We think he plans on killing someone… immediately!"

Van Leer came down from upstairs. "He's on the move?" he asked. "Right now?"

"Yes," Paczecki said. "We have to move out! Pronto!"

"Wait a minute," Grogan called from downstairs. "Come down here for a second. I have to show you something."

The other three detectives ran quickly down to the basement.

"What's up?" Spapper asked.

"Check it out," Grogan said while pointing.

"So what?" Van Leer questioned. "It's just an old freezer with a padlock and chain around it."

"Call it a hunch," Grogan said. "But I'd like to see what he's got in there."

"Right this second?" Van Leer pressed. "We're chasing a psycho killer who's on the move, and you have a hunch about a freezer?"

"Let him go," Paczecki suggested. "Kyle's got a knack for these things."

Grogan shot the lock off the chain. He took a moment to brace himself. Then, he opened the freezer.

The rancid smell was the first thing that hit them. Then, they all gawked in horror at the contents within.

"Holy Jesus!" Van Leer exclaimed.

"Well, I'm glad he put her head on the same shelf as her heart," Paczecki commented. "I'm guessing those see-through garbage bags hold whatever's left of the body. Probably in small pieces."

"Who do you think it is?" Van Leer asked.

"I'm pretty certain it's his mother," Paczecki deduced. "It looks like she never made it to Canada."

"What kind of a sick weirdo does something like this," Grogan winced. "Especially to his own mother?"

"Well, gentlemen," Spapper announced. "If we're looking for Paradox, I'd say we hit the jackpot."

"And he was last seen heading south on Spaulding," Paczecki reminded. "He was chasing Lindsay Bainbridge."

"Then, let's get going," Van Leer said. "It's time to catch us a deranged serial killer."

* * * * * *

Five minutes after the first call went dead, they were still in their apartment. They weren't sure what they should do.

"I've got to admit, Danny," she said. "I'm a little nervous. She hasn't called back yet. That's got to be a bad sign."

"I know," he agreed. "I'm really tempted to drive over there."

"You can't be serious," she argued. "We're talking about a psychotic mass murderer, for God's sake! What are you going to do when…?"

His cell phone interrupted them.

He nervously answered, "Hello?"

"Danny, it's me," she whispered into the phone. "Sorry about what happened a few minutes ago. Something ran out in front of my car. I think it was a dog or something. I swerved to avoid hitting it. The roads are so slippery today. My car slid off the road and wrapped around a telephone pole."

"Are you alright?" he asked as he put her on speaker phone. "I tried to call you."

"I think I'm okay," she whispered. "Listen. I don't have much time. My car wouldn't start and Jeremy was closing in on me. I had no choice. I ran into an old abandoned building on Spaulding. It's called Ratcliffe's Wholesale Distributors. Do you know the place?"

"The old abandoned warehouse?" he asked. "That's where you are?"

"I'm hiding on the second floor," she whispered. "I heard Jeremy come up the steps. You've got to help me, Danny. If Jeremy finds me, he's going to kill me!"

"Why don't you call the cops?"

"I'm terrified, Danny," she whimpered. "He's going to kill me! Please, Danny! I need you! Oops! I gotta go. Please, Danny! Help!"

The phone went dead.

"Oh shit," he proclaimed. "We can't call her back. I'd better go help her."

"You must be joking," Krysten said.

"You heard her," he said. "Lindsay's trapped on the second floor of an abandoned warehouse not three miles west of here in a bad part of town. And Paradox is out to kill her. How am I supposed to leave her there?"

"Easily," she said. "Take me to lunch like you promised."

"Krysten!"

"Call the cops before we go," she suggested. "This is their job, not yours."

"The cops?" he scoffed. "In this town? The cops would never go into that part of town. The cops around here wouldn't go into that neighborhood even if Donut Kingdom opened a new franchise right in the middle of Center Square."

"I'll call those detectives," she said. "They'll be on their way anyway."

"They're at least a half hour away," he said. "I can get there in five minutes."

"Daniel," she averred. "This is a serial killer we're talking about. Not to mention, this is all about Lindsay… again!"

"Oh for God's sake, Krysten," he argued. "This is no time for your childish jealousy bullshit! I put the phone on speaker so you could hear the call. This is no fucking around anymore, sweetie! A serial killer is going to slice her to ribbons! I love you…not her! You have no reason to be afraid of Lindsay! I'm done with her! But it doesn't mean I'm going to stand there and watch her get murdered!"

"Don't you see?" she countered. "This is why she always runs to you. This is why we'll never get rid of her. You always 'take care of things.'"

"Krysten," he assured her. "We can't do this now! I love you, Krysten. But this isn't like helping her move! This is Paradox! I'm sorry, but I have to go!"

"If you're going, I'm going too."

"No you're not!"

"I'm not leaving you alone with Lindsay," she asserted. "Last time I did that, you kissed her!"

"Not this again," he argued. "I didn't kiss her! She kissed me! Oh God! I don't have time for this! I have to go!"

"Then, I'm going too!"

"Oh, alright already!" he heaved a sigh. "You can call those detectives and give them an exact location while we go! And stay out of harm's way! Blackwell is extremely unbalanced…and dangerous!"

"Danny?" she asked sheepishly. "What are you planning to do? You're right about Blackwell. The guy's a maniac."

"So am I," he said. "Remember, I'd be doing this even without Lindsay. That son of a bitch butchered my sister!"

"Just be careful. Okay?"

"I will," he said. "And you stay totally out of sight, Krysten. I mean it!"

There was a moment's pause.

"Danny? By the way, I love you too."

"I know, princess. Let's go."

* * * * * *

She hid behind a stack of boxes in a large room. A continuous patter of rain sounded against the huge windows that lined two opposite sides of the filthy, cluttered enclosure. Light from outside was dim at best.

Vision was nearly adequate, but marred by numerous shadows.

Boxes and crates of all sizes were stacked in haphazard piles all over the room. A layer of dirt covered everything like a grand tarp of grime and grit.

There were plenty of things to hide behind. She planned to find a way to circle around and double back in order to escape. She was frightened.

But it was her only chance for escape.

The stairs to the ground floor were not too far from the door. Maybe fifty or sixty feet. She heard Jeremy step into a smaller room first. She heard him call out her name.

She took the opportunity to silently move over behind the next pile of boxes that was closer to her exit. She was shaking with fear. Tears rimmed her eyes. However, she knew she had to keep her wits about her.

She wanted to stealthily make her way over to the next stack of crates. Did she dare? She was gathering up her nerve when she heard Jeremy enter the room.

"Lindsay?" he called. His voice was louder and closer now. "Lindsay? Come on out, sweetheart! I want to talk!"

The echo in the room made his voice sound more eerie.

She figured if he walked past a certain point in the room, maybe she could try to escape. Perhaps she could quietly make her way down the stairs and out of the building while he was looking for her.

But, where would she go?

"Lindsay?" his voice echoed louder. "I just want to talk. I won't hurt you. I promise. Come on out."

She was petrified. She swallowed hard against the lump in her throat. The urge to scream felt nearly impossible to suppress.

"Lindsay? I just want to explain! Just talk to me! Please?"

He was walking further into the room. He was approaching a point where she might feel safe in moving. She took a silent step backward. She caught her foot on some rubble on the floor. She let out a quick squeal as she caught herself noisily against a crate.

He turned in her direction. She was afraid to look. She couldn't see the expression in his eyes. But she heard the sound in his voice.

"So there you are!"

She could hear him march steadily over to the stack of crates she was using as cover. Her entire body tensed. She began to panic. Even though she couldn't see him, she knew he would be on top of her in a matter of seconds.

In a frightful frenzy, she screamed. She ran out from behind the crates as fast as she could. She was heading for the exit.

As he saw the motion, he instinctively shoved the stack of crates to impede her efforts. The crates crashed loudly on the filthy floor with a maddening echo. She had already come out from behind them as she fled for the stairs.

It only took a few moments before she could feel his arm wrap around her neck. She screamed and cried as he dragged her back to the center of the room.

"No, Jeremy! Please!" she begged with panic in her voice. "Please! Let me go! Please don't kill me! Oh God! Don't kill me!"

"What makes you think I'm going to kill you?"

"The knife in my throat," she cried. "Please don't, Jeremy! I don't want to die! I won't tell anyone, Jeremy! I swear!"

He pressed the sharp blade of the knife against her neck as he held her tightly from behind. "Why did you have to run, Lindsay?" he inquired calmly. "I asked you not to run. Back at my house. Why did you force me to chase you?"

"I was scared!"

"Does this make you feel better?" he asked. "Being in a place like this? Forcing me to hold a knife to your throat? Is this what you wanted?"

"No," she cried. "Please let me go! Please!"

"You should have just talked to me, Lindsay," he said. "You should've just let me explain."

"I panicked," she sniffled. "Those things you said!"

"What things?"

"About your mother," she wept. "About...oh God! I don't remember! I'm so frightened! Please, Jeremy! I won't say anything to anyone! I promise!"

"How do I know you didn't call someone already?"

"I didn't! I swear!"

"Oh well," he said as he tightened his grip around her neck. He let the tip of the knife press sharply against the underside of her chin. "I guess it really doesn't matter. I guess I'll just have to kill you anyway."

"No!"

"If you had stayed and talked to me," he informed her calmly. "I may have been able to explain. I might have gotten you to understand what I'm doing. I may have impressed upon you how important my work is. It's a little late now, though. You're too terrified. In this frame of mind, you would be incapable of understanding the task I am performing on behalf of our Lord and Savior."

"Please, Jeremy," she implored. "I understand. I'll do whatever you say!"

"I don't believe that for a second, Lindsay," he told her. "You never listen to anyone. You certainly never listen to God. Or Jesus. You were living in sin with Betty Stark's son for over two years. Weren't you?"

"How did you know that?"

"Betty Stark is such a wonderful, holy woman," he imparted. "So righteous! And she tried to teach her children to walk in the ways of The Lord. Then you came along and dragged her son down into your world of sin and degradation. And if that's not bad enough, you dumped the poor boy. And for who? It was that drunken slobbering piece of garbage who was hitting you out behind that den of iniquity. What was that club called? Waivers, was it?"

"You saw that?"

"Why do you think that wretched, drunken stumble-bum didn't keep his promise to drag you back home?" he pointed out.

"Oh my God!" she gasped. "You killed Ethan?"

"Was that his name?" he asked. "I just saw the way that pile of human wreckage treated you, and I figured I should do the world a big favor. So I sent the little demon back to Hell where he belongs."

"So, you were following me that night?"

"Of course," he replied. "I wanted to see the kind of woman Betty was setting me up with. I can only assume Betty thought I could help you find the path back to God. She must have thought you were worth saving."

"I *am* worth saving," she begged. "Please let me go!"

"Oh, I'm afraid it's a little too late for that," he said. "You see, I'm doing God's work now. I'm helping Him cleanse his Earth and making it free from sin. Not everyone can understand. And I can't allow anyone to hinder God's will."

"I don't want to hinder anyone, Jeremy," she pleaded. "I just want to live!"

"Believe it or not," he admitted. "I'm sorry it came to this. I would have liked to get to know you better. You're a beautiful, smart woman. You may have made some stupid choices, but you're no fool. You might have been led back into God's flock, with a little patience and guidance. But now it's too late. You have to die so I can go back to doing God's work."

"This isn't God's work you're doing," she wept. "You're just killing people!"

"Oh shut up, you little whore," he threatened. "You don't know nothing! I'll be doing the world another favor by ridding God's Earth of another filthy sinner. Well, I hate long good-byes. Let's just get this over with, shall we?"

She screamed as she felt the blade move against her skin.

Then, she quickly asked, "Wait, Jeremy! If you're going to kill me, don't I get a last request?"

"A last request?" he scoffed. "What do you think this is? Some cheap, old fashioned pirate movie or something?"

"Please, Jeremy," she implored. "I just want you to answer one question for me. Okay? When you killed those people, you always left a note. Each one of those notes had one line in common. They all read, 'I am the paradox that is all mankind.' What did you mean by that?"

"Is that all?" he said while rolling his eyes. "Don't you get it? We're all a paradox. Each and every one of us. God built us all to be a paradox. He built us to be strong and follow his lead. He demands perfection from us, and He can settle for no less from us. But He also gave us free will. And he also made us weak. He made us prone to sin and imperfection. It was His intention to set us up in this cruel trap that is so difficult to escape. We should follow His word, but we are tempted by our weaknesses. We all sin, and that's why we constantly need to ask His forgiveness. Even I have committed these sins. I have craved. I have lusted. I have coveted and even yearned. Don't you see? I killed that prostitute because in a moment of weakness, I wanted her. Even in her cheap, unholy, inappropriate garb of a temptress, she looked so beautiful to me. I craved her. So I wasn't just ridding the world of sin when I killed her. I was expunging my own sins."

She wept gently as she listened. His arm held her tightly. That blade was so sharp and cold against her flesh. Where was Danny? Where were the cops?

"It's the same with the senator's depraved little hussy," he continued. "And Betty Stark's daughter. In their wickedness, they all reminded me of how I have lusted, coveted and yearned. I have even yearned for you, Lindsay. In my weakness, I have allowed myself to think unclean thoughts. So you see? When I kill them, I am not just erasing their sin from God's earth. I am also redeeming myself of my sins. As much as I've tried to be perfect, I am subject to my human weakness. Like everyone else,

I am the paradox that God built us all to be. It is the eternal irony. It is the cosmic joke that God played on all of us in His stern, demanding cruelty. He built us to live up to His standard of perfection. But He built us all to be weak, so we will always fail. He set us all up for failure in the cruel cosmic joke that He imposed on all of humanity."

"But, that's not true, Jeremy," she argued bravely. "God doesn't expect or demand total perfection from us. God knows we're human. He knows we make mistakes. If what you said was true, nobody would have any chance of getting into Heaven. Everyone would just be going around killing everyone, trying to earn forgiveness. God doesn't want that. He just wants us to do our best and be as good as we can. And if we make mistakes, He will forgive us if we turn to Him and try to do better next time. He's not a cruel God. He's a forgiving God. He's a compassionate God."

"Enough!" he growled. "Don't you presume to tell me about God, you sinner! You fornicator! You vile, wicked temptress! You know nothing of God's intentions or His purpose! You have lived in sin, and your death will be a blessing and a comfort to God's earth!"

"No!" she begged. "Please!"

Then, they heard a distant voice. "Lindsay? Lindsay? Are you there?"

"Danny!" she shouted at the top of her lungs. "On the second floor! Help me!"

"Shut up!" Jeremy barked while pressing the blade to her chin. "Keep your filthy mouth shut!"

As he tried to tighten his grip she managed to sink her teeth deep into his wrist. He howled as he released her for a moment. She shouted as she began to run. But he grabbed her after only a second. Again he was holding her from behind. His arm was around her shoulders and neck. The tip of the knife was pressed sharply under her chin.

"If you ever try that again," he snarled. "I'll slice you to ribbons, you worthless slut!"

"Let her go, Blackwell!"

He looked up toward the voice. Danny Stark was standing in front of the doorway about forty or fifty feet in front of him. His feet were apart and he was using both hands to aim a gun straight at Jeremy.

"Get out of here, Stark!" Jeremy ordered. "This doesn't concern you!"

"It does now," he said. "Let go of the girl! The game is over!"

"Drop the gun, Stark!" Jeremy demanded. "I'll kill her! I swear I'll kill her right where we stand!"

"If you harm one hair on her head," he warned. "There won't be any reason for me not to kill you. You'll never get out of here alive. Recognize this gun, Blackwell? I got it off the front seat of your car. You should really lock your doors in this neighborhood, buddy. Is this the gun you took from that hooker you killed, Jeremy? Or should I call you Paradox?"

"I swear I'll kill her, Stark!"

"You ain't killing anybody, pal," he stated. "If you kill her, you're dead! I'll shoot you where you stand. I know how to use this thing. I took a year of police training right out of high school. I'll admit I never finished my training, but I can still put one right between your eyes at this range, pal! You can bet on it!"

"You haven't got the guts!"

"I've got the guts and the incentive," he assured. "You killed my sister. I'm the one who had to identify the body. You carved her up mighty handily. You even took out her heart. I got to hand it to you. You do nice work, in a sick and gruesome way. I'd admire your artistry. But it was my sister, you fucking dirtbag! I'd like nothing better than to return the favor and do the same thing to you. But, I'll make a deal with you. If you let go of the girl, I'll let you walk out of here free as a bird. Just drop the knife. Let the girl go, and I'll let you walk out of here in one piece."

"Why should I believe you?"

"I guess you'll just have to trust me."

"Not good enough!"

"It's all you've got," he said. "You're not getting out of here with the girl. And if you hurt her, I'll kill you. The police know who you are. They're on their way over right now. If you let her go, you can walk. I promise. It's the only chance you have to escape. Take it or leave it."

"No!" Jeremy argued. "You don't call the shots here! I'm in charge! You don't understand! Nobody understands! I'm doing God's work here!"

"This isn't God's work," he disagreed. "God doesn't want people to go around killing each other in His name! He put us on this earth to love one another, be nice to each other and even help each other! It's even in The Commandments that we 'shall love thy neighbor as thyself'."

"Don't you dare try to quote The Bible to me, you loathsome, wretched sinner!" Jeremy ranted. "I know what I'm doing! You have no idea what God wants! Now back away, or I'll slice her from stem to stern while you watch!"

Suddenly, a female voice sounded from out of nowhere. "Jeremy Blackwell! This is God! You are making me angry! Let the girl go! Killing is a sin!"

Jeremy glanced around the room. "Who said that?" he shouted.

"I told you," said the voice. "This is God! You have killed enough, and killing is a sin! Let the girl go and renounce your sins!"

"Who is that?" Jeremy repeated as his eyes darted around the room. "Have you got a girl hidden somewhere, Stark?"

Danny kept his gun trained on his target. "What are you talking about, Blackwell?"

"That voice!" Jeremy called. "That woman's voice claiming to be God!"

"You're crazy, Blackwell," he said. "There aren't any voices! Stop stalling and drop the knife!"

"You didn't hear any voices just now?"

"No!"

"This is God, Jeremy Blackwell," said the voice. "You are making me angry! You have sinned enough for one day! Let the girl go!"

"You didn't hear that?" Jeremy called as he desperately scanned the room with wild eyes.

"Hear what?" Danny said. "There aren't any voices, Blackwell! Drop the knife and let go of Lindsay!"

Jeremy held Lindsay tightly while testing her flesh with the cold steel of the blade. "What about you, Lindsay?" he barked. "You heard that voice claiming to be God, didn't you?"

She was trembling with fear. She couldn't move beneath Jeremy's grip. That knife was a sharp threat that brought horrified tears to her eyes. She couldn't think straight. She glanced over at Danny. He looked so good…so daring as he aimed that gun with both hands at Paradox.

She and Danny had been through so much together. They knew each other so well. She didn't know what he was planning. However, she could tell by the look in his eye that he wanted her to play along.

She swallowed hard against the blade to gather her courage.

"Well?" Jeremy repeated impatiently. "Didn't you hear the voice of God?"

"What voice?" she cried. "I'm sorry, Jeremy! I didn't hear anything!"

"You didn't hear that voice?"

"I'm sorry, Jeremy," she wept. "I didn't hear any voice!"

"Jeremy Blackwell," the female voice reiterated. "I can be a patient God. But I will not be ignored! Let go of the girl, or God's wrath will rain down upon you!"

"You didn't hear that?" Jeremy asked with panic and confusion.

"Hear what?" Lindsay sobbed. "I'm sorry! I don't know what you're talking about!"

"Will you stop with this bullshit about voices, Blackwell?" Danny pressed. "There are no voices. Just drop the knife, let go of Lindsay and I promise I'll let you walk out of here. It's your only hope. You're running out of time. The cops are on their way."

"Jeremy, you wretched sinner!" the voice chastised. "You are securing your eternity in Hell! Listen to God and release the girl!"

"Stop it!" Jeremy screamed. "You are not God! Stop tormenting me! You always do this! Why does God always contact me in the form of a woman? God is not a woman! Why do you do this? It's my mother, isn't it? She was the one who taunted me endlessly with the brutality of her religious teachings! She forced me to kill her! But then, she wouldn't die! Why don't you die, Mother? I won't feel guilty for killing you! You were the sinner, you horrid beast! Not me! Stop taunting me! You are not God!"

In his rant, he forgot to hold his grip on Lindsay. He loosened his hold enough that she rammed his gut with a sharp elbow and quickly wriggled free.

She screamed as she ran in the general direction of Danny near the entrance.

"You bitch!" he shouted at Lindsay. "Come back here! I'll kill you!"

He raised his knife. He was about to start chasing her as Danny opened fire. He just kept shooting over and over until he heard the click, click, click of the empty chamber.

The first bullet hit Jeremy right in the chest right over his heart. The second bullet caught him in the chest again. Each bullet knocked Jeremy backwards. The third bullet tore into him just below the sternum. The next bullet hit him square in the face.

That was the shot that sent him tumbling back against a tall stack of large boxes. The containers he fell against slid out from under him. The large boxes above him dropped onto his fallen frame as he hit the floor. The boxes looked heavy as they bounced off his bleeding carcass.

When the echoing crashes subsided, Danny and Lindsay stood in nervous anticipation. They looked over at Jeremy.

All was silent. Jeremy didn't move. He just bled on the grimy floor.

After a minute, Lindsay turned to the man who had rescued her.

"Oh, Danny!" she cried as she flew into his arms.

"It's okay," he whispered. "It's all over. You're safe now."

She wept into his shoulder as she held him. He finally dropped the gun.

After a few moments, Krysten entered the room. Her eyes narrowed as she watched that girl holding her man. However, she knew Lindsay had just been through a harrowing ordeal. So she allowed the hug to continue for a minute.

When she couldn't take anymore, Krysten placed her hand gruffly on Lindsay's shoulder. A startled Lindsay stepped back in shock. Her eyes grew wide as she took another step backwards away from Danny.

"Krysten!" she gasped.

"Hello, Lindsay," Krysten said curtly.

"Krysten," she stammered. "That was you? You were the voice of God?"

"Yes," Krysten nodded. "It was Danny's idea. He suggested it as we drove over here. The detectives told us that Jeremy was delusional and he thinks he talks to God.

I didn't want to do it. But when I heard how things were going in here, I figured I had to do something to help."

"But, how did you know Jeremy hears God speaking to him through a woman's voice?" she asked.

"We didn't," Krysten explained. "We just figured if he's delusional, any voice might confuse him enough to give us an advantage. I guess we got lucky."

"So," she sputtered. "You did this for me? To help me?"

"Don't get me wrong," Krysten said. "I still don't like you. You've been harassing me and Danny and pissing me off for a couple of weeks now. But you don't deserve to die. Not like this. Not at the hands of Paradox."

Lindsay just stared at her in awe.

"Thank you."

"You're welcome," Krysten said as she put her hand on Danny's shoulder. "Now listen to me, Lindsay. We helped you because it was the right thing to do. Now it's your turn to do the right thing. I know you've had a very bad day. But, it's time to face reality. You gave Danny up all on your own. He has moved on. I'm with Danny now. I love Danny. He's mine and you can't have him back. It's time to leave us alone. Do you got that?"

"She's right, Lindsay," he concurred. "I'm glad you're okay. And we were happy to help you during this crisis. But you and I are history. You have to accept that. I'm with Krysten now. I love Krysten, and that's all there is to it."

Krysten took him into her arms. She smiled sweetly up at him as she said, "I love you, Danny Stark."

Then, she caught him up in a long, passionate kiss.

Lindsay could only stand and watch as they kissed. It was so painful to watch. It hurt more than anything she could remember. She had been through so much this day. But this felt like the most devastating experience she had to cope with.

She could feel her heart breaking. She could almost hear it!

And they just kept kissing!

Reality began to catch up with Lindsay. There was so much to process. So much to cope with. So much to swallow.

Jeremy…the chase…the terror…nearly getting killed…and now, Danny and Krysten! Her head was spinning. There was so much to take in. Her stomach was churning. Her legs could hardly support her.

And they just kept kissing!

Lindsay had to turn away. She looked over at Jeremy. That didn't help. He hadn't moved. He just lay motionless on the floor. A growing puddle of blood spread out around his lifeless body.

Disturbing memories were becoming reality. She had to turn away.

Oh God! Danny and Krysten were still kissing!

Lindsay just had to leave the room. Her whole body hurt. She struggled to walk as her legs just didn't want to function.

Reality was still catching up to her. Jeremy…the chase…nearly getting murdered.

And those two were still kissing as she staggered out of the room.

She steadied herself against the banister as she made her way down the stairs. Her mind was a whirlwind of negative input. She didn't even hear the sirens growing louder outside the warehouse. She just slowly made her way down the stairs.

When she reached the ground floor, she mindlessly ambled out into the main room. She didn't hear the sirens stopping just outside the building. She just wandered aimlessly toward the center of the large room.

Four detectives burst into the building from the street. They were accompanied by a handful of uniformed policemen.

"Ma'am?" Paczecki called. "We're the police! Are you Lindsay Bainbridge?"

She nodded vacantly.

"Where's Jeremy Blackwell?" Spapper asked.

She pointed absently toward the back of the room. "He's up on the second floor," she muttered. "He's dead. Danny killed him with the gun Jeremy brought so he could kill me."

"Blackwell's dead?" Van Leer asked.

"Danny Stark is up there too?" Grogan asked.

"Yes," she sputtered. "Danny's up there with Krysten Salinger. Jeremy tried to kill me. He was Paradox. Danny saved my life. Danny and Krysten. They both saved my life. I don't know why they bothered though. There's nothing left to live for anymore. Danny will never…I mean, I owe it to them to…it's over. Oh my God! It's really over! It's over!"

Reality finally came crashing down on Lindsay. It collapsed on her like a condemned building surrendering to a wrecking ball.

She dropped to her knees and began crying uncontrollably.

After about ten seconds, Spapper said, “We’ll go up and check on the others.”

He and Van Leer ran to the back of the room. The uniformed policemen followed. A barrage of footsteps could be heard racing up the stairs.

Paczecki and Grogan stayed behind to look after Lindsay. They just stood there and watched her as she wept. They felt so helpless. They wanted to help her. But, there was nothing they could do.

She just kept crying into her hands.

And the tears just wouldn’t stop.

About the Author

Donald Gorman was born in Albany NY on September 25, 1961. He grew up in the nearby small town of East Greenbush. and graduated Columbia High School in 1979. He briefly attended a few local colleges and now works for The State in Albany. His love of the horror genre began in high school, and has been heard to say that he finds graphic violence and carnage very soothing and calming. Nothing relaxes him more than a brutal, vicious murder after a hard day. This is his 8th book with AuthorHouse. Check out his website at www.wrongfulsecrets.com.

Printed in the United States
151161LV00001B/11/P

9 781438 990309